Little Sisters

Stuart Perrin

Blue Kite Press
New York

Blue Kite Press
New York, NY
bluekitepress.com
212-721-0305

Cover & book design by Robert Sink
webworksnyc.com

Photos by Claudio Musajo
claudiomusajo.com

Library of Congress Control Number: 2012922109
North Charleston, SC

Perrin, Stuart, 1942 -
Little Sisters / by Stuart Perrin — 1st ed
      p. cm.
ISBN: 978-1480146426
1. Perrin, Stuart — Fiction.
2. Author, American — Suspense novel — Contemporary
3. United States, Kathmandu, Nepal, India — social life and customs,
abduction, human trafficking, sex slavery, forced prostitution, Mumbai
brothel life, impact on the lives of four young Nepalese sisters.

Little Sisters by Stuart Perrin, © 2012 ebook—1st edition

Dedication

To Rudi,

Without whose love and profound spiritual teachings nothing would have been possible in my life.

To my daughter Ania Devi Perrin,

Who has taught me much about unconditional love...

Acknowledgements

So many people helped me with this book, it is with heartfelt gratitude that I thank them all. If I have missed mentioning anyone who encouraged me or shared insightful thoughts, please know I will forever be grateful for your input and for generously giving of your time. Foremost, Edy Selman, my literary agent and friend, who recognized, from its inception, the importance of *Little Sisters* — tirelessly, with meaningful discussions and finesse, she encouraged me through several rewrites until the idea for this dramatic fiction of social concern became a fully-realized novel. Her understanding and relentless drive pushed me to work on this book nonstop for over three years. Without her support, I don't think I could have labored as diligently as I did. Equally important, I'm grateful and give immense thanks to Barbara Gordon, former TV Emmy documentary producer and writer, thinker, friend, whose combination of editorial expertise, political shrewdness, literary awareness and razor sharp critiques inspired me to constantly dig deeper, helping to bring greater clarity and a more seamless structure to the multiple narratives of this complicated story. Special credit goes to Angeli Singh, for her editorial insight early on. To the readers along the way, Kristina Jones, Michael Jaliman, Yonah Daniella Gershator, Bella Rosenberg, Jane Selman, Lanny Kazner, Ann Gray Kaback, Cecilia Rosinger, and Annette Hunt many thanks for taking time to offer reasoned suggestions. My deepest thanks to Robert Sink for doing an incredible job designing the book and cover, Claudio Musajo for his beautiful photographs, Alice Stipak and Anne Kohlstaedt for an amazing copy editing job. Derek and Michelle Lords, Cecilia Alves Pinto, Alik and Devorit Elzafon, Pat Fay, Virginia Jones, Eva Arroyo, Jose Hurtado Prudhomme, Jeannie Neidich, Lisa Berkley, Richard Garcia and many others who believed in *Little Sisters*.

I want to acknowledge the work and courage of Kristina Jones, my dear friend and spiritual sister who spent time on the frontlines combating human trafficking. Aruna Uprety, for her unselfish work that has saved the lives of thousands of young girls who could have wound up in Mumbai brothels, and all those people who are engaged in a daily battle for the elimination of human trafficking in the world.

Other Books by Stuart Perrin:

Rudi: The Final Moments

Moving On: Finding Happiness in a Changed World

A Deeper Surrender: Notes on a Spiritual Life

Leah: A Story of Meditation and Healing

The Mystical Ferryboat

Author's Preface

For more than twenty years I lived, studied and traveled in Nepal and India as an integral part of my learning, ongoing research, and deep interest in the ancient art and religions of South Asia's respective cultures.

In 1992, my distinguished colleague, Kristina Carlson Jones moved to Kathmandu to open a meditation center. She contacted me in New York and told me about children being abducted and trafficked into sexual slavery. She had met a Nepalese doctor, Aruna Uprety, who detailed the horror of how girls between 10 and 14 years were being bought by sex traffickers in the hinterlands of Nepal for transport to brothels on Falkland Road in Bombay (Mumbai).

In an instant I understood.

"That's horrible," I said to her. "This has to be our work. We must find a way to protect these children."

Thus the Bahini ("Little Sister" in Nepalese) Foundation was born, one of the first organizations of its kind in Nepal.

Within a few months, we set up a safe house to provide shelter for the children. We worked closely with Dr. Uprety to identify young girls who were prime targets for sex traders. We went to families in poverty stricken villages and showed them there was an alternative to Falkland Road brothels. At that time, the income of these families was about $15.00 to $20.00 a year. A girl could easily bring $200.00 from a trafficker — and more if she was a virgin. The family would no longer have to worry about raising money for her dowry. She would go to Bombay, Delhi or Calcutta to "work". No one in the village knew exactly what kind of work, but they all hoped she would send money home to help the family survive.

In a matter of weeks, it became clear — the plight of these prepubescent children was heartbreaking. After many difficult months spent looking for and identifying girls who were potential targets for sex traders, we convinced a few families to forgo the money they could make selling their children and entrust them to the Foundation's care, and hopefully a dignified future.

It wasn't easy to do and often we weren't successful, but a number of girls came to live in a large house the Foundation had rented in Kathmandu. We enrolled them in school, fed and sheltered them. Even in the safety of the Bahini House, we had to remain vigilant to keep them from the clutches of sex traffickers. We also welcomed women and their children who had escaped from brothels in Mumbai.

On one occasion, at the risk of her life, Kristina Carlson Jones outfitted as a nurse, went into the Falkland Road hellhole of brothels in Mumbai to document the dismal condition of young girls who were sold to traffickers. Had the brothel owners known what Kristina was really up to, most likely they would have killed her.

The Nepalese Government kept the sex trafficking business under wraps. It was an embarrassment, something no one in Nepal would speak about. Occasionally, a high-ranked politician would furtively show up with tears in his eyes and thank us for helping his people. By and large, the world has until today remained indifferent to the plight of these Nepalese girls and has essentially ignored the most despicable criminal horror ever inflicted on innocent children.

One of the Foundation's goals was to school the brightest of these children in the West. It was our hope that through education, they would return to Nepal as doctors, teachers, economists, mathematicians and scientists, and thus help to raise the economic and social conditions of the Nepalese people and eliminate the sex trade.

The Bahini Foundation disbanded in 1996, but its work in Kathmandu was continued by R.H.E.S.T. (Rural Health and Education Service Trust of Nepal) — a Nepalese NGO headed by Dr. Aruna Uprety whose extraordinary vision (with the generosity of The American Himalayan Foundation) has helped to save at least 10,000 innocent girls from being sold into sexual slavery.

Today, the Internet, mass media, and inexpensive jet travel have shrunk the size of our planet to a global village. We now know that the sex slavery network is as prevalent in the West as it is in South Asia. The subject of sex trafficking has emerged from the back pages of newspapers and has been included in a few public-awareness audiovisual programs. International organizations are taking stock of the situation and will hopefully intervene with some degree of efficiency.

When children (no matter what their nationality, ethnicity or religion) are forced to become sex slaves or are kidnapped so that their kidneys can be surgically removed and sold on the black market, the entire world must take responsibility.

Little Sisters, the novel that follows, arises from my direct experience and awareness of the pain and redemptive passion felt by real people concerned with these issues. I want the reader to become graphically aware of what life is like in the Mumbai red-light district. Beyond revealing the horrors of sex slavery as others have in documentary style, I have endeavored, through fiction, to render the intolerable fate suffered by four sisters at the hands of sex merchants and how each of them is transformed by life in a Mumbai brothel in dramatically different and unpredictable ways.

CHAPTER ONE

(New York City 2009)

Gita rushed down the Juilliard lobby steps after having taught a ten AM dance class. She dashed out of the building onto Sixty-Fifth Street. A crush of people moved in two directions and cars, taxis and trucks jostled with each other for position on the city streets. The late morning sun bounced off the windows of the many splendid buildings that made up Lincoln Center — the grand structures devoted to theatre, opera, dance and classical music rose high above Gita's head; they were her favorite place in Manhattan. Being near Lincoln Center always filled her mind with the image of dancers on a stage; and Gita adored the lush orchestral sounds of music from the first moment she heard them several years before.

Gita had an appointment with Lauren Ransum, the artistic director of the Brooklyn Academy of Music for lunch at Fiorello's. Lauren, the wife of Philip Ransum, a New York State Senator and patron of the arts, had asked Gita to perform her Nepalese sacred dance at a concert in the Spring New Wave Series. It would be her first solo performance in New York City. This was the day she had been waiting for.

On the corner of Broadway and Sixty-Fifth Street, a white-faced mime performed before a small crowd of people. In a black tuxedo and without a shirt, a black top hat, and a bow tie around his neck, he mimicked the walk of a rich matron with her poodle tied to a leash followed by her frazzled husband. Gita studied the nuances of the mime's movement, laughed at his parody then looked at her watch. It was 11:55; she had five minutes to get to her lunch date. After dropping a few dollars in the performer's hat, Gita ran across Broadway.

Many people were on the streets, headed to assorted destinations. Their movements, their shapes and forms, their clothing, the colors of their skin — all of this taught her about them even if they would always remain strangers. New York was such a contrast to Rumla, the small village in Nepal where Gita was born. Less than three hundred people lived there, most of them from the same extended families — a place where cows, goats, and water buffalo walked lazily on an unpaved road.

The hostess at Fiorello's showed her to Lauren Ransum's table.

"I've never showcased Nepalese dance," Lauren said to Gita after they finished their lunch, "but ever since I saw you perform at Juilliard, I am drawn to it more and more. And, Gita, your dancing is nothing short of a miracle. I've been thinking, let's bring it to BAM next spring. It will be a premiere opening in a perfect venue."

"Am I dreaming?" Gita asked with a big smile. She could already visualize the enormous stage and sophisticated audiences that attend BAM productions. She knew this was a fantastic opportunity. "I don't know how to thank you."

"Let me go over it with the board," Lauren said, "and we'll speak in a few weeks."

As she turned north to Sixty-Fifth Street, Gita had a lilt in her walk. She looked across Broadway for the mime, but his festive performance had vanished into Manhattan's busy daytime rhythm. It left an empty space Gita wished someone would fill. She adored street performers, be they rappers or break dancers or comedians or jazz musicians. Their spontaneity, the sense of the unexpected, the lack of pretense and structure, all of it reminded her of life on the streets of Kathmandu.

On Central Park West, Gita walked to Sixty-Eighth Street, greeted Max the doorman, and took the elevator to the penthouse apartment where she lived with her husband Daniel. She threw her dance bag on an armchair, stretched her long lithe body on the living room floor, and gazed at a Camille Pissarro landscape Daniel had recently purchased at Sotheby's.

"What a wonderful day," Gita said out loud, and she thought, all that's missing is a cup of tea.

Earlier that morning, the head of the New York University dance department had offered her a position to teach Nepalese dance as an adjunct at the Tisch School of the Performing Arts in September. Now, Gita had just received this offer to perform at BAM. Her mind spun with joy.

It was a beautiful late May afternoon, one of those precious seventy-five degree days with a clear blue sky and a slight breeze. From her living room terrace window, Gita spotted a young girl flying a kite — an innocent enough daytime activity in Central Park that triggered memories of her own childhood in Rumla — one of the few Tamang Hindu villages in the northernmost part of Nepal.

When Gita was a young girl, and had something important to ask the gods, with her kite in hand, she would run across meadows and along streams at the base of the Ganesh mountain range.

She remembered her mother Kamala's weathered face, and her long graying black hair. A strong and vibrant woman, her mother worked from dawn to dusk milking goats, cooking, farming, and doing whatever was deemed necessary to support her family. Kamala looked much older than her years. Like most Nepalese village women she bore the brunt of day-to-day labor. The very thought of her mother — the memory of how much they once loved one another, was a rare indulgence for Gita. It also evoked other bittersweet and very painful remembrances that she preferred to forget. The only memories she had of her father were of a drunken man who did nothing but gamble and laze away his life.

The kettle whistle startled her. Gita went into the kitchen and made a cup of Himalayan black tea. It had an intense musky flavor with faint hints of vanilla, fig, apricot and peach — a tea Gita loved to drink when the day's work had tired her out. She checked her watch, then showered, dressed, and left the apartment.

In her jeans and a tee shirt, with her long black hair, large dark oval eyes, and the high cheekbones of the Nepalese Tamang mountain people, Gita was a strikingly beautiful twenty-five-year-old woman. She was pleased to have found the ideal anniversary present for Daniel in an Asian antiquities gallery on Madison Avenue where she and her husband had recently browsed — a gallery that displayed a rare collection of ancient Hindu and Buddhist statuary from South Asia.

The dealer had placed on a pedestal a small bronze statue of Ganesha — the Hindu Elephant God, and Daniel had looked at it from all sides. He lifted it with care, examined the statue, pointing out to Gita how gracefully Ganesha danced on one leg. Daniel felt the weight of this treasure in his hand and sensitively rubbed the bronze's golden patina — its smooth and soft feel indicated that it must have been worshipped for hundreds of years.

He told Gita that the large belly symbolized what the Chinese call *Qi* — a fullness of life and spirit, of harmony and balance that enabled the gods to clear spiritual and material paths to wealth and abundance.

Daniel informed the dealer that he would think seriously about the piece. He wanted to see if the energy of the statue stayed with him after he left the shop.

Daniel's reaction had stirred her with waves of anticipation. Gita hurried out of the taxi and panicked, fearful it was too late and that the special piece had already been sold. A gray-haired Indian man greeted her from behind a desk and she asked him about the Ganesha.

"You mean this?" the dealer said. He opened a showcase, removed the six-inch statue, and handed it to her.

Gita remembered how Daniel lovingly ran his fingers over the piece. He had mentioned to her the night before that he wanted to buy it.

"Yes," she told the dealer with a smile.

"It's Nepalese," he replied. "Fourteenth century."

"My husband admired it very much when we saw it last Saturday."

"I remember."

"What are you asking for it?"

"My best price is $7500.00. Actually, there's no way I could replace it at any price."

Gita examined the statue, placed it carefully on the desk, picked it up again and, for the first time, felt its weight.

"That's so expensive," she said to him in Hindi. "I mean I'm from Nepal. How can a statue like this be worth so many rupees?"

"If you rub its belly you will overcome obstacles," the dealer said with a smile.

"Can't you do any better on the price?" Gita said. She rubbed the statue's belly and silently asked the god for a little help on this one.

"$7000.00. I'd rather keep it than sell it for less."

"Oh dear," Gita hesitated, "my husband liked it so much."

She took a deep breath and pulled out a credit card.

"It's a deal," Gita said smiling, "I'll take it. We're celebrating our anniversary tonight."

He took the statue into the back room, checked her credit card, and came out with the bronze Ganesha wrapped in a silk-lined velvet box.

"Thank you Mrs. Gold," he said and Gita signed the slip.

As Gita left the gallery, she wondered how a village girl like her could be so transformed that she was now married to a wealthy American lawyer and living in luxury in New York City. "Karma is so full of inexplicable events," she said to herself. She stashed the gift carefully in the bottom of her tote bag and braced herself for the struggle to find a cab.

It was rush hour, but a cab let someone out right in front of her. Bemused by the thought that the gods were already granting her wishes, Gita entered the taxi quickly and clasped the package on her lap.

"The FBI is working closely with Nepalese authorities to investigate the disappearance of an American woman while trekking alone in Nepal," Gita heard a newscaster say on the radio. *"Chicago FBI spokesman John Lester was quoted by the Associated Press as saying that on Sunday the agency began working with Nepalese authorities on the disappearance of 24 year-old Lorna Bevin from Peoria, Illinois.*

"Could you please make that louder?" she asked the driver.

"Bevin hasn't been heard from since May 21st, when she emailed her parents from Nepal. She planned to finish her trip around May 30, according to AP. Her father, Paul Bevin said that FBI agents have made two visits to his home. He went to Nepal on May 26th to look for his daughter. He told reporters he recovered her laptop computer and journal from the hotel where she had last been seen.

"And in a related story, here's Mark Forester with the BBC report."

As the taxi entered Central Park, Gita asked the driver if they were listening to NPR.

"Yes," he answered.

"This is Mark Forester reporting from Mumbai. I'm here with the Indian health minister, Dr. Adnan Vishnumurti and Amitra Sharma, a Nepalese doctor of sociology who runs the "Children are Precious" safehouse she started for street kids in Mumbai. Beneath the economic boom of India is a conspiracy so devious few talk about it. Like a spider's web, it captures ten-to fourteen-year-old girls in its sticky grasp and sucks the life out of them. Statistics say that up to ten thousand Nepalese children a year are sold into prostitution. These are conservative figures because no one knows for sure, but it's enough to chill the heart of anyone with an ounce of compassion. Ms. Sharma, can you tell us about this horror."

"Yes, Mark," she replied. *"A child's voice cries out from a place so deep in the human soul that few can hear it, a voice that's hidden beneath the chaos of Mumbai streets, the sound of which can carry thousands of miles and pierce a mother's heart. We know little of the pain in a twelve-year-old girl whose life has come to an end in Mumbai's red-light district, we know little about Nepalese children sold into slavery, children bought for a few hundred dollars from poverty-stricken parents."*

"Dr. Vishnumurti," Forester said, *"Falkland Road is one of the worst hellholes on earth. It seems as if the Indian Government pays it no mind. It seems that prostitution and slavery run rampant, that AIDS and other venereal diseases are pandemic. Can you tell us why nothing is being done by the authorities to put an end to this travesty of human degradation?"*

The driver switched to a music station. Gita knocked on the glass divider. "Please don't change that, I was listening...it's important...please go back to NPR," but by the time he did, she had missed the doctor's answer.

"The Nepalese problem is vast," the reporter went on, *"with no solution in sight. These children of the gutter are gripped in an economic vise that's drawn so tight human life has no value. They are truly existential creatures*

living without home or family, they survive on almost nothing every day."

The taxi pulled up in front of Gita's building.

"That'll be $12.30," the driver said. "Wanna receipt?"

"Wait a minute. I want to hear the end of this."

"Lady, I've got to make a living. That story's depressing."

"Keep the meter running. Please, I'll take care of you. Just let me hear this."

"Hear what?"

"The guy on the radio," Gita answered. She listened to the reporter sign off.

"Forty to fifty percent of the Nepalese girls in brothels spread HIV to tens of thousands of Indians every year. The disease is spreading so fast doctors and hospitals can't keep up with it. There's no way of knowing how many millions of people will die. This is Mark Forester of the BBC reporting from Mumbai, India."

Suddenly, Gita was seized by what felt like a spasm in her chest. She could barely breathe and was trembling with a chill that traveled through her body and left her so weak she couldn't get out of the taxi. A tightly sealed shroud had been lifted from a reservoir of memories of her sisters Renu and Prema that Gita couldn't keep from entering her consciousness no matter how hard she tried. When she heard the BBC report, her mind was flooded with long-buried concerns for them both.

Her thoughts were chaotic, rambling, and assaulted her like shots from an automatic weapon. Oh God, Renu? Prema? Are they still in my village or were they sold and forced into a life of prostitution? Would my father sell his own daughters? I have to find out. I've got to get to Rumla.

The very idea that her sisters might be prostitutes while she was living in comfort...overwhelmed her. Many years ago, she'd vowed never to return to her village. The reasons for this were lodged so deeply inside her, Gita never spoke about them, not to Daniel...not to anyone. Not knowing the circumstances of her little sisters and her mother, made the horrible reality of sex trafficking even worse. The choices Gita had made in the past were uprooted by this report, and all she was left with were urgent questions.

The fear of returning to her village was like a ratchet that gripped her heart and refused to let go. Gita wanted to scream, but realized how futile it would be. An inner voice kept repeating itself: "I must return to my home" — a place she thought she had banished from her mind many years ago.

"I loved you, *ama*," Gita said out loud as if her mother was sitting beside her. "You said that you would always keep me in your heart."

Gita could never understand why her mother put her in that rich man's house in Kathmandu. Was it possible that Kamala didn't know what would happen in there; that she thought Gita was just a servant? Did she think that somehow by living there, Gita would have had a better life than in the village?

"You promised, *ama*, but never came back to see me. I don't understand."

Gita pictured her mother hard at work in the fields around Rumla; she pictured her washing clothes and cooking millet and *dahl* for her father and sisters. The poverty was so extreme that the cost of her taxi ride could buy a month's worth of food.

Her mother was old now, maybe sick. Gita could have sent money… something…gotten word to her…gone to her village…she could have done more. Why didn't she return all these years? Gita knew she could have, but was too fearful, too possessed by anger.

Little Prema is fourteen now. Fourteen…a perfect target for traffickers. How could I have been so selfish?

Gita paid the fare and tipped the patient cabbie twenty dollars. Still shaken by the news report, she crossed Central Park West and sat on a bench. She needed to calm herself, but one image from her childhood, more than any other, lingered in her memory. On a lazy spring afternoon, after finishing her chores, Gita flew a kite at the top of a hill, released the string and watched it skip from wind gust to wind gust. She saw her older sister Jamuna with a strange man in the distance.

"Look, Jamuna," Gita cried out. "My kite's talking to the gods."

Jamuna waved to her, but continued to follow the man.

"Jamuna, where are you going?" Gita shouted.

But Jamuna never turned around. It was the last time Gita saw her.

"Jamuna," Gita shouted again, but in response, she heard only the deep and silent hush of mountains and valleys. Gita reeled in her kite and quickly ran to the ridge that overlooked the valley.

"Jamuna," Gita whispered. "Where did you go? Who are you with?"

Nervous and frightened, Gita returned to the family hut and asked her mother where Jamuna went with that strange man.

"To work in the city," Kamala replied stoically.

"In Kathmandu?"

"No, in Mumbai."

"When will she return?" Gita asked.

"I don't know," Kamala said in a sad voice and held Gita close…

* * *

Gita knew nothing about child trafficking while she lived in Nepal. Primitive village life lacked television, newspapers, and telephones or any of the electronic gadgets she now took for granted. Even in New York, stories of sexual slavery were buried on page twenty of almost every newspaper or in the Op-Ed section of the *New York Times* — seldom worthy of headline status or prime time.

I'm not even sure if my mother and sisters are still alive, Gita thought when she rose from the bench.

She had broken into a cold sweat and her head was throbbing. After all this time, she wasn't sure that she would recognize them if they walked past her on the street. What kind of a daughter didn't know if her mother was dead or alive?

She glanced at her watch. It was time for her to dress for dinner. She took a deep breath to calm herself. She couldn't let Daniel see her like this.

She crossed Central Park West and entered the lobby of her apartment building. While she waited for the elevator, her thoughts were becoming more focused, more determined. By the time the elevator arrived, she had made a decision. She would book a flight to Nepal…as soon as possible. If Daniel couldn't make it, she'd go alone.

What choice did she have? If ten thousand girls from Nepal were sold into sexual slavery every year, could Renu and Prema be among them? She hoped it wasn't too late…

CHAPTER TWO

(Twenty-five years earlier in Rumla, Nepal)

A few months before Gita was born, when Jamuna was almost four and still little, she liked playing on the dirt floor of her family hut, where she'd later sleep along with her older bother Sivan and ama and bah; and ama told Jamuna she'd teach her a special temple dance to music played by the priests and composed by ancient village poets in honor of Lord Siva. The priests had trained ama and now ama would train Jamuna when she became four years old. Now still three, becoming four seemed to Jamuna like forever. When sh thought about it, she really wanted to learn to dance more than anything e and ama promised, and the priests promised, and she would learn bec ama had told her it's a good way to pray to Lord Siva…

When Jamuna asked ama why her belly was getting bigger, an her that soon she'd have a baby brother or sister; and Jamuna th would be good to have a sister. If it's a sister, maybe when she's a li ama can teach her to dance too. We can both dance in the villag

※ ※ ※

When Gita was born, all the Rumla priests and an astr in a remote mountain temple gathered around her. They chanting prayers to Lord Siva. They told ama and bah Gita was the incarnation of Saraswati, the goddess of they told them that this child, and she alone, should the temple.

When Jamuna heard this, she began to cry. Sh Gita and wished that Gita had never been born.

Bah took her hand. They walked togethe showing his pretty little Jamuna all the plants She was smart and remembered them all. H Jamuna smell them. He told her that some children of her own.

When bah and Jamuna returned to t

Gita. Bah got down on his knees and kissed the infant's feet and he put a little tikka powder on her forehead. Jamuna also bowed to Gita, but instead of tikka powder, she rubbed dirt on the child's feet and whispered that Gita was not a goddess. "She's just another baby and why can't we both dance in the temple?"

✳ ✳ ✳

When ama began to teach four-year-old Gita the steps to sacred dances, an impatient Jamuna, who was now seven, sat in the temple's doorway and ~tched. For a moment, she wanted to punch Gita because Gita didn't ~e a goddess to her, but just another village girl who flew her kite and ~mes of tag with the other children.

~t ama teach me? Jamuna thought. What do the priests know ~ I want to dance?

~at it didn't matter, but she wanted to anyway. He told ~ Gita and Jamuna would be married if he could find ~vries. Just like ama stopped dancing in the temple ~his hut, so Gita and Jamuna would also go to

~le sister Renu and held her on one knee. ~the steps to a sacred temple dance.

~rabbing her. "Gita is the only

CHAPTER THREE
(New York 2009)

After a day crammed with meetings and phone calls, Daniel's afternoon ended on a high note when the Lockheed Martin CEO invited him to Bethesda, Maryland, to discuss a four billion dollar buyout of a firm that manufactured parts for fighter jets.

"It's in the discussion stage," he told Daniel, "but I'd like you to come here after Labor Day. We'll play some golf, party a little, and draw up a strategy. And why not bring Gita? Suzanne would be more than delighted to show her the town."

"It sounds good to me," Daniel said. "I'll ask her; I'm sure she'd enjoy it — she loves the excitement of a new place."

"Perfect, we'll talk in August," the CEO replied.

"I'll be in touch," Daniel said and hung up the phone.

He left the office early and took a taxi to Tiffany's where he ran into his old Harvard classmate, Leon Wiley and his wife Ursula at the store's entrance. Leon was the president of R.R. Dutton, a large Wall Street investment firm.

"What a surprise," Ursula said as she hugged Daniel.

"It's our fifth anniversary today. I'm getting something special for Gita."

"You handsome devil. I always thought you'd be the eternal bachelor," Ursula said to him. "But, I must say, Gita's a jewel. The other night, at Helen's party, she wowed every woman in the room including me when she described the beauty of Kathmandu. Did you really meet mountain trekking there? I was ready for Leon and me to go the next day. Give her a big hug. We'll see you both at the symphony next Friday."

Inside Tiffany's, Daniel walked through the aisles directly to the custom design section. After telling the saleswoman what he was looking for, he carefully examined the three bracelets presented to him.

"This is the one!" he said. He handed her an eighteen-karat gold and emerald inset bracelet. "I like this one very much. It's perfect for my wife," he added visualizing it on Gita's wrist.

"It's an exclusive Tiffany design," the saleswoman said.

"Have it specially wrapped and please deliver it to John Martin, the *maitre d'* at Le Cirque. My wife and I have an eight o'clock dinner reservation. Mr. Martin knows that it is coming."

"Certainly, I'll take care of it personally," she assured him.

Daniel had been born into a banking family, now run by his father and uncle. Gold & Gold, founded in the early 1920's by Daniel's grandfather, was a Wall Street institution — an anomaly on the street, privately owned and still run by the Gold family, it carried a twenty billion dollar portfolio invested both nationally and internationally in stocks, bonds and securities. It was also heavily invested in the international currency market and in commodity futures. Gold & Gold was a highly regarded brokerage firm catering to the wealthiest Americans.

Daniel had been raised on Park Avenue, but his family had houses in the Hamptons, the South of France, on Star Island in Miami, and Hyde Park in upstate New York. Always a good student, he went to exclusive private schools in Manhattan, and graduated first in his class at Harvard and topped off his brilliant collegiate record by graduating *magna cum laude* at Columbia Law.

After graduation, his father and uncle had pleaded with him to join the firm, but Daniel was fascinated with philosophy, the intricacies of law, and ethics — the constant struggle to uncover deeper truths. He was good at dealing with the warrior-type mentality of multinational companies and used his knowledge of the law to find solutions to difficult financial negotiations. He was driven to look for work with a high-profile corporate legal firm. Throughout his childhood, he'd been exposed to stock, bond and commodities trading to the point where it no longer challenged him. He hated the idea of living each day by rote and chose a profession in which daily challenges would force him to cut his own path through life.

Invited to work at the law firm of Gray, Sternweiss, Dobson & Dobson — a prestigious Wall Street boutique law office that represented his father's company — Daniel used his international connections to bring hundreds of millions of dollars in business each year. Within five years, he was made a junior partner, and by the time he was thirty-three, the lawyers at the firm had decided to make him the youngest full partner ever accepted by the firm.

Daniel would often joke with his sister and cousins that sperm count decided his fate. But, he had no regrets. He loved his own work, and he respected the committed hard work of his father and uncle, work that had provided a good life for all members of the family. He was now thirty-five years old, well-built, with dark, curly, close-cropped hair and brown eyes.

Although he could easily afford it, George Gold, Daniel's father, refused to be chauffeured around New York City. He drove his beloved and somewhat battered Volkswagen bug everywhere. When Daniel was a teenager, his father, driving that same car, had often taken him on brief excursions through blighted neighborhoods.

"We are among the most fortunate on earth," his father would say. "Most people haven't been given your opportunities. Just look around and see how the poor live and remember that there are many ways to be bold. Some here have been bold, and with help, they found a way out of this neighborhood and made something extraordinary of their lives."

In his father's time, FDR had vision and guts. Although he was physically weak, he was a strong-willed man, creative, a fighter…a winner. To this day, he remained a hero to George Gold.

His Uncle Marvin was a different sort of creature. He owned six Porsches, a Ferrari, and two Mercedes-Benz sedans, and socialized with high-level politicians and show business celebrities. He'd fly to Washington D.C. for important events every week or two. His uncle had produced three successful movies and two Broadway musicals, calling the entertainment world a diversion from the pressures of mergers and acquisitions.

When Daniel was fifteen years old, one gray February afternoon, on his way home from a study session at a friend's West Side apartment, he walked past the Alice in Wonderland statue in Central Park. He always enjoyed watching the children climb on Alice and the Mad Hatter. But this cold winter's day, the park was empty except for a gang of teenagers that rushed towards him from all directions, beat Daniel up and stole his pocket money. Daniel was strong and fast, but six of them were too much.

"This will never happen to me again," he promised himself with fierce determination.

Already an avid mountain climber, he enrolled in a karate school. In the years that followed, he mastered the art. Disciplined and committed, he eventually became an outstanding black belt. Daniel's skill sharpened to where his beloved Sensei recognized in him a spiritual need that transcended the basic self-defense that he taught to his other students. He gave him a translated copy of the *Tao Te Ching*. He also asked Daniel to teach a class at the dojo. By doing so, bestowed on him a great honor.

"This book will help you to understand the true nature of the martial arts," the Sensei said.

Daniel engrossed himself in Taoist philosophy. He learned from it how to stay focused and centered in the dojo and applied his knowledge of the Tao to many areas of his law practice and just about every other part of daily life.

✳ ✳ ✳

Daniel returned home, showered, dressed and waited for his wife. It was after five PM. Gita was almost never late, unless she had to rehearse or attend a concert. He wondered where she was. Although they had great wealth, he admired her independence. In addition to the enjoyment Gita took in teaching dance classes at Juilliard, she derived great pleasure in her volunteer work with children in the orphanages that his family supported; and the children adored watching her dance.

Daniel knew that Gita valued their wealth. At the same time, she tried to keep their life simple.

"A housekeeper is enough," she said to him one evening while they lounged in front of the fireplace. "Why should we have someone cook for us? I want to surprise you myself; I want to spoil you at breakfast and dinner. That's our private time. On special occasions, we can hire a cook."

"Where did you learn to make these delicious dishes? There isn't a five-star restaurant in New York that wouldn't want to steal you away from me. But, where did you learn? Did you take classes?"

She gave him a gentle kiss, put her hand over his lips and said, "You like them. That's all that counts."

"The rest is mystery?" he laughed.

"Of course," she said coquettishly. "Every woman needs a little bit of mystery, doesn't she?"

✳ ✳ ✳

"Your table is ready," the *maitre d'* at Le Cirque told them as they entered the restaurant. He winked, bowed his head to them and smiled.

"Thank you, John," Daniel said, slipping the *maitre d'* a substantial gratuity and he and Gita sat down.

The wine steward brought them a specially-ordered bottle of Krug, Clos du Mesnil, opened it, poured a little for Daniel to taste, then filled their glasses with the champagne.

"To you, my love," Daniel said. "Happy anniversary."

"Happy anniversary," Gita said as she lovingly took him in with her eyes.

Daniel nodded to the *maitre d'* to come to their table.

"Oh, thank you John," Gita said to him. She glanced at the covered dish he placed before her.

"Just lift the cover," Daniel said with a boyish smile.

When she removed it, Gita found a Tiffany box circled by a necklace of four red roses with a yellow rose pendant that represented their fifth anniversary. Daniel kissed her hand again, then lifted the box off the silver plate and gave it to her. She carefully took out the diamond bracelet.

"It's so beautiful," she said in awe. "I love it, Daniel, thank you, it's almost too beautiful to wear." She leaned closer and gave him a kiss.

"Let me help you with the clasp."

He took her slender hand in his and secured the bracelet on her wrist. She raised her forearm in the air, bending her dancer's arm with the same movement she'd make in a temple dance created for the goddess Parvati. "Just so beautiful," she said again, looking at the bracelet.

"Happy anniversary." Daniel leaned over and kissed her on the lips. "You know, Gita, I feel like the Mad Hatter in Alice's Wonderland."

"You'll have to fill me in," she smiled.

"That was one of my favorite books when I was growing up. The Mad Hatter wanted to celebrate not just birthdays, but un-birthdays too. And I want to celebrate un-anniversaries. I want every day of our lives to be special."

At that moment, she surprised Daniel by giving him his gift.

"Can we open it together?" he asked.

"No, Daniel," she said mysteriously. "You do it. You must open this yourself."

Daniel slowly took the statue from its silk sleeve, held it in his hand, and admired it. Deeply touched and surprised, he said in a gentle voice, "You remembered."

"How could I forget the way you looked at it and even caressed it with your fingers." She leaned across the table to kiss him on the lips, and whispered, "Daniel, I was almost jealous."

"Our Ganesha will sit on my desk next to your picture and I'll always treasure it," he said. "It's the best anniversary present ever and so unexpected, darling."

"I'm so pleased," Gita responded. "Happy fifth, my love. I hope we have a thousand more."

They left Le Cirque around ten PM, and walked west along Central Park South. She could feel his hand in hers, a hand so warm, so loving it made her stop walking. She put her arms around his neck and kissed him lightly on the lips. "I love you," she said, "I love you so much. You know, Daniel, I'll tell you my secret. Everyday I thank the goddess for you. I thank her because people call me Mrs. Gold. I thank her because we are together in this incredible city."

They continued to walk on Central Park South.

"Let's do something different, tonight," Gita said.

"Okay, what do you want to do? Go barefoot in the park," he joked.

"Let's be tourists. How about taking a horse and carriage home?"

"Done, Mrs. Gold." He helped her into a carriage and told the driver where to go. She snuggled up next to him. He took the bronze Ganesha from his pocket and studied it.

"It's from Nepal, like you," Daniel said as he rubbed its belly.

"We're still going, right?"

"Of course," he said. He moved his hand from the statue to Gita's belly.

"But, when?"

"In four or five months."

"No, no Daniel, I can't wait that long," she said to him quietly.

"But why?"

"The media is full of stories about girl trafficking in Nepal."

"Are you worried about your family?"

"Yes," she answered. "My youngest sister, Prema is only fourteen, and I think she could be in real danger."

"Gita, it would be tough for me get away now," he said. "There are so many pressing cases, I'm up to my ears…"

"I can't wait, Daniel. If I have to, I'll go alone, and you can meet me there. School's out, and I'm free until September. Four or five months from now is no good for me," she pressed. "You don't have to go, but I do. I'm afraid that I'll never see my mother again. I know we planned this trip together, but if you can't get away I'll understand. You've never met my family, Daniel," she said choking up with tears.

"Well, you never talk about them," he said. "It's always been such a mystery to me."

"I know," she said apologetically. "I don't like to discuss my past."

He took her hand reassuringly, "Okay, Gita, love, I'll rearrange things, move some stuff around, and make sure we'll be able to leave in a few weeks. I don't know how the hell I'll do it, but I will. I promise you that we'll do lunch at the Hotel Yak and Yeti by mid-June."

She wrapped her arms around his neck, kissed him, and said, "I adore my bracelet, but the Nepal trip is the most wonderful present. I'll show my sexy, handsome, mountain climber husband the Himalayas he's never seen. It'll be like another honeymoon for us."

"In Shangri-La," he said laughing. "Speaking of honeymoons, Sara is living in Paris with a French painter."

"I know all about it from her emails. It sounds serious. Your niece is madly in love with him."

"And I'm crazy in love with a Nepalese dancer," he said. After a long embrace, she heard him whisper, "I couldn't imagine my life without you."

In their bedroom, Gita and Daniel stood on the terrace looking out at the big black mass that was Central Park at night and the glittering necklace of lights that made its way down Fifth Avenue and along Central Park South — all this a backdrop to the love they had for each other. He pulled her close, kissed her neck and slowly slipped off her gown. He touched the outline of her full lips, opened them and touched her tongue with his tongue in a deep kiss, pressing their bodies tight. They were both aroused. He felt her nipples harden. He kissed and caressed her breasts and enjoyed moving his hands over her long, lean torso, smooth thighs and tight dancer's midriff, wondering all the time how it was possible to love another human being so much. He kissed her gently on the lips. The gentle kiss grew into a passionate embrace in which the two of them were consumed by an uncompromising hunger for each other. He picked her up, easily carrying her to their bed and they made love over and over again till the early morning light came through the window.

CHAPTER FOUR
(fifteen years earlier)

Jamuna and the man walked eight hours over hills and valleys and entered a mountainous forest that led to a road where they met a friend of the agent sitting in a car.

"She's a pretty one," the friend said. "How old?"

" I think about fourteen."

"We'll get a good price for her in Mumbai."

"First we have to get her across the Indian border."

"That shouldn't be hard. We'll go to Nepalgunj. There are many places to cross the border there without being bothered by the police."

"What am I going to do in Mumbai?" Jamuna asked them.

"Work," the agent whose name was Lobsang answered.

"For who? Doing what?" Jamuna asked. "I don't want to go to Mumbai. I don't even know where Mumbai is. Let me out of here. I'm going home."

She struggled with Lobsang, scratched and bit him and screamed that she wanted to go back to Rumla. The driver stopped the car and Lobsang smacked Jamuna so hard that she was knocked partially unconscious. Then he pinched her nipples and put his hand between her legs. "If you don't stop screaming," he said, "I'll rape you, then he'll rape you, and no one in your village will ever want to see you again."

✳ ✳ ✳

Lobsang tied Jamuna's arms and legs and put a handkerchief over her mouth. The insufferable heat made Jamuna sweat until her clothing was soaked through and through. They drove on a one-lane blacktop with recumbent cows everywhere, through a flat, endless plain covered by field after field of maize, where "Goods Carrier Trucks" colorfully painted with images of Siva, Ganesha, Indra, and other gods vied for position on the road with water buffalo-drawn carts, bicycles, a smattering of cars, chickens, goats, dogs, and three-wheeled rickshaws — all creating such dense traffic that it felt as if their car moved along an inch at a time.

Jamuna observed that the people of Nepalgunj in the Terai were strangely different than in Rumla. They had very dark skin and thin faces, arms, torsos and legs, and they seem to be always arguing with each other.

The car pulled into a driveway of a house located on the outskirts of Nepalgunj.

"The border's less than a kilometer from here," Lobsang said to the other man. "We'll cross before the sun comes up tomorrow morning."

He untied Jamuna's hands and feet, took her by the arm and pushed her towards the door of the house that was opened by a pitch-black, middle-aged, and toothless woman, who looked more like a falcon than a human being.

"She's a beauty," the woman said with a smile on her face. "She'll bring us some real money."

✳ ✳ ✳

Lobsang kept staring at Jamuna as she curled up and lay on an old mat in the corner of the living room.

What a beautiful girl, he thought, who will soon be fucked by hundreds of men. She's a virgin that someone will pay a fortune of rupees to sleep with.

He knew her financial value, but, at the same time, her beauty captivated him, and he wanted her badly. He was obsessed by the thought that every man in Mumbai would sleep with her but him.

She was pure, untouched, had no disease, and she offered nothing but perfect pleasure for whomever took her in this state. He had found her, and he would enjoy her first. He was the one who would fuck her all night, then bring her to Mumbai and sell her to a whorehouse.

His obsession with the girl took hold of him. He grabbed her by the arm and forced her to stand up.

"You will be mine," he said, "at least for tonight I will enjoy you." Then he pushed open the bedroom door and threw her onto the bed.

✳ ✳ ✳

"Are you my husband?" Jamuna asked Lobsang the next morning after he raped her, "because no one else will have me now that you've hurt me and made me bleed and did to me what a husband does to his new wife. I resisted you three times, but the fourth time was different. I felt pleasure when you put yourself inside me and I wanted you to do it again and again because each time you stroked me a fire burned in my thighs and belly, and I said to myself that this must be the way a woman feels when she gives herself to her husband."

Lobsang just laughed at her, then said, "You'll pleasure hundreds of men in Mumbai. If you want, you can believe that each of them is your husband."

"But I can have no one else but you," Jamuna said. "No man can touch me because I belong to you."

"You're a little whore now and you belong to no one," Lobsang said and threw her to the floor. "I don't want to hear any of this nonsense. When we get to Mumbai, I'm going to sell you for the best price I can get and go home to my wife and children. It's good business for me, Jamuna, so shut up about belonging to me or any other man."

"I know you took me like a man takes his wife, and now I belong to you."

"Like hell, you do," he responded angrily. "Now shut up, or I'll beat you to within an inch of your life."

She heard his words, but couldn't understand them. There was one thing she understood very well. Whoever she was the night before died in this room. She would never be the same.

✳ ✳ ✳

"You're not to say a word when we get out of this car," Lobsang warned Jamuna as they drove slowly towards the Indian border. "India's about a hundred meters directly in front of us. There are no guards here, but sometimes the police patrol the place. If they catch us, it could mean years in prison."

"And the house where you'll meet Sunil?" the driver asked.

"It's just eighty meters from the border on the Indian side."

Jamuna got out of the car and followed Lobsang across a large rock-filled field illuminated by the twinkling light of a starry sky.

"We're in India," he said after a long silence. "We're lucky, the police aren't on patrol."

They continued to walk across the open field over rocks and patches of maize. "There's the house," he said to Jamuna. "Sunil's waiting for us. He has seven other girls there. In a few hours, we're all going to drive to Mumbai. If you say a word to anyone about this, the police will find you dead in a ditch. Remember, you're just another pretty girl worth a lot money in the marketplace."

✳ ✳ ✳

With barely enough air to breathe, with a periodic handful of rice and dahl to eat, and enough water to keep them from dehydrating, Jamuna and seven other Nepalese girls were fit tightly into the rear of a windowless minivan, all of them between twelve and fifteen years of age. They couldn't stand or move. If anyone complained, Lobsang had the driver stop the minivan. He got out and beat the girl mercilessly. The van made its way over one-lane potholed blacktops that connected villages to towns to cities all the way from Nepalgunj to suburban Delhi where Lobsang picked up more girls, and put them, along with Jamuna and the others, into the windowless rear of the colorfully-painted truck. The girls were forbidden to move or to speak. Lobsang and Sunil drove the eleven-hundred kilometers that separated Delhi from Mumbai.

It was pitch black in the interior of the truck's van, so dark that Jamuna could barely see the girl seated next to her. She heard some of the girls sobbing. Others asked in a whisper for water, for food, for air to breathe, for someone to help them. One girl tried to open the truck's door, but discovered that it was locked from the outside.

I am not Jamuna, she thought as she lay quietly with her back up against a wall of the van, but the ghost of Jamuna.

She was a person who didn't exist anymore — no mother, no father, no more sisters, nothing but Lobsang's paws all over her.

She touched the arm of the girl next to her. "I died last night," she whispered. "There's nothing left of me. There's only a big empty hole that I no longer fit into."

"You're crazy," the girl said.

"No, I'm the ghost of Jamuna."

When they arrived in Mumbai, a strange man who wore a white rumpled linen suit, a bow tie, with a big belly and puffy cheeks, told Lobsang that he wanted Jamuna to come with him.

"She's a beautiful girl," he said. "She'll serve me well. Take the others to Leila's house."

CHAPTER FIVE

(2010 – a few days later)

As Gita and Daniel walked together past the children's zoo in Central Park, the delightful voices of kids filled the air like the contrapuntal sound of laughter and shouts in a late morning piece of chamber music. They stopped to listen, and Daniel said to Gita, "Wouldn't it be great to have a little boy laughing like that in our apartment."

"Someday," she responded.

"Just tell me when," he said. "A girl would do just as well."

"I'm not ready, yet, my love. It's hard for me to forget there are thousands of abandoned babies in Nepalese orphanages that could use a home. Maybe we should adopt one or two of them."

"Not if we can have our own."

Daniel was puzzled by this because Gita's response conflicted with the dream he had of being a father.

"I've seen too much poverty," she responded. "I mean children in orphanages can laugh just as loud and have just as much fun as these kids. And they really need to have a family. We can give them a passport to a wonderful life."

"After the second-born Gold comes to us," Daniel said trying to lighten her up a bit, "I wouldn't mind a few adopted kids."

"In Kathmandu, we can visit the orphanage where I once performed. After I met all those children, I swore to myself I'd never get pregnant," Gita went on.

"That makes me nervous," Daniel replied. "Could there be anything more wonderful than the laughter of our children on a Sunday morning at home?"

She took his hand and squeezed it. "I know, my love, I really know that," she said smiling. "We'll have beautiful children together. I just need some time."

CHAPTER SIX

On their flight from London to Delhi, Daniel was exhausted from the additional hours he had to put in before they left. "Eight hours of sleep with no headphones beeping and you beside me, Gita, is my idea of heaven." He kissed her forehead, wrapped a blanket around himself and was asleep in an instant.

Gita dozed in the window seat. At last, after years, she was returning to the Nepalese countryside of her childhood. Her mind was filled with flashes of memory: faces, places, and like a kaleidoscope, changing images of those youthful days in Rumla. She could picture, as if it were yesterday, where she walked from the river along a narrow pine, oak, and rhododendron-lined path that snaked its way through the forest to her village. It was early in the morning — her favorite time of day, a time when the sounds of the forest were dense and full of life. She wondered about the myriad creatures that lived in and around her village; she wondered about the spirit world spoken of in stories passed down for many generations. Along the path to the river, there were black sacred stone statues of *Siva*, Ganesh, and Durga. The priests had told her that some of these carvings were over a thousand years old. All of them were worn down by wind and rain. They were covered with faded red tikka powder used by local priests performing ritual offerings to the gods. Her favorite shrine was a stone carving of the multi-armed goddess Durga — the great mother who gave birth to everything. During *Dashain*, she'd go with her parents and siblings to the Kali temple on the other side of the river. They'd bring a baby goat with them and give it to the priest who stood ankle deep in blood — the priest who sacrificed hundreds of animals at the altar of the goddess.

"It will bring us good fortune," her mother told them when they left the temple.

She would often meet her cousin Bina on the way back from the river. They'd laugh and giggle together about the possible husbands their parents would choose for them. They were both twelve years old and would soon be married. Each had a favorite boy in the village, but marriages were arranged, and Gita knew that she, like all the girls in Rumla, would have no choice in the matter, and could do nothing but abide by her father's wishes.

The main street of the village was crowded with children dressed in faded old western-style clothing. The boys wore long pastel sweaters or washed jean jackets over threadbare trousers; they also wore baseball caps and multicolored stocking hats. Their bright Tibeto-Mongolian faces, twinkling eyes, and big smiles lit up the street. Many of them were playing tag. Others lounged about casually talking to each other. The young girls wore faded dresses over torn trousers and swept the dirt from the entrances to their huts. Half-naked toddlers crawled in the dust; on the porch of each mud dwelling, a father of these children sat cross-legged on the ground drinking a cup of black tea. An open fire-stove burned dried cow paddies or charcoal, and on the stove, the women prepared *dahl* and millet for breakfast.

Gita stopped to speak with her cousin Yamu — a thirteen-year-old Tamang girl who would be married in a few months. The two of them giggled about Leske — Yamu's future husband. He had a farm and a few water buffalo and a number of chickens and goats, and his family was considered well off by village standards. Yamu's father, Dawa, was hard-pressed to put together a dowry of animals, cooking vessels and textiles. He had borrowed some money without a thought of how he would pay it back, even if it meant, that one day, he would become the lender's slave, and bought whatever was necessary for his daughter's dowry.

Gita put down the waterpot near the entrance to her family's hut. She heard her father, Lal, already drunk, and it wasn't even nine o'clock in the morning, telling Kamala in a loud voice that Gita would be going to Mumbai in about a week.

"But she's only twelve years old," Kamala replied angrily. "The priests say she's the incarnation of *Saraswati*."

"I don't give a damn what the priests say. We haven't a rupee for her dowry."

"I'll speak to them," Kamala said. "I know they will protect her."

"I already have," Lal said. "They told me the moment she bleeds, the goddess will leave her body." He stormed out of the shed knocking over Gita who stood in the doorway.

Frightened and confused by her father's words, with tears in her eyes and shaking, Gita put her arms around Kamala who embraced her.

"First Jamuna, now you," her mother said. "I won't let him do it. Go to the temple, my child, and dance for the goddess. Ask her to help us. Now go, and pray that we can change your father's mind."

Gita ran all the way to the temple. She knelt and prayed before the bronze statue of the Goddess Durga, sensing that her life was about to change. Maybe the goddess could answer the rush of questions that poured through her mind.

"What is this place called Mumbai? Where is it? Does Jamuna live there? Why is my father separating me from *ama*? It had been many years since Jamuna left Rumla with that strange man and no one has heard from her since. But there was only silence — a profound and disturbing silence that answered none of her questions.

"I am your servant, Mother Durga," she said with tears in her eyes. "Protect me. Please help to change my father's mind. This is my home; this is my temple."

She danced a sacred dance her mother had taught her as a child. At its conclusion, she bowed to the statue of the goddess, and said, "You will guide me, Mother. I trust that you will watch over my life."

Gita was fearful of the unknown path that *bah* had chosen for her. The little flame of hope that still resided within her was extinguished when she returned to the hut. Unable to convince him to change his mind, *ama* decided that before the agent came, she and Gita would make a quick trip to Kathmandu. They would say goodbye to cousin Ganga and her family, then return to Rumla. *Bah* didn't know about any of this yet, but, as soon as he returned home, *ama* would tell him.

"*Ama*, are there any mountains in Mumbai? Do ibex and monkeys live there? Will I be able to run through a forest and find another temple in which to dance?"

"It'll be alright," her mother replied in a strong, but quiet voice.

"I don't want to live so far away from you."

"Trust me, my precious child, the goddess will protect you. We'll leave for Kathmandu in the morning."

CHAPTER SEVEN

The voice of the pilot stirred Gita out of her reverie. She had found herself lost in these childhood memories — memories that had been buried for years. The pilot announced that he had turned on the seatbelt sign because of minor instability and assured the passengers that it would last no more than fifteen minutes.

Gita checked to see if Daniel's seatbelt was fastened. He was still asleep and she covered him with a blanket. Once again, she closed her eyes, and returned to her thoughts — some sweet, others laden with childhood turbulence in Nepal.

Her drunken father staggered through the door of their hut, washed his face with water, and lay down on a mat. He tried to sleep, but loudly complained that his head ached, and his stomach was bloated with *rakshi*. He ranted feverishly about his lack of money, cursed Jamuna's life in Mumbai, where rupee notes fell like leaves from a tree. He had no doubt that Jamuna had become so prosperous in the big city she forgot about her parents. Having married a great *Rana*, village life embarrassed her.

"I'm taking Gita to say goodbye to my cousin in Kathmandu," Kamala said to Lal.

"I didn't know you were up," Lal answered in an angry, drunken voice.

"We're leaving early in the morning," Kamala persisted.

"Go wherever you want."

"We'll return in three days."

"Just be sure she's back," he said emphatically. "The agent is coming to get her next week."

"We'll be back," she assured him.

He grabbed Kamala's arm and drunkenly ordered her to lie next to him. "Come," he insisted.

"No, I need to get up early," Kamala answered. She removed his hand and lay down on a mat in a far corner of the hut next to Gita.

Half awake, Lal mumbled to himself: "When a man's got a daughter, he must pay to marry her. Give your daughter to the agent and the gods smile on you. You win at cards. You have thirty rupees to spend on *rakshi*..."

"He thinks I'm stupid," Kamala whispered to Gita. "He thinks I don't know what Jamuna does in Mumbai. Now he wants to sell you, my sweet child. Then it will be Renu and Prema. This time I won't let him. I'd rather die first."

Gita moved closer to her mother who had drifted into a deep sleep. She could hear her father's drunken voice rambling on about money and spent a fitful night wondering what kind of work she would do in Mumbai, where she would live, and if she would ever dance again?

❊ ❊ ❊

It was predawn and still dark. Her father slept like a dead man and the rest of the village was quiet. Gita heard the barking of a stray dog in the distance when she and Kamala entered the forest. They followed a narrow hand-hewn path hundreds of years old and known only to the peasants who lived in Rumla — a path that descended the mountains and made its way from the river's bank into the depths of the forest where they walked along a four-foot wide cliff that dropped sharply a thousand feet into a gully. There was a slight breeze, but the sky was clear, and the majestic Himal loomed high above their heads. They continued their downward trek into the valley through bamboo groves that led them back to the river and Kamala chanted *Aum Vakratundaya Hum* — a sacred *Ganupati* mantra she had learned from the village priests — at first in a soft voice, then gradually, she intensified the chant until Gita could hear an echo in the distance, as if the god himself sat on his mountain throne and responded to the sacred words that would help them on their journey.

At the conclusion of their eight-hour trek, they arrived in a small village nestled high above a valley. A toothless, old woman in a tattered sari informed them that the bus would be there soon.

"It would take five hours to get to Kathmandu," the old woman said. Kamala telephoned her cousin Ganga and told her that she and Gita were on their way.

❊ ❊ ❊

The driver strapped their cotton totes on the bus's roof, where passenger's possessions were piled one on top of the other like a small mountain — everything from TV sets to bedding, rugs, carpets, mattresses, caged chickens, roosters, food, suitcases and rucksacks; and Kamala and Gita found the last two empty seats in a bus that had no glass in the windows, and a door that didn't close.

As the driver navigated the twists and turns and bumps of the unpaved road, a terrified Gita, who had never been on a bus before, looked from the window at a sheer drop into an almost invisible valley below. Every time the bus bounced, she took her mother's hand and smiled nervously.

"It'll be alright," Kamala told her.

"But we're going to fall over the cliff," Gita said.

"The driver is good at what he does," Kamala replied. She put her arm around Gita. "He balances this bus like you balance a waterpot on your head."

"Then he must be good. Does he sing to Lord *Siva*?"

"Like you and me," Kamala replied.

"I wish we'd get there," Gita said.

"In time, my child. Have a little patience."

Ama tenderly stroked Gita's long black hair, and said, "Remember, that no matter where you are, I will always love you. Whatever happens in the future, know that you live in my heart."

"Oh *ama*," Gita said as she put her head on her mother's lap. "I love you, too. You also live in my heart."

The winding dirt road forced the bus driver to make many sharp turns. Gita and Kamala bounced up and down, laughed and trembled, and looked at the valley thousands of feet below the cliff on their left. *Ama* told Gita that Ganga would be waiting for them in Kathmandu — the cousin who had visited them in Rumla last year. She worked in a merchant's house and was married with two children.

Gita wondered if Jamuna was married and if she still lived in Mumbai.

"How far is Mumbai from Kathmandu?" she asked her mother.

"Why?"

"I thought we could visit Jamuna."

"I'm not sure," Kamala said. "But I know it's a long way."

I'll be there soon Gita mused, and Jamuna and I will fly kites in the fields again and run through the forests together like we used to. After we play a little, I'm going to bring her home. It's better to be home with our mother. We can help her milk the cows and do the farming. Who needs Mumbai, anyway? I'd rather dance in a Rumla temple; I'd rather get water from the river, listen to the animals in the forest, and take care of my little sisters. Why does *bah* want me to go to Mumbai? Why do I have to work there? There's plenty of work to do in my village.

In the crowded Kathmandu bus terminal, people waited for passengers, beggars hustled a living, children hawked cigarettes, postcards and candy, and food and gift carts lined the road, in that seething mass of humanity that congregated where buses came from the remotest areas of Nepal, Kamala pointed to a woman dressed in a sari wearing a shawl that covered her head. "There's Ganga," Kamala said excitedly. After many hugs and kisses, they followed their cousin through a labyrinth of side streets to the merchant's house where she lived and worked.

Gita had never seen such large crowds of people; nor had she ever seen bicycles, taxis, cars and trucks, grocery stores or a shop to buy clothing or a restaurant or a place to get a haircut.

"Is this a holiday or some special Durga festival?" Gita asked her mother.

"Is it too much?" Kamala replied laughing.

"It scares me a little," Gita answered.

"It scared me the first time I saw it too," Kamala nodded. "I still don't know how my cousin lives this way."

✳ ✳ ✳

While Gita played jump rope and tag with her cousins in the backyard of the merchant's house, the sound of their laughter could be heard by Kamala and Ganga in the kitchen. It was a delightful sound, so carefree, so worryless — like the songs of birds flitting about a tree.

"Just listen to them," Kamala said sadly. "Wouldn't it be nice if they never had to grow up."

"What's the matter?" Ganga asked. She saw tears in Kamala's eyes and took her hands.

"Lal has arranged for Gita to work in Mumbai," Kamala replied. She was so upset, that it was difficult to get the words out. "He sold her to an agent and she's leaving next week."

"He was a shit when I knew him years ago and he's still a shit," Ganga said. She put her arms around Kamala and asked her if she'd heard anything from Jamuna.

"Not a word since she left Rumla," Kamala answered. "You know the kind of work they do there."

"I have a friend who works as a cook in a Rana's house," Ganga said. "She told me yesterday that a maid left. They're looking for someone."

"See what you can do," Kamala replied. "I'm not going back to the village till I find a place for her."

"Okay," Ganga said. "Just wait here for me to get back."

* * *

In the early evening, Ganga took Kamala and Gita to the house of Mahesh Bhahadur *Rana* — a middle-aged distant relative of the King of Nepal. They waited in the entranceway until his wife Jali appeared, followed by a female servant whose name was Anuja. Jali was a tall Indian woman with long black hair and brown eyes, about forty years old and the daughter of a Bihar Maharaja. As a child, she had suffered from a mild case of polio and now walked with a slight limp. Her facial skin was soft, and her eyes and smile exuded kindness and compassion. She greeted Ganga and Kamala politely, and asked Gita to come closer.

"Are you the one who wants a job?" Jali asked. Gita didn't reply. She had no idea what Jali was talking about.

"She's the daughter of my cousin," Ganga interjected. "She's a good girl and has been taught by her mother to work hard."

"Do you love your mother?" Jali asked Gita.

"Yes, madam," Gita answered shyly.

"You will keep my house clean?" Jali asked. "Someday, if you work hard, I will have a tutor teach you English."

"I cannot read or write," Gita said in barely a whisper. She backed off a little and looked at Kamala.

"Then he will teach you to read and write Nepalese before he teaches you English," Jali said smiling.

"I can cook," Gita volunteered shyly.

"What do you cook?" Jali asked.

"*Dahl* and rice."

"Nothing else?" Jali asked.

"No madam."

"Then we will have to teach you to cook as well," Jali said. She motioned for Ganga and Kamala to come closer. "I like her very much," Jali said. "She can live here and work for me. I'll pay her forty rupees a day plus room and board. You can visit her whenever you like."

"Thank the goddess," Kamala said.

"You have a beautiful daughter," she said to Kamala. "I will take good care of her."

"Bless you," Kamala answered. She bent over and touched Jali's foot with her hand.

"They're all such gentle souls," Jali said to Anuja. "Somehow they live more in the light of spirit than any of my friends who have far more worldly goods."

Gita didn't know what to make of any of this and when Kamala told her she'd be happy here, a wellspring of emotion rose up and she began to weep. "I thought I was going to see Jamuna in Mumbai," she said nervously.

She couldn't figure out why her mother wanted her to live in this house. Who were these people? Why was her mother going to leave her with them?

"No," Kamala said with a sigh of relief, "you're not going to Mumbai. You have to stay here."

"I don't want to be here, *ama*. I want to be with you."

"Trust me," Kamala said. "Please, I'm asking you to simply trust what I say."

"Will you be here with me?," she asked Kamala.

"No. I have to return to Rumla."

"You'll be so far away."

"I know my angel, but I will try to visit you as much as I can."

"No, don't go. Please, take me back with you to Rumla."

"I'm going to miss you, Gita," Kamala said, "but I know that the goddess will protect you. You're *Saraswati*, aren't you, and if what the priests say is true, then the goddess will look out for one of her own."

"You're not going to leave now?" Gita asked her mother.

"Yes, my love. I have to go. But you will be fine here. This is a safe house, a good house. These people will take care of you."

"When will I see you again?"

"Soon…soon. Remember where you really live," Kamala said pointing to her own heart. "You will always be with me."

"Yes, *ama*, I will always be with you," Gita said.

Her eyes were fixed on her mother whom she embraced one last time, and when Kamala moved towards the door, Gita wanted to chase her, but stood frozen in her tracks, not believing that *ama* was leaving. She felt the empty chill of abandonment — a knot in her stomach and tears in her eyes. For the first time in her life she couldn't conceal her emotions — the deep well of sadness of being a child left behind; and when she heard the sound of the closing front door, it was like a death knell, and Gita said to herself in a whisper, *"Ama, ama, why am I here?"*

⁂

"I've worked in the *Rana's* household for over thirty years," Anuja said to Gita.

The size of the house frightened Gita. She had lived all her life in a mud hut in Rumla and couldn't fathom the high ceilings, the marble floors, and the gold-painted furniture. It seemed dreamlike to her, otherworldly — like she had stepped into one of the fables Rumla village elders would tell at night before the children went to sleep.

They walked up a winding marble staircase to the second floor.

"Can you imagine going up and down these stairs twenty times a day," Anuja added as she struggled to catch her breath.

She was a mouse-like woman, about sixty years old, with black squinty eyes and a long nose with skin so heavily wrinkled that Gita wondered if Anuja's years of service as a domestic in the *Rana's* house had taken its toll. She wore an English maid's outfit, and told Gita, in a squeaky, but still imperious voice, that it was her duty to oversee other domestics and report directly to Jali.

"When I first came to the *Rana's* house," Anuja said, "I ran up and down these steps without any trouble. But now — I don't know how much longer I can do it."

Gita had never seen a hut like this before, and she wanted her mother to know about it. There was a shiny stone floor Anuja called marble that glittered in the sun and a light in the entranceway that hung from the ceiling like a giant snowflake; and different kinds of gold-painted furniture, and room after room of beds and glass things they called mirrors, and so many other strange decorations she didn't even know where to begin.

Ama, did you ever see a round bowl with water? Anuja says that's where they go to the toilet. If I push a button, water will flow down like a small stream, and everything disappears.

"Don't ever touch the dishes in that cabinet," Anuja warned Gita. They were walking past a large rosewood breakfront on the second floor. Anuja told her that each of those ugly painted things was worth more rupees than Gita would make if she worked in this house for the rest of her life.

"If you break one," Anuja said in a hushed voice, "it's the quickest way to become the *Rana's* slave. You'll have to work without receiving a rupee until he thinks it's paid for."

"And that?" Gita pointed to a large oil painting of a man who wore a topi and dressed in a military uniform. The stern look on his face frightened her.

"It's the *Rana's* grandfather," Anuja explained. "There are paintings of his ancestors all over the house. I'm told the family is more than five hundred years old."

The servant's quarters were on the fourth floor and Anuja took Gita to a small room with a single bed, a mirror, a table, and a closet.

"You will sleep here," she said, "and there's a clean maid's outfit on the bed. You are to change immediately and meet me downstairs in the kitchen."

Change into what, Gita asked herself when Anuja left the room, this strange costume that no village girl in her right mind would wear. The monkeys in the forest would laugh at me; the priests would never let me dance in the temple. When she finally shed her clothes and put on the maid's costume, she had to laugh when she saw her reflection in the mirror. She looked more like a black and white parrot than a temple dancer from Rumla.

"Your job is to scrub the floors every day from the house entrance to the servant's quarters," Anuja said when she and Gita met in the kitchen. She handed Gita a few rags and two buckets and told her to fill them with water.

While filling the buckets with water, she told herself that she wasn't like Anuja. She won't spend thirty years in this house and become a wrinkled old maid gasping for air with the ghost of a faceless young girl trailing behind her. The very thought of working in Jali's house for one day frightened Gita. She just wanted *ama* to take her home.

CHAPTER EIGHT

Gita opened the airplane window shade and looked out at a star-filled sky. She checked to see if Daniel was sleeping, kissed him on the cheek, placed the rumpled blanket over him again, and continued to muse about her early life in Kathmandu.

From the moment she stepped foot in the *Rana's* house, Jali had been kind to her. Although Gita had a room of her own, and extra money, although she had learned to read, write and even to speak a little English, although she no longer mopped the floors, but was given the lighter tasks of dusting Jali's bedroom, of keeping the living and dining rooms clean, of polishing silver and making the *Rana's* family beds in the morning, and sometimes helping the cook prepare sophisticated meals for guests, she would have traded all of it for the opportunity to dance in a temple in her village.

It was late afternoon — almost a year after Gita began to work at the *Rana's* house. There was a shaded arbor next to a small goldfish pond in the garden — a place she'd go after finishing her chores in order to practice dance steps. Jali had just returned from high tea at the King's palace and went into the garden. She wanted to see the bougainvillea and rhododendron trees, to take in some fresh air and meditate, but instead, she saw Gita dancing in the arbor, and Jali was struck by the delicacy of the girl's movements. She had never seen a Nepalese dancer with that kind of grace. There was spirituality in the girl — something so profound that it touched on the transcendent; and in her excitement, she asked Gita if she would perform for guests that were coming to dinner that night.

"Someone who dances like you," she said to Gita, "should have a role in life more important than a household servant."

Gita was trained to dance for Lord *Siva*, not guests at a party, and the priests in Rumla would forbid her to reveal the sacred steps she had learned to an audience of drunken Nepalese and foreign dinner guests. At first, she refused, but Jali continued to ask until she agreed to perform short village pieces that her mother had taught her many years ago. Her performance was such a success that Jali asked her to do it again; and Gita finally realized that dancing gave her a more important position in the *Rana's* household.

* * *

Jali was taken by how well Gita danced and was drawn to the simple beauty of the girl — a purity she rarely, if ever, found in her immediate circle of friends. She'd treat the child as a confidante and took her on excursions to different places of interest in Kathmandu. One of her favorites was the Swayambunath *stupa* — the so-called Monkey Temple on top of a hill in the western part of Kathmandu — a place where Hindus and Buddhists have worshipped for hundreds of years.

They climbed three hundred and sixty-five steps up a hill path that led to the *stupa*, where monkeys grabbed food from the hands of unwary pilgrims and tourists. They were not like the Rhesus macaques that lived in the forest near Gita's village — their constant chitchat had often entertained her as she walked to and from the river. These monkeys were city creatures, more at home with the intensity of Kathmandu life than Gita was herself and were considered sacred by religious people who visited the temple. When these pesky primates grabbed food from a pilgrim's hands, it was considered an offering to the gods and many benefits would accrue.

Gita gave a slice of cake to a monkey that stealthily walked up to her, snatched the offering, and scampered away. She made a silent wish. "Hanuman...more than anything, I want to see my mother," she said to the monkey who now sat on a stone pillar at the side of the path eating the goody. "Please bring her to Kathmandu."

* * *

She was now sixteen years old. A strikingly beautiful young woman, tall and lithe, strong, and dressed in a sari she had bought with her own money, Gita stood in front of a mirror in her room, admiring herself as sixteen-year-old girls often do.

Although small, her room had become a sanctuary where she could dance as freely as she did in the village temple. Every afternoon, no matter how many chores she had to do, she managed to find time to practice her dance in front of the mirror.

Dashain had ended. It was late in the afternoon on a day Gita would never forget. She had purchased a CD in the market of early Hindu poems that inspired her dance. The singer's voice had touched a place in her heart and reminded Gita of priests chanting in her village. Happy and alive, graceful and joyous, Gita moved her arms and legs in devotion to the goddess Durga, not aware that Mahesh Bhahadur *Rana* stood in the doorway and watched her dance. He was a tall heavyset man with graying hair, dark skin, thin lips, black eyes, a wrinkled brow and slightly hunched shoulders. His face was bloated from excessive alcohol, and his well-fed belly hung over his pants, and his body smelled from the daily use of spikenard and cumin cologne. When she saw him in the mirror, Gita immediately stopped dancing and turned around.

The *Rana* never came to the servant's quarters unless he was paying a visit to his mistress Shanti — a twenty-two-year-old Rajbansis girl who had been working in Mahesh Bhahadur's house for seven years. Her room was down the hall from Gita's. The night before, the cook had told Gita that Shanti ran away with a Newari stonemason, got married, and went to live in his cousin's house in Pokhara. Although the *Rana* had never spoken to Gita nor paid her any mind, she feared this man who ruled his household like a tyrant.

"You dance like no one I've ever seen," Mahesh Bhahadur *Rana* said to Gita. "Like *Devi*, herself."

"Thank you," she replied, as he approached her. She didn't know why he was in her room, but pulled the train of her sari over her face. She could smell the stale odor of cigarette smoke on his breath and the sickening sweet scent of cologne.

He touched her hair and moved his hand slowly from her face until it reached Gita's breast. She pushed his hand aside and backed away.

"Leave me alone," she cried.

"I can make you very happy," Mahesh Bhahadur *Rana* said. His front teeth were stained and had gold and silver inlays with a large gap, and his tongue moved in and out of his mouth.

"Take your hands off me," Gita pleaded.

He put his arm around her waist and pulled her to him. "This can be easy or difficult," he said. "It's up to you."

"No," she gasped, "Get away from me."

"I can love you," he said. His hands were now moving all over her body.

"I don't want you to love me," she said trembling and pleaded with him to stop.

"Easy or difficult," he laughed.

When Gita scratched him and punched him and tried to escape, he grabbed her by the wrist and slapped her in the face. After throwing her to the ground, the *Rana* told Gita in a gloating voice that he had slept with many women.

"Please, leave me alone," she begged, now too frightened to do anything but lie beneath his wide spread legs. He slapped her again and again until she lay barely conscious on the floor. Then he ripped off her sari and raped her.

"If you tell anyone," he said to her after satisfying himself, "you'll be sold to girl traffickers. They'll take you to Mumbai and you'll spend the rest of your life in a brothel as a whore."

Curled up in fetal position, her aching thighs covered with blood, and feeling like he used a knife to cut open the walls of her vagina, she was ashamed and angry and full of fear.

"You're mine now, do you hear. You're my mistress," he said to her. "I'll come here twice a week, but remember one thing, next time don't resist me. I can be gentle. I know how to love a woman, and remember Gita dear," he said just before he left the room, "no one's to ever know about this."

The cracks in the ceiling moved in and out of Gita's fading consciousness. Was she in a dream? Only the unbearable pain in her throbbing vagina reminded her that she'd been raped. No matter how hard she tried to rid Mahesh Bhahadur *Rana* from her thoughts, he was there, all one meter, eighty of him, with his hunched back and big belly; he was there, and she was his mistress — not knowing where to go or how to get rid of him.

No longer a virgin and now the shame of her family, neither her mother nor her cousin Ganga would believe the *Rana* had raped her. Even if they did — so what! Who would want her? Not with Mahesh Bhahadur *Rana* coming to her room twice a week. She wanted to scream, but knew how futile a scream would be, how easily she could be put onto the streets; not having the power to combat him, Gita had to leave his house, but didn't know where to go or who would take her.

In the bathroom, she filled two buckets with hot water and scrubbed her body over and over again to rid herself of the sweet sickening smell of Mahesh Bhahadur *Rana*; and she cursed him and her mother and cousin for having brought her to this house.

"I'd rather live on the streets," she repeated over and over again.

After scrubbing herself, but incapable of washing away the wound that cut deeply into her mind and emotions, she could still feel his penis violating her person like an uncontrollable fire roaring through a forest; and the memory of it drove a sixteen-year-old girl to the limits of her reason.

She could never again look in the mirror without seeing the *Rana's* filthy hands pawing her body, his rock hard penis entering her vagina, and blood splattered all over her thighs.

Gita returned to her room, got into bed, and tossed and turned most of the night. Vengeance is possible, she thought, even killing the *Rana*; but she lay in bed, helpless, alone, frightened, not knowing where to turn or what to do. Unable to erase from her mind the nightmare she'd been through, it was like some brutal force of nature that shifted the very core of her being.

The first light of dawn had filtered through her bedroom window before Gita fell asleep only to wake up a few hours later and run to the bathroom. She scrubbed her body again, but the wound, so embedded in her mind and emotions, left a permanent scar no amount of scrubbing could remove. Timid and wary, afraid that every person in the *Rana's* household would find her culpable and want to toss her out onto the street, she couldn't shake the horrible thought that she was now his mistress. He would come to her room twice a week.

Jali hadn't risen as yet and Gita dusted the living room furniture without being interrupted. Certain that whomever she met would instantly recognize her loss of virginity — her wound was so apparent it could never be hidden — Gita avoided her fellow workers until hunger demanded that she go into the kitchen for some breakfast. She asked the cook if the *Rana* was still at home.

"He left for Bihar early this morning," the cook replied giving Gita a suspicious glance.

"When will he be back?"

"Why do you care?" the cook growled. "You got something for him?"

"No," Gita responded. "I was just wondering." She didn't know what else to say to this difficult woman.

"He'll be back tomorrow at noon," the cook said in a huff, "with special guests. His highness wants me to prepare a feast and I'm going to need your help."

"Just tell me what you want me to do," Gita replied.

The cook's jarring nature irritated Gita who was about to leave the kitchen to resume her chores.

"Jali treats you like her own daughter," the cook said in a jeering voice. She grabbed Gita by the arm and stopped her from leaving the kitchen. "Do you know why?"

"No," Gita answered.

"To keep her husband from sleeping with you."

Gita stared at her without saying a word. She was about to cry.

"Madam once told her sister who was visiting from Bihar that she's got to protect you; she's got to preserve the innocence and spirit she sees in your dance."

"Why?" Gita asked in a whisper.

"Because the *Rana* always has sex with the most beautiful young peasant girls that work in this house," the cook said laughing maliciously. "Now that Shanti's gone, you'd better watch out."

Gita just stared at her. She was angry and frightened, but didn't know how to respond.

Madam Jali can do nothing about her husband's philandering, the cook told Gita. Her marriage contract stated that if they ever divorced, the *Rana* would sever her family's business connections in Nepal. There was nowhere for her to go but into the bed of a filthy pig that always stinks from another girl. If she divorced him, Madam Jali would become an outcast. Her family would never take her back.

Jali is also a prisoner in this house, Gita thought, and it's so easy for the *Rana*. He's always off to Bihar, back with guests, having dinners and parties, off somewhere else, and we're trapped in this cage.

Gita went upstairs to Jali's room, knocked, and when no one answered, she entered and began to make the bed.

"Oh, Gita," Jali cried out from the hallway. "Where are you?" She entered the room and said, "There you are, my precious. I want you to go shopping with me. Let one of the other servants finish here."

"Yes madam," Gita replied in a timid voice.

"Is there something wrong?" Jali asked her.

"No. Nothing is wrong. Just let me finish making the bed."

Does Jali know what her husband did to me? Can she see it in my face? Why did she ask me if something was wrong? She wondered how a woman as kind as Jali could be married to such a brutal man as the *Rana*.

"There's the car," Jali said looking out of the bedroom window. "Let's shop for saris today."

Determined to hide her feelings, Gita forced a smile and hoped to conceal last night's horror. For her to spend the day with this kind and caring woman whose company she usually enjoyed, was nothing short of anguish.

"Can you dance at my party tomorrow night?" Jali asked Gita after they settled into the back seat of the car.

"If that's what Madam wants."

Jali told Gita that most of her guests would be foreign, and they knew nothing about the customs of Nepalese villages. She had an antique Nepalese dress that would fit her perfectly.

She knows about the customs of her husband, Gita thought bitterly, and can do nothing about them?

"I want to buy you a sari," Jali said. "You're so beautiful, Gita. If you were born in a wealthy family, a smashing match could be made for you."

Like your animal of a husband? Gita thought. I'd rather be dead than married to a rich man who rapes his servants. Again, she wondered how Jali could have married such a beast. Adrift in her own thoughts, Gita was startled by Jali's cheerful voice announcing, "Here we are. Let's look at saris."

There were many shops in the marketplace that sold saris, but Jali liked a particular one where the owner always welcomed them like long-lost relatives. He asked Gita and Jali to sit on large cushioned bolsters at the edge of a room. The floor was covered with stark white sheets of paper. He ordered an employee to bring the finest Benares silk saris and tossed them one after another onto the white paper. As they unrolled, an array of dazzling hand-woven floral prints and gold and silver-threaded brocade stood out like a kaleidoscopic color fantasy. He unrolled sari after sari until Jali chose six of them and told the owner to send the bill to her husband.

"Which one do you like?" Jali asked Gita.

"It doesn't matter," Gita said.

"No, choose one. It's a little thank-you for dancing tomorrow night."

Gita wanted to tell Jali that all the wealth, the large houses, the foreign guests, the saris and parties could never change what Mahesh Bhahadur *Rana* had done to her.

"This one," Gita said pointing to a very colorful one with a floral print.

"That's my favorite, too," Jali said. "Now let's go get a sweet."

They went into an ice cream parlor and both of them asked for a scoop of vanilla. Not having an appetite, Gita ate half the ice cream and left the rest in the dish.

"Is that all you want?" Jali asked.

"I'm sorry," Gita responded. "I just don't feel well today."

"Then let's go home. You can rest a little while I prepare for the party."

Never in her young life had Gita felt so alone. She tried to conceal the deep sadness that had engulfed her, but despite many efforts to ward off emotion, she began to cry.

"What's wrong?" Jali asked her.

"I miss my mother," Gita said. "I wish I could see her."

"I'll send a message to your village," Jali said and stroked Gita's long black hair.

"No. I don't want to worry her."

"If you need to talk about something, I'll be happy to listen."

Gita wiped the tears from her eyes and said, "It's alright. I just had a bad moment."

Jali studied Gita's unhappy face — the same sadness she had seen in other girls that worked in her house. "It's my husband," she gasped out loud in horror, now fully understanding Gita's problem. "You poor child. Shanti's gone, and my pig of a husband has gotten to you. Someday," she said through her own tears and looking for words, "someday, I will kill that man."

* * *

Late the next afternoon, Mahesh Bhahadur *Rana* came to Gita's room. She didn't fight him this time. When he finished and had buttoned up his pants and put on a kurta, she rolled over to face the wall.

"I brought you a present from Bihar," Mahesh Bhahadur *Rana* said to her. "I thought it would look nice on you." He gave her a very beautiful printed Kashmiri silk scarf. "But don't wear it when my wife is around."

With hatred in her eyes, she stared at him, and said, "I'll rip it to shreds if you don't take it back."

He just looked at her without responding.

"How do you wipe off a spot of dirt so embedded in your soul that nothing can remove it?" she asked.

"What?"

"Nothing, Mahesh. Do you mind me calling you Mahesh? Are we familiar enough so I can do that?" She threw the scarf at him. "Take it. I don't want your filthy presents."

He picked up the scarf. "I'll be back Thursday afternoon," he said menacingly. "Don't give me any trouble. I can be a very dangerous person."

That evening, after she danced for Jali's guests, Gita bowed graciously, smiled, and thanked everyone. She hurried back to her room, packed a few belongings, paused for a moment, then descended the long staircase, made her way to the pantry and quickly fled the house through a rear door. She disappeared into a maze of pitch-black streets in Kathmandu's old city.

CHAPTER NINE
(June 2010)

Indian Airlines flight 2107 landed in Kathmandu at ten o'clock in the morning. Daniel and Gita gathered their belongings, and left the airplane and stepped onto the tarmac. Intense heat and high humidity greeted them, a heat so unbearable it reminded Daniel of the worst August days in New York City.

They entered the crowded Tribhuvan International Terminal — a place where Indian, Tibetan, and Nepalese families traveling to Pokhara, Calcutta, Delhi, and Lhasa, nestled together on tattered blankets, where beggars and hustlers and taxi drivers vied with porters for people's luggage, where birds fed off scraps of bread on the floor, where half-starved dogs walked lazily from garbage pail to garbage pail, and hoards of beggars harassed tourists for rupees.

On the other side of a glass partition, Daniel spied his sister Diana, and her husband Bob, the American ambassador to Nepal with a Nepalese man dressed in an army uniform. The three of them wove their way through a seemingly impenetrable mass of people and moved quickly past customs and immigration to where Daniel and Gita waited on line with passports in hand.

"You look marvelous," Diana said to Gita. "So chic. New York living really suits you."

"Wherever Daniel is, that's what suits me," Gita replied.

Daniel gave Diana a big hug and kiss. "Amazing," he said. "It's been almost five years and it feels like a few days have gone by. Mom and dad send their love."

"This is Ashok," the ambassador said, introducing the Nepalese man. "He's the airport manager."

"Come with me," Ashok said. He led them to the front of a long line and showed the immigration officer their documents.

"Have your boy collect the luggage," the manager said to the ambassador. "I've arranged everything. He'll be able to clear the bags through customs. Now, let's get out of here."

"Sara's in Paris," Diana said to Gita as the car pulled out of the airport parking lot.

"She's with Jacques," Gita replied.

"You should see them together. They're madly in love. They left Kathmandu a month ago, and oh, Gita, how I miss her. But Bob and I are thrilled that she's so happy."

"I'm not surprised," Gita said playfully.

"Why?"

"She wrote me a long email about his exhibition at the French consulate gallery, how they met there and fell in love."

"Confiding in her best friend?" Diana asked with a smile.

"As girls will do," Gita answered.

"It all happened so quickly."

"What's he like?" Gita asked. "Is he gentle?"

"You can see the love he has for Sara in the beautiful sketches he's done of her dancing."

"C'est la vie," Bob sighed. "I've lost my little girl."

"Oh Bob, it's about time she left Kathmandu," Diana said. "I didn't know it would happen this way, but I'm happy she's living with the man she loves in a city as beautiful as Paris."

Diana reached into her purse and took out a letter. "It's for you," she said to Gita. "From Sara. It arrived by post yesterday."

Gita opened the seal and read it.

My precious sister,

I think about you so much. I remember the times we had together, the dances you taught me, and the concerts we went to. Without you, my growing up in Nepal would have been empty. I can't tell you how much I love you, how grateful I am for all you taught me about dance. I wish I could have met your mother, and that I could have danced in the temple you danced in as a child. If you ever go back to your village, please place a flower for me on the altar. Thank the goddess for having given us the opportunity to be her little sisters.

Know that I miss you Gita, and I can't wait till we're together,
Sara

P.S. I'm performing a solo dance concert next week at an Asian Cultural Center on Boulevard Saint-Michel. Wish me luck — S.

"This is a hell of a time to come to Nepal," Diana said. She took both Gita and Daniel's hand.

"Yeah, I know," Daniel, replied. "It's like taking a vacation in a steam room."

"But why?" Diana chuckled.

"To have lunch with you and Bob at the Hotel Yak and Yeti," Daniel answered, "then visit Gita's village tomorrow. You know better than anyone, Diana. She hasn't seen her mother or sisters in years.

"That's quite a trip," Diana said.

"We're hoping it will be a second honeymoon," Gita replied.

"I'll arrange for an air-conditioned SUV and a driver," Bob said.

When they arrived at the Marshal's residence, the chauffeur pulled the car into the driveway.

"You know I was a little worried at first," Diana whispered to Daniel. They were walking together towards the front door of the house.

"About what?" Daniel asked.

"Your marriage," she winked and took his hand. "There was a great cultural divide and I was afraid you wouldn't make it."

"We crossed that bridge a long time ago," Daniel said to her. "It's funny how love has a way of making things work."

"I can see," Diana smiled after kissing Daniel lightly on the cheek.

✳ ✳ ✳

The trip to Rumla…

Daniel looked out from the tinted window of the Toyota SUV at jagged snow-covered peaks that hovered over them like a painting done by a visionary artist depicting the earth touching the sky. He recognized that time had no relevance here. If he were to die now, it would be okay, because life and death were woven together like ancient Chinese brocades. Some demon god constructed these mountainous citadels, caring less about human wellness than building a path to eternity. If there were living gods, they must reside in the Himalayas.

He was like a pup licking the feet of ancient history, trying to understand how a coterie of gods and goddesses could create destiny in the minds of true believers. It made him turn inward; it frightened him and inspired him to such a degree that he was forced to reevaluate his very existence…

Gita took Daniel's hand, squeezed it, and watched the rugged landscape move past them. For her, the towering peaks and deep chasms acted like a timer on an explosive devise that ignited her cache of memories, memories that she had kept buried even from herself for a long time. Why did Kamala abandon her in the Rana's house? Why did she never see her mother again?

Gita couldn't understand what *ama* had done. She was her daughter and you don't leave your daughter alone in a stranger's house — a stranger who raped young girls.

A bus came down the narrow mountain road and their driver pulled the SUV to within inches of the edge of a cliff that dropped thousands of feet into the unknown. Gita and Daniel giggled nervously and waited for the bus to creep past them and continue its descent.

His Sensei talked about the same nothingness Daniel saw in the vast spaces that separated the mountains. How did he discover this? Did he live in the Himalayas? It was clear to Daniel that ambition was a hopeless thing when confronted by the remoteness of mountain life, by a culture that believed survival was the most the world had to offer. He saw peaks of such monumental proportion they towered above the other mountains like giant trees shading saplings. He wondered if any of them were Everest or the Annapurna massif.

It's the earth flexing its muscles, he smiled — the power of youth showing off...

Could Daniel deal with the poverty of Rumla — her father's drunkenness, the mud huts, and the day-to-day struggle to survive? Gita thought. Could her parents ever accept a westerner as her husband? And Prema and Renu? Were they married? Did they have any children? Were they happy with their lives? She wondered if Jamuna was still in Mumbai? Wouldn't it be great if she were home? Wouldn't it be great to see her once again?

Gita couldn't shake the fear of once again meeting her mother. She had always loved Kamala, but after she was raped, the trauma was so deep, Gita never wanted to see her again. She swore that *ama* and the rape would be erased from her memory. For so many years she was afraid to go back to her home...

Daniel observed that everything here waited patiently for the universe to take its course. There was nothing to do, nowhere to go, and it was all perfection in and of itself, it was all part of the evolution of consciousness. He would have liked to practice law in these mountains, to find justice where there wasn't any, to negotiate contracts with time, to balance nature's long-term investment in evolution, to find man's rightful place...

Oh, my dearest *ama*, Gita thought letting go a little of her deeply held anger. If you are still in Rumla, if you are still alive, let's hold each other and drown out the past. Shanti ran away. You couldn't have known anything about that hideous *Rana*. I will forgive you and hope you will forgive me for not coming home all these years...

"Daniel, I don't know what to do," she whispered.

"Tell me darling. Do about what?" he asked coming out of his reverie.

"My mother, my sisters, the village I left behind so many years ago. I'm frightened, Daniel. What if my mother's dead? What if my sisters no longer live there?"

"It'll be okay," Daniel said softly.

He put his arm around Gita and kissed her gently on the cheek, hoping that his warmth would calm her anxieties.

"It's probably better to wait until we get to your village and see what's happened after all these years," he said to her.

"You really are a dear," Gita finally smiled. She kissed him on the lips. "With all your wisdom in law, you're still an innocent. I know you so well, Daniel. You're trying to make sense of this place, but the moment we think about it we destroy its essence, we take away its beauty, we try to become gods."

"But men create gods," Daniel said laughing.

"No, my love, men are not powerful enough to create gods. All men die one day, but the gods live in these mountains through eternity. They make sure that our prayers find a channel to the Infinite."

"Then why are you afraid?"

"I'm human, aren't I? I love my mother and I want to help her live a better life."

"She can live with us in New York?"

"Perhaps," she said, "or someplace like Kathmandu where we can buy her a house and pay for servants."

"Maybe near Boudhanath," he said, "or in Patna. Let's see what happens when we get to your village."

The car pulled into a small town nestled against a mountain. Daniel made arrangements with the driver to wait for them no matter how long it took to return. They got out of the SUV and put on their backpacks.

"Are you ready? Gita asked. "Now the real trip begins. It's an eight-hour walk through the forest to Rumla."

CHAPTER TEN

The village of Rumla — frozen in time — no different than Gita remembered it thirteen years ago — the mud huts with thatched roofs, the piles of cow paddies, the chickens, water buffaloes, goats and dogs moving and waddling about, the unpaved road, and a handful of villagers working in the fields. Thirteen years had gone by, and Rumla still had no electricity, plumbing, telephones or any of the hundreds of other modern conveniences.

Gita and Daniel walked slowly to her family's hut among familiar childhood faces: her uncles Ram and Pemba, her aunts Najju and Pima, and even the parents of childhood friends, wrinkled with age, somehow seeming tiny as if the world she remembered had shriveled up and become microscopic.

"I'm Gita," she said to them. "Gita. Do you remember me?" But, they just stared at her with inquisitive eyes. She was nothing to them but a stranger. Some of the men and women gathered around Daniel. They were, after all, poor peasants who had never seen a white man. One elderly woman squinted to see Daniel better, moved a little closer, touched his hand, and giggled before running to hide behind a sleeping water buffalo. The other peasants laughed.

Gita recognized her father — the man who had dominated her household when she was a child, the man she had once considered godlike and omnipotent. Now he sat cross-legged in front of the family hut — his thick black hair had thinned and grayed, his bloated face was covered with red pockmarks, and his wiry arms and legs were like string.

She gasped and took Daniel's hand.

"That's my father," she said to him in English. "He's gotten so old."

Lal continued to stare into space as Gita approached him.

"*Bah*," she said.

He didn't look at her, but drooled over himself, and quickly ran his hands through his hair and made screeching animal sounds like a monkey in distress.

"*Bah*," she said again, without getting an answer. She knelt before him and touched his foot. "I've missed you and *ama* so much," she said to him in Nepalese. "It's been a very long time since we've seen each other, over thirteen years. Oh! *Bah!*" Gita's eyes filled with tears, frustration, sadness, and disbelief. She was assaulted by waves of powerful emotions. "What happened, *bah*, what happened?"

"Too much *rakshi*."

The words came from a woman standing behind Gita. With a belated shock of recognition, Gita realized it was her Aunt Gauri — a thin woman, about five-feet tall, with black hair, brown eyes, and a nose like a hawk. "He drank so much, he destroyed his own mind," she told Gita.

"Aunt Gauri?" Gita said, still taken by surprise.

"Who are you?" the woman asked.

"I'm Gita. Gita. I'm Kamala's daughter."

This aged woman leaned on a makeshift cane carved out of devdar wood. She shook her head and replied, "Gita was killed in a landslide."

"Is that what my mother told you?"

"Yes. Ask anyone in the village."

"No, it's not true. *Ama* took me to Kathmandu where I worked in a *Rana's* house. Now I live with my husband in America."

"It can't be," Gauri said. She looked carefully at Gita, examining her face and hair and hands. "All these years I believed Gita was dead." She lifted her hand and gently touched Gita's face. "But it is you, my child. It is you," she said with tears in her eyes. "I thought you were buried in a landslide," she gasped. "Your mother told me you were dead."

"Why?" Gita asked. "Why would she do that?"

Gauri stopped short, looking at Daniel.

"It's alright," Gita said. "Tell me more. He doesn't understand our language."

"She was afraid of him," Gauri said pointing at Lal. "She had to get you out of the village. If you stayed, she knew what was in your father's head, and that would have ruined your life."

"What?" Gita replied trembling. "What was in my father's head?"

"He would sell you to girl traffickers."

The shock of this revelation forced Gita to withdraw into herself. She stood in front of her Aunt Gauri without moving, without saying a word. A fleeting image of herself living out her father's plan crossed her mind. She took Daniel's hand and squeezed it. "It's unbelievable," she finally said out loud in English. "Just unbelievable."

"What is it?" Daniel asked her. "What's going on?"

Without answering him, Gita stared in stony silence at Gauri. She realized that her aunt had just confirmed the fear that always lurked deep within — one she had never wanted to face.

"Come, my child," Gauri said. "Let me hold you. I won't believe you're real until I put my arms around you."

The two of them embraced.

"She was afraid you'd wind up in a Mumbai brothel like your sister Jamuna," Gauri said.

No, Gita thought with horror. Could it be possible?

She clung to Gauri as if she were a child — her body trembling, shaken by the horror she had just heard.

"What," Daniel interrupted again impatiently. "Tell me, Gita, what's happening?"

"In a moment, Daniel, in a moment."

"Jamuna's still in Mumbai," she said to Gauri. The very idea that her sister had been sold into sexual slavery sent shivers through Gita's body.

"They sold every young girl in the village," Gauri went on. "Then they drank *rakshi* day and night and gambled away the money. Look at him. He's become exactly what he was in his life — an animal, a filthy beast."

"Did my father sell my younger sisters, too?" Gita asked breathlessly in disbelief. For a moment she wanted to run away, to disappear, to make believe this was all unreal.

"Yes," Gauri answered. "Thank the goddess that your mother put you in that *Rana's* house."

Ama, Gita thought with tears in her eyes. How courageous she must have been to bring me to Kathmandu. If *bah* knew, he would have beaten her — maybe killed her.

And how wrong Gita had been all these years? How blind? How selfish? She had to see her mother; she had to beg her forgiveness.

"Where's *ama*?" she asked her aunt.

"In the hut," Gauri said sadly. "She's very ill, my child. The goddess could take her at any moment."

"No," Gita said. "First my sisters and now my mother. It can't be true."

"Yes, it's true," Gauri, replied. This tiny woman, strong and loving, held Gita in her arms.

The ground beneath Gita felt more like quicksand than solid clay. She clung to Gauri not wanting to believe that her entire family had disassembled; somehow believing that she was to blame for having spent so many years away from the village.

Lal began to squeal again like a sick monkey.

"What's going on?" Daniel asked Gita again. "Can't you translate for me?"

Gita struggled with her thoughts. She didn't tell Daniel about her sisters, but she managed to blurt out through her tears, "My Aunt Gauri just told me that *ama*'s very ill. She's in this hut. Please, come with me to see her."

The interior of the hut was dark, humid, and hot, and Gita's mother lay on a cot beneath a closed window. Her thin, old, skeletal body, her entire appearance reeked from a liver ailment. Gita walked up to the dying woman's bed, knelt before her, kissed her hand, and touched her foot.

Shocked by the frail, sickly appearance of her mother, Gita spoke in a tearful voice, "*Ama*! Oh, *ama*! It's me, Gita. It's your daughter come home."

But Kamala didn't respond. Barely breathing, she stared at the ceiling, her eyes glazed over, her skin parched and dry, her delicate body looked like it would shatter if touched — this skeleton of a woman who was once so vibrant and alive lay dying in front of her daughter.

"*Ama*, it's me, Gita," she said again.

"Gita?" Kamala asked in a barely audible voice too weak to even move her lips. "How can it be you? Am I dreaming?"

"No, *ama*, it's me. I will take care of you. I will help you get better."

"No, my angel. I will not get better."

"I will take you to live with me in America," Gita said.

"America? Where's America?"

"I came here with my husband to visit you."

"It's too late. Perhaps the goddess will see to it that I'm born in America in my next lifetime."

"Can we take her to a hospital?" Daniel asked. He put his arm around Gita as they both kneeled on the floor next to Kamala's bed.

"It's ten hours from here, Daniel," Gita answered. "She won't survive the trip."

The smell of death filled both Daniel and Gita's nostrils — the frustration of not being able to call a doctor was unbearable to both of them.

"Where are my sisters?" Gita asked her mother.

"Your father sold Renu to girl traffickers years ago and your brother sold Prema last month," Kamala said in barely a whisper. "They are both in Mumbai."

"How could *bah* and Sivan be so cruel?" Gita asked.

"I have nothing to live for," Kamala went on.

"I missed you so much," Gita said.

"I didn't know you were alive," Kamala replied. "You disappeared from the *Rana*'s house and Ganga had no idea where you went."

"I know."

"Why did you leave, my child?"

"He wanted me to be his mistress."

"The *Rana*?" Kamala asked in a surprised voice. "But his wife was so gracious and kind. She welcomed you like her own daughter."

"Yes," Gita said. "Jali was wonderful. I could never figure out how she married such a demon."

Kamala sighed and closed her eyes. She squeezed Gita's hand and said, "My life is over, but the gods have performed a miracle. They've brought my daughter home to me; they let me know that you are still alive."

She pointed to a framed photo of Prema on the wall and whispered to Gita, "Prema is such a beautiful girl, so good to me and everyone in the village. I want you to find her. You see how kind she is. I want you to get her out of that place. Take her to America. Give both her and Renu a life. Promise me you'll go to Mumbai and get them...promise me," Kamala said as she slipped into a very deep sleep.

"*Ama!*" Gita cried. "Please, don't go away!"

Gita bowed before the sleeping body of her mother.

"I promise, *ama*, I will find my sisters and bring them to America. I will do as you ask."

"She's so peaceful, Gita," Daniel said. "Look at her face. It's like she's slowly moving from the pain of this world to a place where she can have some rest."

"Yes, but I wanted to forgive her; I wanted her to forgive me. It's been so long."

"It's done," Daniel said. "'There's so much forgiveness in this room it could heal the human race."

"Oh, Daniel," she said. "You don't know what's happened here."

"Then tell me."

She paused for a moment to regroup her thoughts and told him that her sisters were all in Mumbai. "They're prostitutes," she said, so angry she could barely get the words out. "They were sold into sexual slavery." Then she told him her mother's wish and how she couldn't betray her. "I've got to find Prema and Renu in Mumbai."

"Who did this?" Daniel asked.

"My father and brother. Can you believe it? They sold both my sisters and spent the money on *rakshi*."

Without saying another word, she showed Daniel the framed photograph of her sister Prema, and her eyes filled with tears.

Her worst nightmare had come true, Daniel thought. He tried to comprehend the horror of parents selling their children; he looked at the mud huts of Rumla, the dirt street, the cows and dogs and chickens and thought he was in the stone ages — poverty that defied all human comprehension. He had once told his sister that one of Kathmandu's charms was how easily a person living there could move in and out of the tenth century. But this was different. How could governments let such poverty exist? How can people suffer like this without anyone giving a shit? What's more precious than one's own child? he asked himself. What's more beautiful than raising someone who's your own flesh and blood?

"Thank goodness you're here," he said to her in a muted voice. "You knew how important it was to come home."

"Yes," she answered in barely a whisper.

"I'm sorry, so sorry, Gita, but I promise, I'll do whatever I can to help."

When Daniel and Gita left the hut after her emotional reunion with *ama*, they heard a group of jeering toughs taunting Gita's father. They were all gathered around Sivan, Gita's twenty-eight-year-old brother, who swigged some *rakshi* from a ceramic pot and shouted for his mother to make lunch.

Gita fixed her eyes on him and realized that Sivan didn't recognize her. "*Ama's* very sick," she said to him softly in Nepalese.

"So what," he shouted. "She should fix lunch anyway." Taken aback by the presence of Gita, he asked, "Who are you?"

"I'm your sister, Gita."

"Gita died years ago in a landslide."

"That's what *ama* told you after she put me in the house of a Kathmandu *Rana*."

"Well, if you're my sister," Sivan said. He paused for a moment and looked at Gita like a merchant examining merchandise in a bazaar. "I can sell you." He grabbed her by the arm and pulled her towards him.

"What the hell," Daniel said without a moment's hesitation, and forced Sivan to release Gita.

"Who's this guy?" Sivan asked her.

"He's my husband."

"Don't give me that," her brother replied. "No one from this village has a white husband." He grabbed her arm again. "A beautiful woman like you is worth many rupees."

"I'm warning you. Don't touch her," Daniel said as he pushed Sivan away from Gita.

"He's a dead man," Sivan said to Gita, angrily.

"Tell them to keep away," Daniel said to Gita.

Before Gita could open her mouth, Sivan pulled out a knife and circled Daniel.

"Don't," she cried to Sivan.

"Shut up, whore!" Sivan leered. "I'm going to kill him, then sell you to traffickers."

Gita's brother lunged at Daniel, but Daniel twisted Sivan's arm and kicked him in the head. As he fell to the ground, his wrist and hand crushed, his head throbbing; he lay in the dust, unable to move, feeling intense pain. Two other men lunged at Daniel and were knocked unconscious. Daniel motioned for the rest of them to come, but they backed away from him, and ran quickly into the forest.

"A great fighter never hurts his opponent," Daniel remembered his Sensei once saying. *"His Qi is so strong, no one will attack him."*

Maybe I'm not a great fighter, Daniel thought, but I'm sure happy to see those shits lying on the ground. Never could he have imagined testing his karate skills in the hinterlands of Nepal — in his wife's village, by a gang of creeps he didn't even know.

"He's my brother," Gita said sadly in English to Daniel, "and he wanted to kill you."

"I'm okay," Daniel said to her. "But, your brother. That's a hell of a way to greet relatives."

"He's drunk," Gita responded, not wanting to tell Daniel Sivan's real motives. When things calmed down, she'd explain it all to him.

"You crazy boy," Aunt Gauri said to Sivan. "Just like your father; just like my husband, you've sold all the women, and now what? Look at him," she pointed to Lal. "Look at the way you'll be in twenty years."

Sivan told his aunt to mind her own business.

"Slime," Gauri replied kicking a stone at Sivan who lay on ground. She told Gita there was no excuse for the way her brother treated guests. "A miracle sister, no less, who all these years I thought was dead. What a foolish boy! He deserved what your husband did to him."

She invited Gita and Daniel to stay in her hut.

"Of course," Gita replied. "Thank you. We'd love to stay there. I can get water from the river or help you prepare dinner. Tell me what I can do."

"Nothing, my child," Gauri said. "Just eat with us."

It was a one-room hut with two open windows, a dirt floor and benches surrounding a small fire pit. The only decoration was a multicolored print of Lord *Siva* nailed to a wall. Gauri lived there with her drunken husband

and two sons who had become part-time agents in the sex trade. Both her daughters had been sold long ago. To support herself she embroidered small textiles that she'd sell to traders who came through the village. It was a meager living, but one that enabled her to breed goats and chickens and raise them for food.

Gauri built a fire from dried cow paddies. She cooked *dahl* and rice and curried goat in honor of her special guests. The usual family fare was *dahl* and rice. Only on important occasions that honored the gods and guests would there be chicken or goat. The smell of curry and cumin filled the hut. It reminded Gita of *Dashain* festivals when she was young.

"Special guests must be treated like gods," Gauri said. She took Gita's face between her hands and shook her head in disbelief. "I can't believe you're here. You don't know how many tears I cried when I heard you were dead."

After dinner, Daniel and Gita sat on a straw mat outside the hut. Dark clouds had formed in the sky foreboding afternoon rains, and the village street was empty, most of its people taking a customary nap to help digest their large midday meal.

Daniel could in no way fathom the journey Gita must have taken from Rumla to a penthouse apartment on Central Park West. He knew so little about her — this beautiful, charming, and talented woman who was his wife — a woman he loved like no other woman, who, in many ways, resembled a lotus flower emerging from muddy waters. Although they'd been sleeping in the same bed for over five years, it was only a few hours ago that Daniel discovered there was more mystery in her than any person he'd ever known.

"You have to tell me what's going on here," he asked her again.

"Sex merchants," she answered sadly. "All the young women in this village have become commodities."

"What about the police?" He asked.

"Here?" Gita responded. "It's a joke. There's no authority in this part of Nepal."

"Poverty certainly twists people out of shape," he said.

"Yes," Gita replied. "The income in Rumla is maybe ten to fifteen dollars a year."

"Couldn't the government do something about this?" He took a few steps onto the deserted street, kicked a rock and scattered a few goats and chickens that were feeding nearby, looked at the mud huts, thatched roofs, fire pits and the abysmal poverty of the place. "Can't the people here get any help?" he asked Gita. "I mean, who the hell would want to live under these conditions if they had a choice?"

Gita said with a note of exasperation, "It's all they know, Daniel. This is their home. Where are they supposed to go?"

"But their village is dying," Daniel replied with some reticence. "All their young women have been sold into slavery. It's too horrible for me to even think about, Gita. In ten years, Rumla will be nothing more than empty huts."

"I'm going to Mumbai to find Prema and Renu," Gita said after a moment's pause.

He knew that Mumbai was a city of sixteen million people — a busy anthill with more secrets than New York. He had been there for three days once. When he thought about the crowded streets, pollution and impossible traffic, he shook his head in disbelief.

"How are you going to do that?" he asked her.

"I'm not sure yet," Gita replied.

She learned today that her mother was a noble soul whose children had been ripped away, who was dying because she had nothing to live for.

"What would you do if it were your sister?" she asked Daniel. "Would you go to Mumbai?"

"We'll go together," he said a little taken aback. He sat down next to Gita. "I want you to know that I will do whatever I can to help you find Renu and Prema."

The village street was empty, except for Gita's father, who sat on the ground in front of his hut. When Gita kneeled in front of him, he began to squeal again. She tried to take his hand, but he pushed her away, jumped up and down, and shouted incomprehensible words sounding more like the shrieks of a monkey than a human being.

"*Bah*," she said softly. "It's Gita. Your daughter."

He continued to jump up and down, and beat his body violently with his hands until he fell into a deep and impenetrable silence.

"Can you believe it? My father was once a respected elder," Gita said to Daniel who sat down next to her. "Too many daughters, no money for dowries, no hope — a perfect target for traffickers."

It pained her to see him like this, but even more painful was the knowledge that *bah* had destroyed her family. She didn't know what to do.

"Just love him," Daniel said, "and forgive him. This village has turned him into an animal."

"How can I forgive what he did?"

Daniel didn't know, but he told Gita that if she didn't forgive him, she would carry these feelings for the rest of her life.

"I just wanted you to meet my parents," she said. "Do you forgive me?"

"For what? Having a past?"

"For getting you involved with my family. Let's face it Daniel, this isn't a second honeymoon."

She had dragged him to Nepal and they found ruins — not like the ruins of Ankor Wat or Pompeii, but the ruins of a family — a village that was turning to dust and children that had been trafficked into slavery.

"Maybe you're right," he said to her. "Maybe this village won't exist in ten years, but it produced you, Gita, this family produced you, and you and I will continue to love each other and the children we're blessed with for the rest of our lives." He put his arms around her and said in a gentle voice, "Take me to the river I've heard you talk so much about. Maybe it will bring some respite."

✳ ✳ ✳

The river's crystal clear water formed pools, eddies, and waterfalls, as its slow, but forceful and contiguous currents cut a path through the mountain — a sacred river worshipped by inhabitants of Rumla. The non-stop sound of its turbulent waters quieted Gita's mind. She kneeled and began to pray. She asked the god *Siva* for help to find her sisters, to take care of her mother, to heal her father, and to give her aunt Gauri and the other villagers a better way of life.

Daniel also kneeled, but he didn't pray. He thought about his Sensei who once told him that there were many paths through life and they all led to the same place. *"It wasn't for us to judge, but to respect diverse beliefs,"* his Sensei said. *"If we all just learned to listen, each path would teach us exactly what we must know to perfect ourselves as human beings. But, there's no one true path. There's only life's multifaceted avenues leading us into the bosom of eternity..."*

If my own heart were as pure as this river, Gita thought, the goddess will guide my mother to a better incarnation.

"Perhaps in New York," she said to herself, "perhaps as my own child. I could love *ama* and take care of her like she once took care of me."

In the distance, Daniel saw a large bier covered with ashes and surrounded by logs. He assumed that it was the cremation grounds — a sacred place where the souls of the deceased are supposed to cross over to a higher plane and commune with the gods. Daniel was fascinated by the simple manner in which the villagers took care of their dead. He had never seen anything like it in the States. He kneeled and washed his hands in the river, and listened to Gita, who told him the following story about the day her cousin Vishnu died:

Her sisters and she had followed the funeral procession to the cremation grounds. They spent an hour praying to Lord *Siva* while the priests burned the body. After the ceremony was over and they were on their way home, Jamuna wanted to return to the biers. *Ama* had once told them that the goddess Kali sanctified the place after every funeral. She would sit there in deep meditation and make sure that the dead person's soul enters the house of Lord Siva.

"But we're not supposed to," Renu said. "It's forbidden to watch the goddess in deep meditation."

"No one will know," Jamuna replied. "Gita could always dance in the temple and ask the goddess to protect us."

So they returned to the cremation ground. They didn't see the goddess Kali there, but instead, seated on the funeral pyre an *Aghori Baba* with blazing black eyes and matted hair down to his waist, a trident painted on his forehead and white and orange stripes painted horizontally on his cheeks and chest. He wore a tiger skin and rudraksha bead malas around his neck, sat in lotus position and chanted *Om Namah Sivaya*. He lifted some ashes from the pyre with both his hands and rubbed them into his hair, his chest, his arms and legs until his entire body was covered, all the time chanting in a soft haunting voice, *Om Namah Sivaya*. They hid in the bushes and watched until the *Aghori Baba* finished his prayers, rose, left the funeral pyre, and disappeared into the forest.

"'I think he lives in a cave on some remote mountain,' Jamuna said.

"'But where is mother Kali?' Renu asked.

"I don't know," Gita answered, "but maybe that was her; maybe she came to the cremation ground in the form of an *Aghori Baba*."

After the next funeral, the villagers returned home, and the three of them went to the pyre to look for the ascetic. He wasn't there. They never saw him again.

"It's like a fairy tale," Daniel said to her, but quietly, and to himself, he mused that Gita had become a strangely different person than he had known before.

"My mother's next incarnation will be a better one," she said, "if I go to the temple and offer myself through dance to the god Yama."

He kissed her gently on the lips and thought that the more he learned about his wife, the more beautiful and mysterious she became...

The wooden temple at the village edge had carved Apsara pillars at its entrance, a small stone statue of Durga and a larger one of Yama — the god of death. Gita and Daniel walked up the front steps to its entrance, took off their shoes and went in; and after Gita bowed before the statue of Yama asking him to help Kamala's soul move through the cosmos to a future life, she rose and commenced her dance.

Daniel watched her every step as if it were a cosmic force — pure, untouched, yet a sentient being, but more godlike than any carving he'd ever seen in a temple, she moved with the grace of a sylvan nymph in an ancient tale.

By the time the dance finished, night had settled on the village. They returned to Gauri's hut, rolled out a mat, and lay down next to each other, snuggled a bit until Gita could hear the slow, rhythmic breathing of Daniel fast asleep. She knew how important family was to him and tried to imagine what Daniel felt about a place like Rumla where poverty and greed had eaten away the very fabric of family tradition. These thoughts evoked memories of her own past; and no matter how much she tried to sleep, Gita, in her own mind, was no different than a traveler on a train moving into the endless night, gazing out a window at one lit image after another darting past.

CHAPTER ELEVEN

Gita stared into the black liquid of the lampless village night and thought back with trepidation of the moment of her escape from Mahesh Bhahadur's *Rana's* house.

The Kathmandu shops were shut, and the maze of dark, narrow streets caused her to lose all sense of direction. She decided to lie down in a doorway and sleep. Before she closed her eyes, Gita chanted in a hushed voice an old *Saivite* mantra that her mother taught her. It asked the god to help and protect her family.

Fearful that the *Rana* would find her, Gita slept in short semi-wakeful periods at a time. She rose at dawn and walked quickly through Old Kathmandu. Dressed in a lungi and trousers, her hair knotted and tangled, her hands, legs and face dirty, she carried a small bag that contained one change of clothing, the sari Jali had given her, some money she had saved, and a photo of her mother. Hungry and unfamiliar with the markets and restaurants of Kathmandu, Gita wished that she'd taken food with her from the *Rana's* pantry.

There were many beggars washing themselves at a fountain. Gita waited in line for her turn, scrubbed her hands, legs and face, and used her fingers to clean her teeth and gums, and was startled when a man approached her who resembled Mahesh Bhahadur *Rana*. She quickly gathered her belongings, but realized that the man was just another beggar who'd come to wash himself. He put his hand out and asked Gita for ten rupees. She scrutinized him carefully, then shrugged her shoulders, and walked away. She entered a labyrinthine network of streets, and continued to walk until she found a square in a remote quarter of Kathmandu's old city. She bought food in small open-air markets, drank water from public fountains, and spent the nights in courtyards of buildings where copper gilt Hindu statues were mounted on walls. Many homeless people slept in these courtyards. They believed that the images of *Siva*, Parvati, and other gods in the *Saivite* pantheon, would protect them from marauders. But on every street and alleyway that Gita walked, in every courtyard and square, like spectres in a bad dream, she saw men that resembled the *Rana*. She couldn't shake herself loose of him no matter where she went.

Gita learned early on that beggars and prostitutes were territorial. On more than one occasion, she was chased from a street corner by ferocious indigents wielding sticks or clubs. They protected locations that gave them easy access to tourists — the prime targets for food and money.

Two months had passed since Gita left Mahesh Bhahadur *Rana's* house. She found a regular place to sleep in a crowded Thamel district courtyard. She lived among street people who congregated there to protect themselves from gangs of kids that roamed Kathmandu. She looked for maid's work every day, but young and alone, without references, in a tattered and dirty sari and threadbare sandals — no one would hire her. She'd often think about wearing the silk sari Jali had given her, but was well aware that the courtyard indigents would rip it off her body or steal it from her bag. She waited for an opportune moment to sell it without being seen by them.

Late one morning, on Durbar *Marg*, after Gita had applied for and was refused maid's work at the Hotel Yak and Yeti, she mingled with crowds of foreigners and discreetly sold the sari to a German tourist for eight hundred rupees.

Her only friend, a sixteen-year-old girl named Devi, slept on a straw mat next to Gita — a half-starved, pregnant urchin who had lived on the Kathmandu streets since she was a child — a girl who'd been raped repeatedly by homeless men, whose mind was almost gone, who sat for hours on her mat and stared into space. Gita would bring her food and water, but Devi refused to eat.

"No!" she screamed. "Why are you feeding me? I'm just going to die anyway. Me and my baby won't live out the day." She pointed at a gilded statue of *Siva*. "Look at the tears in his eyes," Devi said. "He's crying for me and my baby. Each tear is a river, and when I die, I want you to burn my body and throw the ashes into the water. Don't you think it would be a blessing to spend eternity in a teardrop?" She'd laugh another high-pitched laugh until she fell asleep.

One evening, Devi rose from her mat, went to a fountain at the center of the courtyard, and filled a copper pitcher with water. She anointed and blessed each and every beggar telling them she would heal all their ills.

"I am the daughter of Uma," she chanted. "I will bless you. And this child in my belly, it's the baby Indra, the king of the gods. You'd better bow to me if you want to live out the day."

She grabbed a stick from the hand of a blind man and beat herself. "There is pain," she screamed, "and the more pain, the better. I will die, yes, I will die this evening, and when I die, the gods will come and make you rich. Do you want to be rich? Do you beggars want to be rich? Then come and beat me! I tell you it will happen if I die tonight."

"Go back to your mat," Gita whispered to Devi. "You will hurt the baby."

"She's already hurt," Devi said, "but I will heal her. If you beat me with this stick, my baby will be born a god. You! You!" she pointed at two beggars who lay on mats near the courtyard wall. "What are you waiting for? The goddess commands you. She wants you to throw my ashes into the river."

"Come with me," Gita said to her.

"Where?" Devi screamed. "Into the teardrop? Where do you want me to go?"

"To the mat," Gita said softly. "I brought you some food."

Devi ran wildly around the courtyard. She beat beggar after beggar with her stick, until they all got up from their mats, caught her, and threw her to the ground.

"Hit her," an old man screamed. "Give her what she wants."

The indigents beat Devi until she lay unconscious. They cut the head off a live chicken, squirted its blood on the mad girl and continued to beat her until she died.

Gita hid her face in her hands and cried like a scared child. Devi and her baby would be cremated, she thought, and their ashes thrown into the Bagmati River; and Lord *Siva* would shower the world with tears.

Gita rolled up her mat and left the courtyard. Afraid the beggars would beat her as well, she hid in the swarm of people that made its way through the shop-lined Thamel district. She couldn't stop the flow of tears that soaked her sari. The thought of Devi — the traumatized girl beaten to death, the blood that flowed from the headless chicken, the cries of the indigents, and the malevolent looks on their faces — Gita couldn't shake the scene from her mind. She sat on the rim of an ancient, black stone four-niche *chaitya* at the center of a small Thamel square. In each niche there was a carved figure of the Buddha with ceremonial flowers at its base. It was getting dark. The tourists had all disappeared into hotels and restaurants. The few scattered people that remained on the streets were mostly homeless. A teenage boy, legless and seated on a four-wheeled board came up to her and motioned to follow him.

"I will find you a place to sleep," he said. "My name is Aadesh."

He took her through a maze of back alleys into a courtyard full of armless and legless cripples. Lepers, beggars and prostitutes lived in this enclave for the forgotten ruled by a three hundred and fifty pound entrepreneur named Sonam who collected money from indigents he forced to work the streets.

"You come," the legless boy said to Gita. "I'll introduce you to the boss. He'll help you make money."

Aadesh brought her to Sonam.

"What is your name?" the entrepreneur asked her. He shrewdly appraised Gita. To him she was merchandise to be bought and sold.

She didn't answer.

"Where did you come from?

Again, she didn't answer.

"You will work for me," Sonam said with a greedy smile on his face.

"No!" Gita screamed.

She backed up to the entrance of the courtyard. Sonam came after her, but she turned and ran into the alleyway like an ibex chased by a leopard. She ran through streets and alleys until she came to the Royal Palace on Durbar *Marg*. It was after midnight. A homeless family slept outside its walls. Gita lay down on her mat, but a tall woman with a club in her hand threatened to beat her.

"You're not a member of our family," the woman cackled. "You're not welcome."

Gita rolled up her mat and walked from Durbar *Marg* to New Road. The street was empty save for a car or truck that would drive by every few minutes. Tired and not knowing where else to go, she unrolled her mat in the doorway of a building, laid down on it, and closed her eyes. The nighttime silence of this strangely quiet enclave in the center of a noisy city lulled her into a restless dream-filled sleep, where Devi's face and her unborn child appeared and then receded into a limitless void.

CHAPTER TWELVE
(Rumla – June, 2010)

Daniel's steady breathing told Gita that he was fast asleep. She covered his arms and neck with a blanket. On the other side of the tent, Aunt Gauri, her husband, and sons slept like they hadn't a care in the world. The silence was profound, almost deafening. The song of a bird, a dog's bark and the cry of a rooster would occasionally break the stillness on this pervasively starry night. Across the dirt street, in the family hut, her mother's life ebbed away. Gita prayed that with the coming of dawn, she'd have one last chance to tell *ama* how much she loved her. She closed her eyes and tried to sleep, but Gita's mind drifted back to the dramatic events of herself adrift in the indifferent chaos of life on the Kathmandu streets.

✳ ✳ ✳

When she awakened the next morning on New Road, the first thing Gita saw was a sign directly above her head: *St. Christopher's Orphanage: All Are Welcome To The Living God.* She knocked on the door, waited a few moments, and knocked again. After what seemed like an eternity, the door slowly opened, and a white woman dressed in a black robe and coif, greeted her in Nepalese. At first Gita backed away. She had never seen a nun before, and wondered if this strangely dressed person would do her any harm. But the woman had a kind face and soft brown eyes. She smiled and asked Gita to come in.

"I have nowhere to go," Gita said nervously.

"When did you last eat?" the nun asked.

"I don't know," Gita replied.

"My name is Sister Anne," the nun said. Beneath the dirty face and torn sari, the nun recognized in Gita's eyes the familiar sight of a lost soul on the Kathmandu streets.

"Tell me about yourself," she said to Gita in a gentle voice.

"There's nothing to tell," Gita replied.

"Are you from Kathmandu?"

"No. I ran away from a small village in the mountains."

"Why, my dear? What happened?" Sister Anne asked putting her arm around Gita's waist.

"All I want is some food and a place to sleep," Gita said. "I am a good worker."

"Come with me," the nun replied.

With trepidation, Gita entered the orphanage, then followed Sister Anne up a flight of stairs to a small room with a cot, window and cupboard. Its walls were whitewashed and its only decoration was a plastic figure of Jesus on a cross that hung above the cot.

"You can sleep here," Sister Anne said to Gita. "The bathroom is across the hall and someone will bring you a change of clothing. After you wash up, meet me in the kitchen for breakfast."

"And work?" Gita asked. "I want to earn my way."

"There's plenty of work," Sister Anne smiled.

"Thank you," Gita said. "I will not let you down."

Upon receiving a clean sari, Gita went into the bathroom, filled a pail with hot water, then lathered her hair and entire body with soap, scrubbed herself and rinsed off. She cleaned her teeth, put on the sari and looked out the window of her room at the orphanage courtyard. Many children milled about. Boys were playing games of tag and football, and the girls were jumping rope, playing hopscotch, and brushing each other's hair. The sound of children laughing made Gita think about her life in Kathmandu — how lonely she had been, how it had been years since she'd played with other children, how her life there had been full of so much sorrow and pain.

"I am an orphan, too," she said to herself.

Lonely and afraid, unsure of herself, not wanting to see anyone or anything, she lay motionless on the bed and listened to the birdlike sounds of children's laughter rising from the courtyard, until pangs of hunger forced her to get up and go to the kitchen. Sister Anne greeted her with a warm smile and had already prepared breakfast.

✳ ✳ ✳

At least sixty boys and girls lived in the dormitories at the orphanage, all ranging in age from five to sixteen. Most of them were street children picked up by Nepalese and foreign non-governmental organizations that brought health care to the poor and identified homeless children in need of shelter. They attended school on weekdays from early in the morning until mid-afternoon.

Gita's daily work included cleaning the courtyard, washing dishes, and helping to cook lunch and dinner. She also baked bread and did many other tasks the nuns at St. Christopher asked of her. At first, she had little or no interaction with the other children, and spent most of her time alone in deep thought. She tried to reassure herself that the nuns would continue being kind. Not wanting to get close to the other children, fearful that some unforeseen incident would force her to live once again on the streets, she'd find an isolated place and practice her dance. She'd often sit for an hour doing *mudra* — the sacred hand positions the priests had taught her. Sometimes she'd pose like a Dakini or Mother Kali or Lord *Siva* and hold that pose for many minutes.

At first the other children ignored her. Some even poked fun at Gita calling her stuck-up and conceited because she never talked to anyone. But, in time, a few children watched her dance, then more and more of them gathered round and applauded when she finished. Her evening practice sessions became so popular that Sister Anne asked her to stage a performance.

When the children gathered in the courtyard, they were wide-eyed and expectant and sat quietly on the grass waiting for Gita to dance a special dance that commemorated Kali. Each movement would reveal another aspect of the goddess — from her wrathful to most-peaceful modalities; and when Gita finished, the children applauded and their happy faces filled her heart with joy.

At *Dashain*, Sister Anne had invited many friends and sponsors to attend Gita's performance in celebration of the holiday. Among those present were Diana Marshal and her thirteen-year-old daughter Sara. Diana, an attractive woman in her late thirties, was the wife of Bob Marshal, the American Ambassador to Nepal. She'd often volunteer her time to the orphanage and donated considerable sums of money to help run the place.

The dance began with simple hand movements that evoked the eight Tantric Goddesses people worshipped during *Dashain*. The combined movement of her hands and feet told the story of each of these goddesses and how devotees worshipped them to obtain good fortune: the young girl finding a husband and having children, men earning money, and women preparing food from a fertile harvest. The audience sat in rapt silence, and watched Gita recreate the magic of Hindu mythology.

When the performance ended, Sister Anne introduced Gita to Diana and Sara, and Sara, who studied Nepalese and Indian dance at a Kathmandu studio, asked her if she spoke English.

"A tiny bit," Gita replied.

Overwhelmed by the performance, Sara wanted to know where Gita had learned to dance like that.

"In my village when I was a child," Gita replied. "My *ama* taught me."

"Were you a temple girl?" Diana asked Gita.

"Yes," Gita answered shyly.

"Tell me Gita, what is it that brought you here?" Diana asked.

"I ran away from my village."

"Oh, my dear child," Diana said, "why did you do that — your mother must be so concerned. Kathmandu is no place for a young girl as beautiful as you to be on her own."

"I mean…It's nothing…nothing…I don't talk about it," Gita said with a pained expression. She had promised herself that she'd never speak to anyone about events from her past. She wanted to erase them from her memory.

Sara and Gita spent a little time together talking about dance, and Gita showed her a number of simple steps in a piece that praised Krishna.

"How beautifully you move," Sara said. "I'm going to ask my mother if I can take lessons from you."

"I'd like to teach you," Gita said, but with some hesitation.

"Can I study dance with Gita?" Sara asked Diana and Sister Anne.

"Well, why not if that's what Gita wants to do?" Diana said, "and if Sister Anne thinks it's alright."

Sister Anne smiled; she knew this was a match that could only have been made in heaven. "You have my blessing," she replied.

"We have such a big house, mother, with so many rooms," Sara said, "that there has to be a place in it for Gita. How great it would be to learn from her every day."

"Of course," Diana said a little taken aback. She shook her head and smiled at Sara. "But first, I'll have to talk with your father. He's in Bangkok and won't return for a week."

"I'm sure he'll be happy to have Gita live with us," Sara said.

"Let's see," Diana replied.

"Whenever Gita dances," Sister Anne said to them, "I see something so spiritual in her that it brings tears to my eyes."

She didn't even know how to describe what it was, but Gita's dance — it was like some kind of profound and beautiful life force that the nun couldn't even find in herself.

"Take care of her, Mrs. Marshal. Give her a home. Love her and be kind to her. I don't think you'll ever regret it."

Sister Anne was familiar with the plight of many poor, lower-caste village girls without dowries who had to work to help support their families. They could be found in every nook and cranny of Nepalese society, and most of them didn't last long at their jobs. Some disappeared on the streets of Kathmandu; others returned to their villages; and others got married to a member of their own caste and ran away. Thousands of them were adrift in life's economic cesspool, indigent, afraid, and many of them homeless. They were like swarms of insects, with nothing but the food given to them, a place to sleep, and forty rupees a day. Her abbot had talked of charity, of performing good deeds, of being kind to the poor, and there had to be a way for these young people to share in the world's vast wealth. Sister Anne had sheltered scores of homeless children in the orphanage. They came for many different reasons, but all of them were desperately in need of love and shelter; and she was wise enough not to ask them any questions.

"What else can I do to help?" Diana inquired.

"To give this child a home would be a great blessing," Sister Anne replied.

"Yes," Diana replied compassionately, "it would be a blessing."

That evening and the next day, Gita wondered if it was wise to leave the orphanage and live in a strange house. She felt safe with the nuns. There were no men to hurt her, and she had a place to sleep and food to eat. For the first time in many months, she lived a quiet, happy life. The orphanage was a safe haven. Why leave?

But Diana and Sara seem like good people, she thought. They donated time and money to help the street children, and Sister Anne very much wanted them to attend the performance today. Did she arrange all this on purpose? I don't know. Maybe, I can ask her later.

"It would be a dream to live in the Marshal's house," Sister Anne told Gita. "Sara would be like a younger sister."

But they are so rich, Gita worried, and she was a girl who had lived on the Kathmandu streets. What if they left Nepal? What if they decided that Sara should no longer study dance? What if she and Sara didn't get along? What if they knew Mahesh Bhahadur *Rana*? Would she be back on the streets again? Would Sister Anne let her return to the orphanage?

Gita's mind turned these thoughts over until she exhausted herself without getting an answer. Her mother had told her to trust in the goddess because she works in ways none of us will ever understand. I mean, look at what's happened to my life, Gita thought. When I was a child in Rumla, no one could have predicted my future.

She had no idea what it meant to live with rich people from the West. It was like some strange spiritual force was guiding her through a door that she never knew existed.

CHAPTER THIRTEEN

From the first day that Gita moved into the Marshal's residence, she and Sara studied and rehearsed together, took long walks, and behaved like sisters who had know each other since early childhood. Along with Bob and Diana, they visited Boudhanath, Swyambunath and Pashupatinath. The two girls studied the religious and artistic heritage of Nepal, went to Buddhist ritual ceremonies, and sought out Hindu holy men to receive teachings that would give them deeper insights into sacred dance.

At Pashupatinath they met an ancient guru — a direct disciple of Swami Nityananda — the great Hindu saint who had taken *samadhi* in a village near Mumbai. He taught them to use breath and mind to tap internal energy and strengthen chakras. They also discovered the power of *yab-yum* in meditation practice and dance from a Rinpoche who lived near Boudhanath.

It was a magical time for both of them. The joy they shared, the knowledge they gained of the dance, the mystery of their search, and the adventure of discovery — all helped them to grow with grace and beauty.

Although the Marshals spoiled Sara — a single child who was given just about anything she desired, Gita never said a word. Instead, she adored Sara's innocence, her frankness, her disdain for class distinction, for the doodads and gadgets that money could buy; and how could Gita not be delighted by Sara's fascination with every facet of Nepalese dance?

Gita's new life at the Marshal's often amused her, sometimes intimidated her, and always evoked interest in subjects that were foreign to her limited experience. From email and telephones to a large satellite TV, there were also electronic gadgets for everything from can openers to cork screws to pencil sharpeners to food processors and blenders and juicers. It was a world Gita couldn't conjure up in her wildest imaginings.

She watched American movies with Sara — romantic love stories, comedies, musicals, horror films, mystery stories and some films that often made her blush. At first, she'd cover her eyes when men and women kissed or made love on screen, but later, she wanted to know if Sara had the strange and wonderful new feelings Gita felt while watching people embrace.

"Yes," Sara answered, "but also when I see boys at school or at night before I fall asleep."

Romantic movies weren't easy for her. Men kissed women in ways she'd never seen before. Maybe it's supposed to be this way, she thought; maybe I'm not supposed to hide from my sexual feelings. When she told Sara that her parents never kissed, the latter replied, "But, it's part of life, isn't it? I can't imagine being married and not kissing?"

Her favorite movie was *An American in Paris*. She watched it again and again until she memorized every song and dance movement, and would often entertain Sara by imitating the actors in the film.

"Gene Kelly," she laughed. "I want to meet him."

"I don't know if he's alive," Sara answered giggling.

"Impossible," Gita replied. "He's right here on the screen."

Diana arranged for an English tutor, and Gita studied mathematics, geography and history at a private school, every day discovering complexities in a world that was so different than Rumla. She wanted, more than anything, to learn to play the *Saraswati veena* — a stringed instrument Gita discovered at a concert she attended with Sara and Diana — an instrument used to play *Carnatic* classical music in South India.

When Diana asked her what present she wanted for *Dashain*, Gita replied that nothing would please her more than a *veena*. She would like to play raga and sing ancient Hindu poetry.

On a trip to Delhi, Bob bought Sara a guitar and Gita a *Saraswati veena*, and the Marshals arranged with one of the king's master musicians to give Gita lessons. He instructed her several times a week at the Marshal's residence. She learned quickly, often practicing late into the night. The maestro also taught her ancient Hindu songs. He told Diana that Gita had the potential to perform concerts in the not too distant future.

She would often play the *veena* for the Marshals after dinner and bring to their household the beauty of classical Indian music and poetry. It was Gita's way of saying thank you to these people who had opened her up to myriad life experiences. They had so lovingly changed her that it was the least she could do in return. Gita was now an accomplished twenty-year old. She spoke English, Hindi, and Nepali. She had also mastered the *veena*, continued to dance, and sang early Hindu poetry.

Every Wednesday afternoon, Diana and Gita would go to the orphanage, visit with Sister Anne, and Gita would perform for the children. Diana often spoke to Gita about her own past: an ambitious woman in her late thirties, she had graduated from the Georgetown University School of Foreign Service with honors and went to work on a global hunger project for the US Secretary of State. She was promoted to a position of seniority by the State Department, where she and Bob met at an international hunger conference. They were workaholics, he an Ambassador and Diana a senior advisor on the project. Soon they became inseparable. Six months later, they were married, and within a year of their marriage, Diana gave birth to Sara, their only child.

"Do you have any brothers and sisters?" Gita asked, and Diana told her about Daniel who lived and worked as a lawyer in New York. "I'm sure you've seen him," Diana said. "His picture is on the mantlepiece in my bedroom. Sara also has one on her desk."

"And your family?" Diana asked cautiously. "Tell me more about your brothers and sisters."

"They're all village people," Gita replied in barely a whisper. "It's been many years since I've seen them."

Diana could feel Gita's reluctance to speak about her family and didn't press the subject any further. She was no stranger to the plight of Nepalese indigent children. She had established a not-for-profit organization called "Child Care" with Nepalese doctors that worked diligently in remote villages to bring healthcare to the local people. One goal was to pinpoint young girls who were prime targets for sex traffickers, to approach their parents, and give them alternatives to selling their daughters. Diana rented a large house from a wealthy land owner, renovated it, and made it a home in which village girls between the ages of ten and thirteen were housed, fed, clothed, and educated — girls who otherwise would have been sold to a brothel in Mumbai.

"I just want you to know," Diana said to Gita, " that in our household you have two jobs. One is to study and do well in school and the other is to teach Sara to dance.

"And if you leave Nepal?" Gita asked.

"You can come with us," Diana responded warmly. "You're my second daughter."

"I can do maid's work to earn my food," Gita said.

"You don't have to," Diana responded. "We hire servants to take care of the house."

✳ ✳ ✳

After a dance concert at a local school, Diana introduced Gita and Sara to Cecily Drummond — an old college friend who had recently arrived in Kathmandu. They were seated in a small café drinking mango *lassis*, and

Cecily asked Diana where these girls learned to dance so well.

"Sara learned from Gita," Diana said, "and Gita was trained by her mother at an early age."

"Do you speak English?" Cecily asked Gita.

"Yes. I've learned it from Sara and at school." Gita answered.

It turned out that Cecily had been hired to produce a multicultural Asian event in conjunction with the United Nations, the Metropolitan Museum of Art, Lincoln Center, and a handful of other venues in New York City. She took a sip of her *lassi*, thought for a moment, and asked Diana if Gita could come to New York for a month in September.

"To do what?" Diana answered, a little surprised.

"To teach Nepalese dance — to be part of my event," Cecily said excitedly. "She's authentic, Diana, she's the real thing. I'm positive I could arrange it with Juilliard."

"Why not?" she replied. Diana thought it was an amazing opportunity, and Bob could easily get Gita a cultural exchange visa.

"New York!" Sara screamed knocking over her *lassi* on the table. "Oops!" she said laughing. "I mean…that's great! That's great! Oh my sister. Did you hear what Cecily just said?"

"But, New York? I don't even know where it is," Gita answered.

"We'll show it to you on a map," Sara said. She gave Gita a big hug. "I'm so happy for you. You should be happy, too," she exclaimed convincingly.

"It's so far from Nepal," Gita reacted to Sara with a nervous smile.

"Have you forgotten that you're part of our family," Sara said. "We'll always be here for you. You don't have to worry about anything."

"And you?" Gita asked Sara. "Will you come with me? I don't want to leave you."

"If my mother thinks it's okay and I can arrange to get out of school. We'll see…"

"There's nothing to worry about," Diana said. She took Gita's hand.

"But it'll be a whole different world for me," Gita protested.

"My parents have a wonderful apartment in New York where you can stay," Diana smiled. "It's exciting, my dear, not only for you, but for others to learn about real Nepalese dance. Just think of New York as a village — but it will be the biggest one you've ever seen."

"I still don't understand, why me?" Gita asked suspiciously.

"Because you dance like a Nepalese angel and I can arrange for you to teach at Juilliard for a month," Cecily replied.

"Juilliard?" Gita asked. "Is it a temple?"

"Not exactly," Cecily smiled. "It's a school for the performing arts. You'll be part of a big Asian cultural event."

"Oh, this sounds special," Gita said nervously, "but I've never even been in an airplane, I've never even thought of being that far away from Nepal..."

CHAPTER FOURTEEN

In mid-August, about five weeks before Gita's trip there was great excitement in the Marshal residence. Diana's brother Daniel was coming to Kathmandu. It had been many years since he last visited.

Sara and Gita were sitting in the garden behind the house. They sipped fresh lime sodas and were resting after several hours of rehearsal. Sara told Gita that she was going to love her Uncle Daniel.

"He's quite good-looking," Sara said, "and he's a mountain climber and martial arts buff. He's got black belts wrapped all around him."

"Black belts?" Gita asked, laughing.

"Yes! Yes! He's like a karate dude...an expert. He spends most of his spare time learning to fight."

"Is he a soldier?" Gita asked.

"No," Sara replied. "He's about as peace-loving as anyone you'll ever meet, but he's addicted to the martial arts."

"When is he coming?" Gita asked, slightly bewildered. She wondered how a man who loves peace fights all the time.

"Pretty soon," Sara said. "He'll be staying with us for a few weeks. Mom and dad have promised to take him trekking. They've hired Sherpas and want to walk the trails in the mountains near Kathmandu. It's gonna be fun to camp out. You'll love it."

"Sounds okay to me," Gita said. "You and I can share a tent."

"I can't wait," Sara replied. She and Gita clicked glasses and finished drinking their fresh lime sodas.

Gita had seen a picture of Daniel Gold on Sara's desk. He was just another face to her among many of Sara's family members. She paid no attention to the photo. Occasionally, Sara would talk about him. It seems that she had spent a great deal of time with her uncle as a child. Since her family had moved to Kathmandu, Sara saw him only on her yearly visits to the States. Her Uncle Daniel was pretty good-looking, and girls went crazy for him. But he worked at his international law practice, studied and taught martial arts, traveled with friends, and was a great mountain climber, that's all.

"Just like my dad, he's a workaholic. He loves kids, and yet, he never got married."

"He's like us too," Gita laughed. "We dance and dance and haven't time for anything else."

❋ ❋ ❋

On a dry, dusty, and very hot morning in late August, Daniel walked slowly on the Kathmandu airport tarmac. He listened to the songs of parakeets flitting among the branches of parched pine, banyan, and chialune trees, and stopped walking for a moment to watch a family of Rhesus macaques climbing on the terminal rooftop. An eighteen-hour trip had come to an end; and the airport's gritty smell, the lack of rain, the sun beating down without relief, a dead dog and a starving cat in the shade, a hawk circling above, the sound of a flute and drum in the distance, and a saddhu sitting in meditation and praying for rain — Nepal, he thought with a smile; no matter how many times I visit here, it always turns my head.

The monsoons hadn't arrived as yet. The meteorologists had predicted a virtually rainless summer — a drought that would provide no relief from overbearing heat and pollution. Nepalese priests had performed ritual ceremonies and had sacrificed goats and chickens to an unyielding god, but crops still withered and the people withered and not a cloud appeared in a clear and endlessly blue sky.

It was a rare vacation for Daniel whose client list was so extensive that there wasn't time in any given day to finish his workload. He needed a break, if for no other reason than to clear his mind from the complicated corporate legal proceedings on his plate. He would return to New York in a few weeks, fresh, and ready to deal with the pressures of work.

Nepal was the perfect place for him to vacation. Far enough away from the corporate rat race and the New York City social scene — a very beautiful and primitive country, he'd be able to visit family, trek, and just take some time to relax.

❋ ❋ ❋

Tribhuvan Terminal — an air-conditioned building with a hodgepodge of people from both east and west crowded together and waiting for passengers to clear customs; and in the mix, Diana, Sara and Gita looked for Daniel — both the girls were dressed in saris and carried garlands of yellow and white flowers to place on Daniel's neck. And when they saw him carting two valises and a trunk, Diana waved and Sara shouted;

Daniel made his way through the thick crowd to where they stood and hugged his sister.

"Oh, how I missed you, Diana."

"Well," she chuckled, "it's been five years."

After both Sara and Gita each placed a garland around his neck, he gave Sara a huge hug and politely pecked Gita on both cheeks.

"How's the Ambassador? How's everyone *chez* the Marshals?"

"You know, Bob's Bob," Diana replied. "He's in Dubai and should be back tomorrow morning. But, look at you, my ageless brother. You don't look a day older."

"Can you imagine? I finally dragged my tired butt out of the office. I don't have one appointment today; there's not a client I need to see."

"This is Gita," Sara said. "She's my closest friend and 'sister.' Though you've already kissed her on both cheeks, I think the two of you should be formerly introduced. Gita — my uncle Daniel. At least shake hands."

"You've become mature in your teenage years," Daniel said to Sara after he shook hands with Gita.

"What's in that thing?" Sara asked pointing to the trunk.

"Presents, my dearest niece, for the entire Marshal household."

"That's my Uncle Dan," Sara said to Gita. "I just adore him."

"Come on," Diana said. "Let's go home."

They drove along Ring Road, and the oppressive heat and dust forced pedestrians and bicycle riders to wear protective masks.

"It's got to rain," Diana said, "or there'll be nothing to eat."

"It's that bad," Daniel replied without much interest. He was so jet-lagged that the impending doom of the Nepalese people got lost in an inner haze.

"If there's no monsoon," Diana replied, "thousands of people could die."

Daniel didn't respond. He looked at the crowded Kathmandu streets, the ancient houses, *stupas* and temples that lined Ring Road — an amalgam of buildings that were many hundreds of years old; and the cars, motor scooters, and buses that brought one into the modern age — people going about their daily lives, but different than the crowded streets of New York. The movement was less sharp, less determined, and less frantic. It was bathed in an off-beige colored light that filtered through pollution from car exhausts and dust that never stopped rising from the streets.

"It's like some of these people still live in the fifteenth century," he said in barely a whisper.

"The poverty is so severe," Diana, replied, "that sometimes I wonder if anything can be done about it."

"But, it's more than just poverty," Daniel said. "There's something so basic here, so simple, something these people can teach those of us in the West who want to learn."

"You're the eternal romantic," Diana kidded him. "I agree with you, but a little rain would be a nice addition to wisdom emanating from the East."

※ ※ ※

While Daniel showered, a servant unpacked his clothing and hung the trousers, jackets and shirts in a large walk-in closet connected to the bedroom. The shower's lukewarm water washed away the tired almost grungy feeling he had from eighteen hours of air travel. A quick session of Hatha yoga stretched his muscles, relaxed his joints and shook off some of the jet lag. When a servant knocked at his bedroom door and announced that lunch would be served in fifteen minutes, he put on a pair of khaki trousers and a dark blue tee shirt and skipped down the stairs to the living room where the Marshals and Gita waited for him.

"Three meals a day of airplane food makes a home-cooked lunch sound terrific," Daniel said. He walked to the center of the living room where the servants had left his trunk. "Now for more important things."

"What can be more important than lunch?" Sara asked.

"Presents," he responded in a cheerful voice. "This trunk is full of them. Diana, the only thing I didn't bring is mom and dad, but they're doing great. Dad's buzzing around New York in his sixty-year-old Volkswagen bug and mom's on the board of every charity ever invented."

"That news is better than lunch," Diana said. She asked a servant to open the trunk and Daniel removed gift after gift, everything from bottled jams and jellies for Diana, an Apple Notebook for Bob, and scarves and blouses for Sara. When he handed Sara a pair of silver-chased bracelets, Daniel suggested that she give one to Gita.

"Because we're sisters," Sara smiled. "One for her and one for me."

"Yes, we are truly sisters," Gita responded. She put the bracelet on her wrist, thanked Daniel, and thought that she had uncles too, but none of them were like him.

※ ※ ※

Sara confided in Gita as the two of them entered the dining room,

"Uncle Daniel just loves Indian food."

Almost on cue, the cook covered a table with a cotton cloth and laid out a cornucopia of Indian dishes. The spices titillated Gita's senses: cumin, curry, masala, coriander and turmeric coming from an assortment of dishes like chicken *tikka*, curried and *biryani* rice, *dahl*, *tandoori* fish, spinach *korma*, *raita*, garlic *naan* and assorted chutneys. "It's so great to have my uncle here," Sara said to Gita. The family served themselves and sat down to eat.

Daniel sat next to Gita. He dipped the garlic *naan* into a dish of *dahl*, put it into his mouth and chewed slowly. "It's delicious," he said to Diana. "Umm...ambrosia. Is there any way I can steal your cook? There are maid's quarters in my new apartment."

"It's problematic," Diana answered. "I mean there's immigration and language problems. She comes from a small village in the hills, and has kids. I think we'll just leave the cook in my kitchen."

"You're right," Daniel said smiling, "but there's no Indian restaurant in Manhattan that comes close."

After lunch, Daniel asked Diana to take him to Thamel to check out antique and crafts stores. He had just purchased a new penthouse apartment in New York, and wanted to accessorize it with a few painted Tibetan chests, some wood-carved architectural pieces as cabinet doors, and perhaps a statue or two of Hindu or Buddhist divinities.

In the days that followed, the family took short trips to many of the temples in Kathmandu; they lunched in Thamel and visited marketplaces in and about the city where ancient Hindu and Buddhist sculptures of gods and goddesses were mounted on buildings and in courtyards; and the endless stream of women dressed in colorful sari-like costumes and men in tunics and vests over tight-fitting pants walked past cows and goats and water buffaloes on crowded, dust-filled streets. It was all so ancient, primitive — a place where merchants sold loom-woven textiles, hand made crafts, metalwork, gold and silver. "Just look at this," Daniel said to Diana. "There's nothing like it in the U.S."

"Not even in Kansas," Diana joked.

"No, I don't think so," he laughed. "It's just that time doesn't exist here."

"In Kathmandu," Diana replied in a droll voice, "it doesn't."

"It would be fun to lose myself in the Kathmandu hustle and bustle," he said, "to actually live with these people and be a part of Nepal's seamless flow."

"For an hour or two," Diana said, "until you have to eat the food and drink the water and get stomach cramps, fungi, amoebas, and an internal battle with parasites that will last forever."

The next morning, they went to the Pashupatinath temple complex on the Bagmati River — a sacred place where the Hindus worshipped the god *Siva*, where ancient stone sculptures of *nandis*, *lingams* and cobras lined the steps that led down to a tributary of the Ganges, where priests burned the bodies of Hindu corpses and scattered the ashes in the river's flowing waters. Monkeys abounded and tourists took photos; *saddus* in orange robes with long beards and matted hair smoked *ganga* in small alcoves, *saddhus* that waved to Daniel and asked him to join them. Diana took a photo of him seated with a half-dozen of these *nagababas* — their long matted hair covering Daniel's arms and shoulders, their eyes aglow and their foreheads painted with tridents and other signs of *Siva*.

When they returned to the Marshal's residence, Diana and the girls watched him work out in the backyard: strong and agile, focused and swift, he wore a tee shirt and drawstring pants, and he performed karate movements like a master — his *karateka*-type energy unfazed by either the heat or by servants who stopped their work to spy on Madam's brother cutting a path through a host of nonexistent enemies that tested his every move. His *kata* finished, Daniel bowed to Diana and the girls, and sat down on a garden chair. He thanked a servant who brought him a towel and a fresh lime soda, and when the ladies joined him, he remarked to Diana that she seemed a little tired of Himalayan paradise.

"It gets to me," she said. "The worst is the water. But, there's also the cow and buffalo shit on the roads, the acrid smell that clings to your clothing, the food and the poverty. No one does anything about it. As a matter of fact, no one does anything about anything here. Sometimes I long for a little western civilization."

"It's up to Bob, isn't it? He needs to get a transfer."

"But he likes Nepal," Diana said with a sigh. "Still, lately, he's been getting edgy. That's a good sign. It means he's thinking of moving on. If it wasn't for these girls and my foundation, I would probably split my time between here and New York."

"And my darling Sara?" Daniel asked. He motioned for her to sit next to him. "My niece has grown up to be quite a young woman." He patted her lightly on the cheek.

"I'm learning so much about dance that it takes up my entire day," Sara replied. "I have the best teacher," and she pointed at Gita.

He had heard about Gita for months from Diana and asked her when he would get the chance to see the magic of her dance?

"Whenever you'd like," Gita blushed.

"Maybe tomorrow evening," he replied smiling.

She placed her hands together in a graceful, prayer-like position and told Daniel that she'd be honored to dance for him.

The following morning, while Sara was in school and Daniel had taken time to visit a Rinpoche at Boudhanath, Diana and Gita were chauffeured to the orphanage.

"My brother's something," Diana said. "Nonstop, energetic, interested in so many people and things."

"Is he like this in New York?" Gita asked.

"Kind of," she replied. "When he's not working at his law practice or teaching martial arts at a dojo. I remember him as a child. He'd always poke his nose into exotic stuff. He'd read comic books that detailed the life of Buddha or Vedic stories and he knew the names of half the gods in the Hindu and Buddhist pantheons."

Gita thought that Daniel was very handsome and easygoing, but still a westerner, so different from Nepalese people. Their worlds were far apart, yet she loved his sister and niece like no people she'd ever known before... and he was a member of their family.

CHAPTER FIFTEEN

At lunch in the Marshal's house, Daniel spoke about the glitterati world and the film scene in New York. They all laughed when he painted a verbal picture of women and men dressed in long gowns and tuxedos, marching like full-feathered peacocks on red carpets at theater and movie openings, pretending not to gush over numerous celebrities that bathed in their own glow of self-importance as they left their limousines.

"The egos of these people are so huge," Daniel said, "that you could compare them to inflated rubber balloons in Macy's Thanksgiving Day Parade — like Mickey and Minnie Mouse waltzing to the tune of their own importance."

"I mean, if Johnny Depp or Brad Pitt was there, I wouldn't mind some of that ego rubbing off on me," Sara said.

"Me either," Diana agreed.

"Mom!" Sara scolded. "I don't believe I heard what you just said."

"And the contemporary art world," Diana asked avoiding her daughter's stare.

"I don't know much about it."

He had bought a Sisley landscape at a Christie's auction a few months ago and an important ninth century Kashmiri bronze of a Bodhisattva. But he had no taste for the contemporary art scene. It was a little empty for him — a different aesthetic.

At first it drove him crazy, he went on, but he finally learned that the mediocrity he found in contemporary art didn't stop modern day artists from becoming very rich and famous. All it took was a PR person with a fully-loaded rolodex to tout the artist's genius and the rest of the world bought right in. He wondered if collectors looked at what they were buying; he wondered if the price of a painting was the only thing that determined its merit, if people invested in art like they did in the stock market.

"It seems, Diana, that galleries and museums have stripped themselves bare by showing contemporary art that was created from just about anything but spirit."

"Spirit?" Diana asked thoughtfully. "We've got plenty of that here. Would you like to hear some raga?"

"Of course," he answered.

"Gita, dear," Diana winked. "I'm sure Daniel would enjoy it if you played the *veena* for us."

"I'll have to get it from my bedroom," she replied a little embarrassed.

She left the lunch table and returned a few minutes later with her *veena*, and they all went into an alcove that the Marshals had set up to resemble a *Saivite* shrine. There was a large statue of a *Siva* Nataraj at the end of the alcove that Bob had bought in a Delhi crafts market. On its right was a bronze statue of *Siva's* consort Parvati, and on the Nataraj's left there was another bronze statue, this one of *Siva's* elephant headed son Ganesha. Above the altar, Gita had hung a Nepalese painting of the goddess *Saraswati* playing the *veena*.

Gita sat cross-legged on a Tibetan tiger rug in front of the Nataraj statue. As she tuned the instrument, the others made themselves comfortable on the carpeted floor.

"This is the opening part of a morning raga," Gita said. Her fingers lightly touched the strings and produced a slow, haunting and very melodic sound that filled the room. When she finished, Daniel stared at her, and barely whispered, "Just beautiful. Beautiful. Where did you learn to play like that?"

"Right here," she answered with a big smile, "in this house, from one of the royal musicians, who also happens to be a great teacher."

✳ ✳ ✳

Years of martial arts training had taught Daniel to maintain a quiet mind and keep his emotions under control — all so necessary when negotiating with CEO's, lawyers and financial managers of multinational corporations. He'd often think that there was no other way of dealing with people that operate in that snake pit. Everything was so complicated and required clarity of mind to act in the best interests of his clients.

When his ex-fiancé, Janet Lipton, skipped from his bed to the bed of a professional basketball player and broke off their five-year relationship, he was able to bury the hurt in a flurry of corporate activity. Though depression would often sneak in and try to poison his day, though anger upset his routine, he managed to keep the imbalance at a minimum. He told himself that in the future he had to be more careful. The heart is a very fragile place and can be broken on another person's whim.

At first, the warm thoughts he had about Gita frightened him.

She's twenty years old, Diana and Bob's "adopted" daughter, Sara's clos-

*est friend, he shivered. It's like incest to be attracted to her. I've got to forget
about this. It'll never work. I didn't come to Kathmandu to upset my family.*

*He used every Taoist technique he knew to regain inner balance. But,
a strange sensation overcame him from the moment he heard her play the
veena. He had never known that a human being could radiate such beauty.
Who is this young woman? Not only is she physically attractive, her music
touches on the divine.*

*He asked her to play the veena again; and when she danced, Daniel
mused that her movements were akin to the highest forms of the martial arts
— a meditation on spirit, something so sacred that even his Sensei hadn't
mastered it. She was unapproachable, yet, so terribly human that her presence opened Daniel and exposed him to feelings he had never known before.*

*She's like a member of my family, he thought, untouchable — a person
I can't get involved with. He tried his best to avoid her, but, no matter how
much of an effort he made, he couldn't take his eyes off Gita when they were
together; he couldn't stop thinking about her when they were apart. She had
found a place in the very fabric of his heart.*

✳ ✳ ✳

"He must really like you," Sara said after Daniel and Diana went out
crafts shopping in Thamel.

"Why do you say that?" Gita asked her.

"My glib, witty, self-confident, charming uncle doesn't know what to
say to a Nepalese girl," she responded giggling. "I probably shouldn't say
anything, but he told me that you're like a goddess."

"And what did you answer?" Gita asked playfully.

"She's my best friend and sister, Uncle Dan, and if she's a goddess, so
much the better. And those were my very words."

Gita just laughed.

"My Uncle Dan can't stop looking at you," Sara teased.

Gita knew this. His eyes were always on her. Sometimes it frightened
her and she wanted to hide. She didn't want to tell Sara that she was
uncomfortable whenever Daniel was in the room. At first she worried
about him. Was he another Mahesh Bhahadur *Rana*? But that couldn't
be. He was Diana's brother, Sara's uncle, and obviously, a beloved member
of their family.

"In my village," she explained to Sara, "there's no such thing as
romance. There's no love. My father would choose a husband for me and

I would move into his house."

"Yuck," Sara said. "Thank goodness we don't live in your village."

"I'm glad we don't live there too," she hesitated, "but I do miss my mother very much."

"If you still lived there, I wouldn't have a sister, and you'd never have gotten to meet my Uncle Daniel."

"Sara, if you're thinking what I think you're thinking, it's simply out of the question."

"It's not out of the question," Sara said. "First you have to talk to each other and then we'll see what happens."

Gita didn't want to get involved with anyone. She was grateful to the Marshals for her life and had no need to complicate things.

"Your uncle will leave in a few weeks," she said to Sara. "What happens then? Come on Sara." She grabbed her by the arm and turned on some music. "Everything's going to be fine. Let's just dance."

Daniel's intense stare was almost like a child wanting something yet too scared to ask. It made Gita uneasy. He'd bring her a flower or a sweet and tell her how beautifully she played the *veena*. He was distant, almost frightened of getting too close to her, of talking about anything but superficial things.

What Gita couldn't tell Sara, as close as they were, that trusting a man, being friends with him, let alone having him touch her instantly conjured up memories of Mahesh Bhahadur *Rana*. The very thought of making love to a man who expected his wife to be a virgin also haunted her. After one night, he'd toss her out. She'd be the disgrace of his and her families. And what would happen after that? Gita didn't know. She hadn't thought about a husband for years, ever since she left the house of that *Rana*.

Gita understood very little about Western culture. She had seen in movies that unlike life in her village, virginity didn't seem to be a matter of great importance when men and women married. She couldn't quite grasp the idea, but felt deep in her heart that if the terrible truths of her past were discovered, Diana and Sara would be crushed. She loved them too much to hurt them.

✳ ✳ ✳

The next day, the Marshal family, Gita, Daniel, a few Sherpas, and a Newar guide, drove into the foothills of the mountains. They had planned a four-day trek: to camp, fish, and swim. Diana and Bob were eager for them to experience days of family bonding. It was the first vacation they'd taken in a long time.

Gita and Daniel walked together on a path up a steep incline that took them from the foothills into a cluster of scraggy cliffs and dense evergreen forest. Intrigued with the raw and primitive nature of the mountains — the scale of things and how humanity was dwarfed by nature's potence, Daniel told Gita that Nepal was an awesome place.

"I don't know any other," Gita replied.

"Where were you born?"

"Oh," she answered, "in a little village very, very far from here. It's a long bus ride from Kathmandu. Five hours, I guess, and then an eight-hour walk over narrow paths that border cliffs and make you cross streams that have no bridges, and trees, so dense that you can barely see the sun."

"Sounds like a fairytale to me," Daniel replied.

He tried to imagine the remote place of her birth, but, it seemed strange to him that a woman with her charm, her sophistication, her beauty, could have lived so far from civilization.

"When is the last time you were home?" he asked her.

"Over eight years ago," she replied sadly.

This mysterious lady, Daniel thought, who seems to walk gracefully in a divine light, this woman whose music and dance stretches the limits of my understanding. I have to find out more about her.

"What did you do before meeting Bob and Diana?" he asked with some caution.

"I don't talk about it," Gita said in a tone that demanded they end the conversation. She didn't know what Daniel wanted from her, but he was getting too personal and her past was no one's business.

"Don't you miss your village?" Daniel asked her after a few minutes. His tone was gentle and compassionate and truly concerned about her.

"Not really," Gita answered in a calm voice that covered the deep pain she felt whenever the subject of Rumla was mentioned. "The Marshals are like family to me."

"You're the sister Sara never had," Daniel said. "At least that's what she told me."

"I love her very much," Gita responded. "It's amazing for me to see how much she has grown as a dancer and a person."

Like Sensei and myself, Daniel thought, but there's more. There's love here, gratitude — a certain kind of wisdom that family closeness brings, that one can only understand if they have suffered a great deal.

"I've never seen anyone dance like you before," Daniel ventured.

"Thank you," Gita replied blushing.

It was strange for her to receive a compliment from a man. It threw her off balance and made her suspicious of Daniel's intentions.

"I once wanted to be a temple dancer," she replied.

"A temple dancer?" Daniel asked her.

What an exotic notion, he thought, coming from this woman who has lived her life outside the realms of my own experience...

"Yes. My greatest wish was to offer myself through dance to Lord *Siva*. I could appease the gods; I could be a link between people who worship in the temple and the divine. The priests asked my mother to train me at an early age and told her that I was born to dance."

He was being drawn deeper into the world of Gita — a mysterious soul, so spiritual, yet, there she was, perhaps the most physically beautiful person he'd ever met — flesh and bones, feminine charm — a woman who attracted him like none he'd known before.

"What happened?" he asked. They stopped walking for a moment.

Why does he go on? Gita thought. What does he want from me? Why do I keep answering him?

Her face dropped and she looked at the ground.

"I went to live in Kathmandu," she replied. There were tears in her eyes and she turned from Daniel and began to walk again. He caught up to her and asked, "Where do you dance now?"

"In lots of places," she answered. "I love dancing for the children at the orphanage, at schools and temples here in Kathmandu, for Diana and Sara, and maybe even in a place called Juilliard."

Oh, he thought with a smile. The gods are with me and I didn't even ask for their help. She's coming to New York.

They walked single file on a cliff-like path that meandered up the side of the mountain. Gita was just ahead of him. She slipped a little and he grabbed her hand. But the moment she regained her balance, she drew it away.

"Be careful," he said. "The bottom of this cliff is a long way down. It's funny, you know, the two of us walking together in these mountains and I'm at a loss for words. I mean...I don't know what I mean. I'm an attorney. I get paid to talk and I don't know what to say."

"There's nothing to say," she replied. They continued to walk and she broke the silence by asking in a very innocent voice, "What does an attorney do?"

"I get paid to talk my way through other people's problems," he replied somewhat embarrassed, "and I've never been tongue-tied before."

"Your tongue is tied?" Gita asked with a smile.

"In little and big knots," he replied.

"Then maybe you shouldn't talk; maybe we should walk quietly and listen to the mountains."

A range of distant peaks soared high above a large valley; streams trickled down a slope into a river, cutting their way through rugged-looking hills and forest. Soft white puffs of cloud dotted the sky, and the sun began to descend behind the mountains. Herdsmen with flocks of goats appeared in the distance and disappeared just as quickly. All Daniel could see was wild and barren land. Gita explained to him that there were many small villages in the mountains and these people lived there.

"Tell me more about your own village," he asked her.

"There's not much to say. It's poor and small, and there's no electricity or plumbing, and I had to walk for miles every morning to get water from the river," she told Daniel with some hesitation.

When I think about it…but I can't, no it's impossible for me to comprehend what experiences turned a young village girl into this strikingly sophisticated woman. Kathmandu is ancient enough, but a village in the Himalayan Mountains, so remote that traces of civilization barely exist. It's more than my mind can grasp. It's another Pygmalion tale, some kind of fairytale that doesn't exist today.

"It's hard to believe that people still live like that," he said to her.

"I know," Gita replied.

They lapsed into silence again and followed the others along the trail that led them beneath a magnolia tree in full bloom. Gita picked one of the large white flowers and gave it to Daniel. "It's my favorite," she said. "I've loved them since I was a child."

It was late afternoon when the Sherpas set up camp. They found a clearing at the side of a steep hill, erected canvas tents that were held together by yak hair ropes, wooden poles, and metal spikes. There was one main tent in which they did the cooking and smaller satellite units in which the trekkers slept. In the distance, there were mountains like giant citadels that hovered above vast and seemingly endless stretches of valley. The thin air made it difficult to breathe and the shadows from a setting sun brought a chill that forced them to put on parkas.

While the Sherpas prepared dinner, Gita and Daniel sat together on a large rock outside his tent. He took her hand. At first, she pulled back, but quickly decided to let him hold it.

"My Sensei told me that to master the martial arts I have to become nothing," he said. "It's easy to understand that here."

"He's a wise person," she said.

"Yes, but so are you."

Gita didn't answer. She untwined her hands from his, stood up and asked Daniel if he wanted some tea. All the while her thoughts dredged up memories of the beatings her father gave her mother — and Daniel was a man — like her drunken father was a man, like her uncles and cousins were men — and all of those men in Rumla treated water buffalo better than they treated their wives and daughters.

"I'll make some," she said. "Let's go in."

"Can't we sit here a little longer?"

"Yes," she said. "It's getting cold, but I'll bring the tea in a minute."

Is she frightened, Daniel thought, of some old hurt that's lodged in her heart that our touching brought out? My goddess is a human being, after all. He felt she'd suffered in her past, but her suffering hadn't diminished her beauty nor kept her from being radiant.

While she brewed the tea, Gita told herself that Daniel wanted something she couldn't give. He was becoming too intimate, and it scared her. Nothing could come of all of this, and he'd be gone in a week. Yet Gita was attracted to this man; she felt emotions that she'd never experienced before. She didn't know what it was, but Gita liked the touch of his hand and the sound of his voice. He was kind to her, and sometimes he even acted like a young boy.

She returned with black Nepalese tea and *momos*. They sat in silence, sipped the tea and ate the dumplings; and Gita couldn't shake the feeling that somehow, in her heart of hearts, she enjoyed being with this unusual man who treated her gently, who made her feel so warm. Her emotions were mixed and deep. One moment the image of herself being raped crippled her thoughts and made her want to cringe and hide, and the next she wanted to hold Daniel in her arms.

"Is anything wrong?" Daniel asked.

"No," she answered. "It's getting cold. Let's go inside."

He took her hand again and kissed her lightly on the lips, but she drew back, removed her hand from his, stood up, and just stared at the horizon unable to forget the *Rana*. It made her want to cry. Instinctively, she withdrew into herself, at a loss for words and incapable of getting more intimate with Daniel.

"What is it?" he whispered.

"It's too fast," she answered trying to hold back her tears.

"But why?"

"I can't talk about it," she replied. Her voice was sad and full of pain. "I can't give you what you want from me."

"I apologize," Daniel said. He squeezed her hand reassuringly. "If it's too soon, I understand. I have patience. If love means waiting until you're ready, then I'll wait."

The sun was setting behind the mountains, and the cold air forced them to go into the tent, where the Marshals were seated on pillows scattered about the floor.

"I'll never forgive you, Uncle Dan," Sara said, mischievously. "You're taking Gita away from me." She grabbed her friend by the arm and the two of them left the tent.

"Are you falling in love with him?" she pressed.

"I don't know," Gita replied softly. "No man has ever treated me the way he does. He's so kind and gentle," she giggled. "But I'm frightened, Sara. I don't want to get involved with anyone. I don't." Then she smiled with tears in her eyes, "I never knew that a man's lips could taste good."

"Hum, Gita. His lips taste good. How did you find that out?"

Gita broke down and started crying. "I can't do this, Sara. I can't ever trust a man. There's so much pain inside me that his very touch makes me want to run."

"I don't understand," Sara said.

"There's nothing to understand. He'll go back to New York and this will all be over with. I just want to dance. That's all. I don't want anything else." She wiped the tears from her eyes and took a deep breath. "Come. It's cold out here. Let's go inside."

❋ ❋ ❋

After dinner, Daniel retired to his tent. Restless and unsure of himself, he tried to fathom what deep hurt kept Gita from getting closer to him. She was a goddess of sorts, but a troubled one, perhaps scarred by her family's primitive views on marriage, perhaps hesitant because he was from the West — a white man who'd never fit into her Nepalese way of life. But, she had lived with his sister and her family for four years; she was Sara's buddy and her teacher, and the love she has for them all is right on the surface. I've never seen such gratitude, such simplicity, and such grace in a person. He began to question his own inner self and what strange force kept him from finding the woman he could spend his life with — something he had wanted for many years, but couldn't attain. He wanted to kiss Gita, to hold her in his arms, to be intimate with her, to fully give his love to this beautiful woman — his heart felt it but he didn't know what to do. He decided that it's all too rushed. He'd have to wait and give her time to learn to love him. There definitely was an attraction. He could feel it from her. Yet, every time he tried to kiss her, she drew away.

There was a knock at the entrance to his tent and Bob came in.

"Can't sleep?" he asked Daniel who was sitting crossed-legged on a stool.

"No," Daniel replied. "It's Gita, Bob. She's gotten into my blood. I can't stop thinking about her."

"That's exactly what I wanted to talk to you about."

"What do you mean?"

"Gita. She's ten years younger than you and like a daughter to us; she's Sara's closest friend, and you've come here from New York to sweep her off her feet."

"Wait a minute," Daniel said.

"No I can't," Bob, replied. "I've got to find out what's going on. Is it some craving in yourself that you're trying to fill with a woman? You can't do it with an innocent girl from Nepal. I know she's exquisitely beautiful and has outstanding grace beyond a person of her age, but what the hell is she going to do in New York? After you sleep together, what're you going to talk about? The whole thing's crazy, Daniel. Just forget her and go home. Just chalk it up to a fascination with a pretty girl in an exotic country."

"I'm trying," Daniel said, "but I can't.

"Try harder," Bob demanded. He stood up to leave.

"Wait a minute," Daniel said. "I am going back to New York without Gita. I'm going to give it a little more time. Dammit, Bob, she's afraid to kiss me. There's some kind of fear that lives inside her that keeps her from becoming close to me. I've never met anyone like that woman and I'm madly in love with her, but I'll wait. I'll give it time. I won't force her to do anything."

"You're serious about this," Bob said to Daniel.

"Yes," he replied. "As serious as I've ever been about anything in my life."

"I don't know," Bob replied. "It's bizarre to me."

"How do you think I feel?" Daniel asked.

"I don't know anything about her past," Bob said. "Neither does Diana or Sara. She never talks about it and it's always been a mystery to us."

"The only one who knows is Gita," Daniel replied, "and someday, maybe

she'll let me in on her secret. I'll just have to wait and see what happens."

"Okay, my brother," Bob said putting his arm around Daniel. "It was all just a little too quick. Have patience, if she loves you and you her, then the whole thing will work itself out."

After Bob left the tent, Daniel lay on his cot and stared at the canvas ceiling. *Gita and I aren't so different, he thought. I've been hurt and so has she, and we're both struggling with hurts from the past. There's got to be a reason why we met. Something changed in me from the moment I heard her play the veena. All the pain went away; I wanted to reach out and hold her and say to her that the music she played had healed my heart. Call it love, call it infatuation, call it whatever you want. I really don't care. She's found a place inside me. It's almost like she's always lived there.*

In New York, Daniel had many friends but not much of a social life. After his last girlfriend broke it off with him, he had brief flings with socialites, models, and professional women that he met at cocktail parties, but Daniel no longer took the reservoir of eligible females seriously. To him, they all had a frenzied look, betraying an insatiable hunger for the right man — that mysterious stranger who would provide them with a passport to a perfect life. In a threatening world, beauty faded, and love hid behind a wall of too much tension and obsessive need, and Daniel discovered that he no longer knew if the person he danced with had her own body or was sculpted into an odalisque-like doll by a plastic surgeon who specialized in perfect proportions. He had no interest in the frantic New York social scene. He spent most of his spare hours at the dojo with his Sensei where he'd learn to master the secrets of karate and Taoism.

"The less there is of you, the better," the Sensei once told him. "It's not you fighting. If you get out of the way, the Qi will master any opponent."

"But how do I get out of the way?" Daniel asked him.

"Let go. Surrender your ego, your will...meditate so deeply that you become nothing..."

CHAPTER SIXTEEN

A few hours after they returned from the trek to the Marshal's residence, Daniel received a call from a Swiss banker client who was in Delhi on business. It was important to see him. He flew out early the next morning. While in Delhi, he telephoned Gita three times. He missed being with her, and, she had discovered, much to her surprise, that she missed him too. As much as she tried to move on with her life, she couldn't stop thinking about this kind and gentle person who professed to love her. To Gita, men were a dark and evil presence she had to put up with for no other reason than they don't go away. Her father had treated her mother like a slave. He was no different than all the other men in Rumla who had beat their wives and treated their daughters as if they were no better than starving dogs; and she couldn't for a moment forget Mahesh Bhahadur *Rana* — his hands and smell, his penis tearing her insides — that brutal night that transformed her from a child into a broken woman. She'd never known kindness in a man before and somewhere, deep inside her scarred and wounded psyche, she thought of Daniel with a smile. It was different with him.

His presence makes me feel so good — as if something inside me can heal, as if I can be a woman around him and not be frightened of men anymore. She enjoyed being with him even if he sometimes had trouble talking to her. If his tongue was tied, so what? Did it matter if he acted like a young boy? It was fun and she liked him that way. The wounded child in her desired someone that could help her find a touch of innocence again.

He returned the following night, reserved a chauffeured Land Rover at the airport, and the next morning he and Gita toured Kathmandu. They went to Boudhanath, where they stopped in many craft shops to look at *thangka* paintings and bronzes of divinities. One dealer showed them an exquisite gold-embossed *Gau* box with a small gilt bronze Buddha peering out of an altar-like window. After examining it carefully, Daniel bought it for his collection. The shopkeeper then showed them a silver necklace with fine turquoise and coral stones he claimed once belonged to royalty.

"My dear," Daniel said to Gita. "You are the queen of the dance. You must have this necklace."

He put it on her neck and bowed.

"No, Daniel," she said in awe.

"Why not?"

He told her that the necklace would be a small token of his love, and she should always remember it as his first gift. Hopefully, there will be many more, but this one would be the most precious.

"You're a crazy man," Gita said.

"Drunken crazy in love with you," he replied.

Across the crowded plaza, at the base of the Boudhanath *stupa*, where Tibetan pilgrims circled its circumference and chanted *Om Mani Padme Om*, each pilgrim fingering japa beads and turning large prayer wheels, Daniel and Gita joined the line, and silently, and with deep respect, they walked together around the *chorten*.

"Would you like to know what kind of a wish I made?" Daniel asked Gita.

"Yes," she responded shyly.

"There'll come a day when you'll give me your heart," he said, "and I can cuddle up there and spend a great deal of time."

Daniel took her hand in his and its very touch ignited a lightness of being inside her — a joy she'd known only as a child and a trust in life that had vanished when she was sixteen years old. Can it be, she thought, that my heart is his home; that I can love him and let him into my life?

"How about lunch at the Hotel Yak and Yeti?" he asked.

"Yes, yes," she answered smiling. "It's one of my favorite places. I love the gardens there."

✳ ✳ ✳

Their table at the Yak and Yeti's Sunrise Cafe overlooked beautifully landscaped gardens and pools where colorful bougainvillea, roses, bamboo, birds of paradise, jasmine, magnolia and jacaranda trees created a dazzling background to the restaurant's décor. There were sparrows, magpie robins and golden-throated barbets darting back and forth among the flora that covered the well-tended gardens. A lone gardener plucked the weeds from soil that needed excessive watering for the lush plants to continue to thrive.

"Why us? Why did we meet now?" Gita asked Daniel. The waiter had just brought two rose water lassis to their table and they ordered lunch.

"Only the gods know," he answered her.

"It must be our karma," she whispered. "No one in my village ever told me that it was possible to love someone else."

"What we have is truly an arranged marriage," Daniel replied. No matter how much he thought about it, he couldn't find another way to put it. "Not by the rules of your village, but by the same gods that rule the Himalayas. They brought the two of us together."

"I love you, Daniel," she said softly. "I never thought that I could say that to anyone."

After lunch, they strolled along Durbar *Marg* to Thamel. Its main street had a crush of dense pedestrian traffic — mostly tourists that spoke a cross section of languages from different parts of the world. Gita felt a tug at the hem of her skirt and discovered Aadesh, the legless boy who had brought her to the beggar merchant, Sonam — the same boy who had promised her money and a place to sleep if she worked for his boss.

"Gita," he said to her in Nepalese. "It's been awhile."

She tried to walk away, but Aadesh continued to pull at the hem of her skirt.

"Have you forgotten your past?" he asked her.

"How could I forget living on the streets?" she said to him angrily. She took a hundred-rupee note from her purse that he immediately snatched from her hand.

"You've become very rich," the boy said with a sneer. "I'll tell Sonam. He'll find you."

Unable to understand what they were saying, Daniel interrupted them to ask Gita what was going on.

"Nothing," she answered. "I'm tired. Let's go home."

Daniel took a step towards the legless boy, who immediately let go of the hem of Gita's skirt.

"Do you know him?" Daniel asked.

"Yes," Gita answered.

"What do you mean?"

"From a million years ago," she said, "from a different life." From a time, she thought unhappily, that could haunt me until the day I die.

"Sensei once told me that the past doesn't exist," Daniel said. They were now walking together towards Durbar *Marg*. "It's just a shadow without substance that trails after us."

"I would like to meet your Sensei."

"You will," Daniel replied. "When you come to New York."

"Maybe in a few weeks," Gita smiled.

"There are no accidents," Daniel said. "You and I have probably known each other for many lifetimes."

"You're more Nepalese than I am."

"No," he answered. "Just a man in love."

"And I am a woman in love," Gita blurted out in a loud cheerful voice. She threw her arms up in the air, circled him, and danced a light, airy dance. "A woman in love," she laughed. "I've never known what that means, but now that I do know, I really like the feeling."

He didn't try to touch her or kiss her or do anything that would make her move away from him. He was also a man in love, but he had to wait. He had decided to return to New York without Gita and only time would tell whether or not they'd ever be permanently together. If they loved each other, he thought, the strength of that love would more than overcome their fears.

✳ ✳ ✳

Later that night, after Gita retired to her bedroom, she replayed the events of the day in her mind. It was all so perfect, she thought, the walk around the Boudhanath *stupa*, the necklace Daniel had given her and the lunch they had shared at the Hotel Yak and Yeti.

But, he's leaving for New York in a few days and he'll forget the village girl he met in Kathmandu, she mused with some trepidation.

There was a hollow ache in her stomach and she began to shiver and wonder why she ever got involved with him. Maybe the people in Rumla are right: love is nothing more than fleeting moments that unhinge young women; moments that make us happy and sad and force us lie in bed at night and cry. New York is so far away…Daniel has a life there…and he'll remember me as a silly person who danced for a moment in his heart. He's nothing but a man, she thought, and he'll move on to someone else who's a better fit than me. I'll become a fond memory — his niece's friend — a person who could never find a rightful place in New York City; and she wondered to what depths of foolishness she could possibly sink. But at least he didn't touch me; at least we didn't make love. I'd rather die then remember Daniel the same way I remember Mahesh Bhahadur *Rana*.

She stared into the pitch-black darkness of her room and listened to the familiar sounds of night birds and crickets and the voices of people shouting in the distance, and thought that Daniel's world was so foreign to her — the newness of it — this man who wanted to take her in his arms and share his life with her; the newness of it made her tremble and kept her from falling asleep.

What would happen if we did marry? Her thoughts continued. What would happen the first time we slept together and he discovered that I'm not a virgin? Although most westerners say that it doesn't matter. It might to Daniel. Then what would happen? She didn't know, and it scared her... it really scared her...

⁕ ⁕ ⁕

Though Gita rehearsed with Sara at the Marshal's house for hours every day in preparation for her concert at Juilliard, though the excitement of a trip to New York kept building, though Daniel telephoned her almost every other morning and they'd talk for at least twenty minutes, she couldn't help feeling that something was amiss. The idea of being in New York frightened her; the idea of flying in an airplane, of leaving Nepal, of meeting Daniel again, all of these ideas were so overwhelming that they upset the equilibrium of her day-to-day reality.

"I'm just a Nepalese girl," she said to Sara after one rehearsal, "and what do I know about New York, about Juilliard, about love, and these sensations that come at me like a river overflowing its banks."

"It's a great river," Sara responded, "and I'm glad to navigate it with you."

"You make a joke about everything," Gita said. "But, none of this is funny."

"What's wrong with any of this?" Sara asked. "Love, success, dancing in one of the great theaters in the world — any other woman would die for the chance."

"I'm not any other woman," Gita replied, "and maybe, all of this will kill me."

"I doubt it," Sara shrugged. "Come. Let's get a *ras malai*."

What troubled Gita most was her relationship with Daniel. She couldn't understand how two people could live a lifetime together without getting in each other's way. Eventually they'd have to grow tired of it. It was so new to her, so overbearing, what with Daniel, Juilliard, and New York at the same time, she wanted nothing more than to disappear and not be heard from again. She had to laugh at herself — the village girl stepping into a new life, frightened and happy at the same time, not knowing how this all happened, but trying to embrace it and trying to let herself be taken into unchartered territory.

In late September, Gita and Diana flew to New York. When Gita saw

Daniel waving to them from the Delta Terminal — smiling with a bouquet of white magnolias in his right hand, a childlike exuberance that embraced her and told her how happy he was that she had come.

"I never thought I'd live to see this," Diana said while looking at them embracing. She stepped aside. "Never," she smiled, "but it makes me very happy to be here with both of you. It's like," she thought for a moment, "an impossible dream has finally come true."

"You remembered," Gita said to him and took one of the magnolias and put it in her hair.

"How could I forget your favorite flower?"

This is the man I want to live with, she thought. This is the first man who's shown me that intimacy is possible. I'm lost in his world and I don't want to come out. She looked into his eyes and kissed him on the lips.

"I was afraid to come here," she whispered .

"And now?" he asked.

"You're Daniel," she said smiling at him, "and I'm learning what it means to be in love."

CHAPTER SEVENTEEN
(Rumla – June, 2010)

With the first trace of dawn, Gita rose from the mat where she and Daniel had spent a restless night. She stepped out of the hut, and walked across the village commons now bathed in the orange, pink and white light that peeked over the mountains and created patches of sun and shade blanketing the street. Gita entered her family's hut where Kamala — whose eyes were open and breathing labored — was lying face up and staring blankly at the ceiling.

"Good morning, *ama*," Gita said.

She kissed Kamala's hand, sat cross-legged at the foot of the cot and gently massaged her mother's feet. She could feel the rough, almost leather-like texture of *ama's* soles. For Gita these were the battle scars of village life — the many years of hard, grueling work picking lentils and millet, milking goats and water buffalo, cooking and cleaning — survival work that put food on the table for her entire family. Gita soaked Kamala's feet in warm water and massaged her ankles and calves.

"You have come home to me," Kamala said in barely a whisper. "My miracle child."

"Do you forgive me, *ama*?"

"For what, my daughter."

"For having stayed away so long."

"It feels like only a second to me now that I know you are still alive. You're here, my love. You're with me. All I want to do is take a walk with you around the village. Somehow I'll find the strength if you help me to stand up, Gita, angel; if you help me to walk with you."

"But, *ama*," Gita said, "you must rest."

"I will have plenty of time to rest when the goddess prepares me for my next incarnation," Kamala said in barely a whisper. "Now I want to take a walk with my daughter. Come. Help me to stand."

Gita placed her mother's feet on the floor, and gently lifted her until Kamala stood erect, making sure that her mother's right arm was secure around her neck.

"Let's walk," Gita said.

"Yes," Kamala responded. "I want to walk through the village with my daughter who's come home at last. I want everyone to see us together."

So they walked slowly out of the hut, step by agonizing step, they walked through the light and shadow patches blanketing the village, past many friends and relatives who watched them from their doorsteps, past Daniel who sat in front of the door to Aunt Gauri's hut, and the whole village listened to Kamala repeat, "My daughter Gita is alive. She has come home to me. She has come home to me..."

* * *

Kamala died three days later. Gauri and Gita met with the priest and made arrangements to cremate her. Four pallbearers carried her body wrapped in a shroud to the cremation ground near the river. They put the body on a three-tiered base of dried wooden tree trunks. Sivan started a fire and Gita and Daniel placed a sacred shawl on Kamala while the white-robed priest chanted Hindu mantras. As the fire's intensity grew, it consumed the body and turned it to ash.

Every member of the village, except Gita's father, had come to the cremation grounds to look on in silence. While listening to the priest chant prayers for the dead, Gauri remembered her own daughters whose lives she had neither the courage nor cunning to save.

"Your mother was a brave woman," Gauri said to Gita. "She deserves to have some rest."

The smell of burning flesh, the priests in white robes, dogs and goats scavenging near the pyre, the laughter of children bathing in the river, and many of the villagers praying to the goddess — the entire spectacle transcended Daniel's limited Western experience and he stood in awe from the beginning of the ceremony to its end.

"*All that dies is the body,*" Daniel remembered his Sensei once saying. "*The soul continues to live through eternity. We shed our clothing. We go naked before the universe. We dress in another costume, then another, until we finally realize that coming and going is also an illusion.*"

After the cremation ceremony ended, Gauri told Gita that all the young men had either become traffickers or moved to Kathmandu to find brides. They wanted nothing more to do with Rumla. The old people were the last vestiges of life in the village.

"When we die," she said tearfully, "there will be nothing left here."

Gita didn't know how to answer Gauri. The idea of her village becoming extinct was so imminent and real that she had to face the truth: the steady loss of young people would turn Rumla into a ghost town. No one wanted to live here anymore. The men had gambled and drank away the soul of the village. But at least the goddess had spared her mother's witnessing the demise of Rumla; and Gita decided, from this point forward, whenever she danced or played the *veena*, a prayer would be said for the people of this vanishing community.

"You're the image of your mother," Gauri said. "I see her in your eyes and smile and the way you walk. I'm not sure where America is, but I hope it blesses you with a good life."

After the priest placed Kamala's ashes in the water, Gita told Aunt Gauri that she and Daniel had to leave for Kathmandu. Once they'd taken care of *ama's* final wishes, they would return to America.

"Come back to your village," Gauri said, "but if you can't, just remember you will always be in my prayers."

"I would have liked to have known your mother," Daniel said to Gita.

"That would have been a great blessing," Gita answered. "She was an extraordinary woman who slaved unselfishly for every member of this community."

For so many years, Gita had hidden her love for Kamala behind a wall of anger, not realizing that she'd probably be dead today if it weren't for her mother.

"I also love this village," Gita told Daniel. "I'm begging you to never let me forget where I come from."

"I don't think I'll have to," Daniel replied.

He looked one more time at the spot in the river where the priest had placed Kamala's ashes — a custom so foreign to him, but nonetheless, so moving that it touched the core of his being. She was born here, she lived here and died here, he thought, and how knowingly the river's current has taken her ashes into its keep.

They left the cremation grounds, walked eight hours through the forest to the village where the car and driver waited for them, and drove back to Kathmandu.

CHAPTER EIGHTEEN
(June 2010)

In Kathmandu, there were cows, Brahman bulls, goats, water buffalo, dogs, and other creatures resting on the sides of the roads in a bit of shade. They refused to move for hours on end. The dust and pollution forced many inhabitants of the valley to wear masks when they ventured outdoors. It was the height of summer and the beginning of the monsoons. The infernal heat, humidity, and torrential rains made life in the valley unbearable.

Bob had just returned home for lunch from a busy morning at the American embassy of meetings with the Nepalese and Indian Prime Ministers, local businessmen, and a few members of parliament, where immigration and water rights, military alliances and trade agreements were discussed in depth. He and Daniel were seated on the living room couch, drinking cold beer, and enjoying the air-conditioned comfort of the Marshal residence.

"What can you do about Gita's little sisters in a Mumbai brothel?" Daniel asked Bob.

Bob replied, somewhat embarrassed, "It's beyond my control. If they were American, I could do something. But they're Nepalese and the whole situation is outside of my jurisdiction."

"They're her little sisters, dammit," Daniel replied. "Laws are one thing, but we're talking about children enslaved in the sex trade."

"International treaties suck," Bob answered sarcastically. "But that's the way life is here."

"You mean trade and water rights can be discussed with the Nepalese and Indian governments, but not the lives of children living in brothels."

"It's about money and image," Bob said. "Just about every Indian knows there are thousands of girls held captive in Mumbai, but if you ask the Indian Prime Minister, he'll shrug his shoulders and deny everything. His country is beyond reproach, and its people are upstanding citizens of the world."

"Gita wants to rescue her sisters," Daniel said.

"She'll get herself killed," Bob replied without flinching. He took another sip of his beer.

"That's what I thought you'd say. Isn't there anything you can do?"

"Not directly," Bob answered. "The whole freakin' Indian and Nepalese governments are on someone or another's payroll. I hate it, Diana hates it, but there's nothing that can be done."

"And the American authorities stand by and watch?"

"We have no authority in this part of the world. There's *baksheesh*. That's it! People get paid a dollar a day to work. It's barely enough to put food in their mouths. Believe it or not, slavery is alive and well on the South Asian subcontinent. If it means selling your daughter into a life of whoredom, so be it. If it puts food on the table or provides the money for another daughter's dowry or some *rakshi*, then it's a bargain."

"What about Gita?" He asked Bob.

"Go home, Daniel," Bob said. "You both have good lives in the States. You don't want any part of this."

He knew that Gita would never turn her back on her mother's dying wish and the last thing he wanted was for Bob to tell him to go home.

"There's must be someone in Mumbai you can call," Daniel said. "If bribery runs this place, then we can buy Prema and Renu's freedom."

"Possibly. But first we've got to find them."

Bob told Daniel that the red light district in Mumbai resembled an anthill that teemed with underaged prostitutes — a typical working class neighborhood where poor men went to get laid at forty rupees a hit. For that you got one orgasm, syphilis, gonorrhea, AIDS, and any other venereal disease known to mankind. It was truly the lower depths.

"You've painted quite a picture."

"It ain't Upper West Side living," Bob replied with resignation.

"I'm going with her," Daniel said.

"I think you're both crazy."

"Just get us a few contacts in Mumbai. I know you can do that."

"I beg you to think about it," Bob said. "It's a viper's nest that no one can untangle."

"Do you have any contacts?" Daniel kept pressing.

"Yes, I have contacts."

"Then please make some calls for us," Daniel said and left the room.

He opened the front door of the house, but the heat was so oppressive, he decided to remain indoors, and shoot pool in the playroom.

What if it was my own sister or niece, he thought.

He racked the balls and prepared to take a shot. As much as he tried, he couldn't quite grasp the horror of fourteen-year-old children being sold by their own fathers to smugglers of human cargo. The very thought made him angry. There had to be a ring in Dante's inferno for creeps that preyed on helpless people; there had to be a fire that scorched their minds and bodies and turned every vestige of their being into ash. He could have easily lined all those sons-a-bitches against a wall and blown their brains out.

Gita watched Daniel at the pool table. He was attempting a shot and she didn't want to interrupt him. He nodded at her, put the cue stick down, and said with trepidation, "Bob's unable to do anything for your sisters. They're Nepalese and outside his jurisdiction."

"If they were the daughters of an American senator, you'd see how fast he'd do something," Gita said angrily.

"I know," Daniel answered without moving.

"They're my sisters," Gita pressed on. "I promised my mother I'd find them."

"You haven't seen your sisters in thirteen years," Daniel said. He cued up again and broke the racked balls scattering them all over the table. His mind and heart were so full of anger that he had spoken to Gita in a voice he had never used before.

"So?" She answered somewhat taken aback.

"You probably wouldn't recognize them if they walked into this room," Daniel said visibly upset.

"What else do you have to say?" She paused for a moment and waited for a response, then walked quickly towards the door.

"Wait," he said. "Don't go. I'm sorry I spoke to you the way I did, but whatever happened to Prema and Renu could have happened to you."

"Or Sara," she interjected. "I'd rather die than break my promise to *ama*." She walked up to him and sat on the edge of the pool table.

"I know. I understand," he said. He put his arms around her and kissed her lightly on the forehead. "I will do whatever I can to help you find them."

"Do you know what they do with fourteen-year-old virgins?" she asked him. "They're toys given to slimy rich men who can get anything they want. You want crazy! Well, that's crazy! That's beyond crazy."

"I could never have dreamed any of this," Daniel said.

"Do you think I come without a past?"

"No," he answered, "but it's the first I've heard about it."

"There's much more that I've never told you," she said with dampened eyes. "I've got to go to Mumbai. It's my family matter and I will take care of it."

"I know," Daniel, said, "I'll go with you. We're married…"

"Yes. For better or worse…"

"Gita, I'm on your side."

"Then, let me do what I have to do."

"I'm not stopping you."

"You know nothing about my demons."

"Then tell me. You've never spoken to me about any of this."

"I don't know if I can. It's so painful I promised myself I wouldn't talk about it to anyone."

Daniel reached out and gently touched her face. "Did you forget who I am?" he asked.

"No," she said tearfully. Something opened inside her and she put her arms around Daniel. "I've never loved anyone. I never thought I would find a person like you on earth. I love you. But, I'm still afraid you won't understand."

"Then tell me," he said. "Trust me."

"You may not want to touch me again. You might ask me to leave, Daniel, and I couldn't bear living without you."

"Just let it go, Gita. It will only make us closer."

She told him about her life in the *Rana's* house; she told him about the rape, about how she ran away in the middle of the night and lived by her smarts on the streets of Kathmandu.

"After many months of sleeping in a courtyard, miraculously, I found the St. Christopher orphanage, Sister Anne, and then Diana and Sara later. I never told your family about my past. You're the only one who knows."

"Why did you go to the *Rana's* house?" Daniel asked her after a moment's pause.

"I found out the other day from my Aunt Gauri that *ama* put me in that house to keep my father from selling me to traffickers. If it weren't for my mother, I would have been a prostitute in a Mumbai brothel."

Daniel's eyes began to moisten. He realized that all of his education, money, business acumen and martial arts training gave him no insight into Gita's past. There are hundreds of kids like her living on the Kathmandu streets, he thought, simple village people driven by centuries-old religious customs and extreme poverty. These conditions forced their parents to commit horrendous acts that in the eyes of the world are nothing more than a societal nuisance.

"I was afraid you'd leave me if I told you any of this," she sighed. "In

Nepal, I would be kicked out of my village."

"It's not possible for me to ever leave you," Daniel said.

"But, my past?"

"It's dead. It's over. It will never get between us. I mean that, Gita. We have our lives now. We have each other and there's nothing more important than that."

His words relieved her of a pain that had gnawed at her heart for more than five years.

"And Mumbai?" she asked him. "I have to go."

"We'll go together," he said softly. "But, let me speak with Bob again."

"What for? He told you there's nothing the American government can do. But what if Prema was his daughter? What if...?" She broke down again. Daniel held her close for a long time.

"I don't know what I can do for Prema and Renu," she finally said, "but I have to try something."

"Of course."

"And I have to do this alone."

It didn't matter to her that Daniel spoke the language of the law courts. She spoke the language of the streets. She could also speak Hindi and Nepali. Gita promised Daniel that she'd go into the brothels and come out with her little sisters.

There was a knock on the game room door and Diana and Bob entered.

"Why don't you lovebirds go back to New York?" Bob said. "There are no Mumbai *gundas* on Central Park West and you can live peaceful lives."

"Knowing my sisters are in a brothel," Gita replied, "I don't see how it's possible for me to live a peaceful life."

"I understand," Bob said. After a moment's hesitation, he told them in a serious voice that he had called an Indian friend in Mumbai who knew the ropes. His name was Balaram Gupta. He would meet them at the airport and take them to an apartment where they would stay. "He will also act as a liaison between you and the Indian government."

"I know you're going out on a limb," Daniel said.

"I don't know what he can do," Bob replied, "but he's smart, well-trained, retired from a confidential position and a good friend. He'll keep his mouth shut and give you whatever help is possible."

"How can I thank you?" Gita asked.

Bob just shrugged his shoulders as if both Gita and Daniel were crazy.

"When do you want to leave so I can alert him?" Bob asked them after a moment.

"In the morning."

"You're like Don Quixote," Bob said. "You're chasing windmills in South Asia."

"Who's Don Quixote?" Gita asked Daniel.

"A character in a book. He was mad and fun. He made the decision to become a knight errant and battle evil in the world."

"I don't want to battle the world's evil," Gita said. "I just want to get my little sisters out of Mumbai."

"It's enough to qualify you and your husband as two characters from Cervantes' book," Bob said. "You don't have to do this."

"What if it was Sara?" Gita asked him.

"I'd go to Mumbai and kill every one of the sons-a-bitches," Bob admitted. He shrugged his shoulders again, and hugged them both.

"Be careful, huh," he said. "They're dangerous people."

"We will," Gita said.

"I've got to go to my office now. I can't be late. But, hey, Don Quixotes, there's still time to reconsider. You've got until tomorrow morning."

"Thanks, Bob," Daniel said. "Thanks for what you've done."

After Bob left the room, Diana took Gita's hand and gave her a coral amulet of the god Ganesha.

"You're like my daughter," she said to Gita. "This will protect you, but remember, you're not Durga, you're just another human being."

"I'll remember," Gita replied. "I'll also never forget that you took me into your house without ever asking questions and made it possible for me to have a life. You showed me that love exists in this world."

CHAPTER NINETEEN
(The next day)

The Mumbai airport was a crowded fluorescent shell full of soldiers and police officers and quasi-important government officials sitting around doing little or nothing at all.

When Daniel and Gita disembarked from the plane, they were greeted by Balaram Gupta, a short, dark-skinned, bundle of energy, dressed in a rumpled white shirt and rumpled white trousers, who took their passports, and ushered them through immigration as if they were heads of state.

"You live up to your reputation," Daniel said when Gupta returned their passports. "Do you have any connections at New York airports?"

"No, Mr. Gold, but I am a master magician at this airport especially for the brother-in-law of my good friend Bob Marshal. I welcome you and your wife to Mumbai," Balaram Gupta said with a big smile. His hands were together prayer-like and he bowed to Daniel and Gita.

"My car is outside, but first, I have to get your luggage. Follow me."

They went to the luggage carousel where Daniel pointed out their bags. Balaram's man put them on a cart and they all proceeded to walk through the green-lighted custom's exit. Gupta stopped for a moment and chatted with a few of the officers on duty. He waved at some others and joined Daniel and Gita in the airport terminal.

They left the terminal and were hit by a blast of hot humid air. It felt more like a steam room than a crowded pickup area where they had to wait patiently for the driver to return with Gupta's car.

"The weather in Mumbai is very unpleasant this time of the year," he said. "It's so hot you can't go out after noon. One never gets used to it."

He purchased three copies of the *Hindustani Times*, gave one to Daniel and another to Gita and kept the third for himself. "Fans," he said laughing, and waved the newspaper in front of his face creating a slight breeze.

"Last summer, when I met Bob in Manali, we enjoyed the cool mountain air together. Bob, Diana, my wife and I spent a month there. We forgot about the heat. But now the crows and kites stay in the shade, and people are panting for a breath of fresh air."

"Me, too," Daniel joked as he fanned himself with the newspaper. "I'd give anything for a cold shower."

"There's too much pollution in Mumbai," Gupta went on in a disgusted voice as he continued to fan himself. "The government does nothing about it and the entire city is going to die from emphysema and lung cancer."

"We had to come here," Gita said almost apologetically.

"I know," Gupta replied, "but when Bob informed me that you were coming, I told him that no one should visit Mumbai now. Even the rats leave. They have more sense than us humans."

They entered an air-conditioned car and were driven through the Mumbai slums near the airport — one sheet metal shanty after the other lined the road and countless half-naked men slept in the shade.

"It'll rain this afternoon," Balaram Gupta said. "The monsoons cool things down."

The car pulled away from the slums and onto Mumbai's boulevards where large, garish billboard posters on building tops advertised Bollywood's latest offerings. Many of the edifices were built by the Raj. Most were soot-covered, dark, ornate, Victorian structures in need of repair.

Gupta had a guest apartment in the Colaba District. It was fully air conditioned and on the tenth floor of a building that faced the Arabian Sea. There was also a servant in the apartment to help them with all their needs. In case of an emergency, he lived just around the corner. They could text him or telephone him and he would be at their service.

"You should be comfortable there," he said to Daniel and Gita, "you'll find that it's a blissful retreat from this infernal hot weather."

"That's so kind of you," Gita said. "There's a great deal we need to talk about."

"But, later," Gupta replied. "When we have dinner."

There's a mystery that always lurks behind the obvious, Daniel thought as he looked out the car window at the streets of Mumbai. It was behind the glistening smiles of actresses in Bollywood movie posters, behind the helpless look of shoeless, half-naked lepers begging on street corners, and young girls holding infants in their arms and poking their expressionless faces into car windows; it was in Gita's beautiful eyes, her suffering lurked beneath the surface in a mind that couldn't forget, in a broken heart, in a mother's dying wish, in a desire to do the impossible.

It was always a mystery to him why human beings suffered the way they did, a mystery why one person was born on the streets of Mumbai and another in the lap of Park Avenue luxury. It was a mystery why people, no matter where they were born, never seemed to be happy.

After what seemed to be an interminable tour of the boulevards and seashore of Mumbai, Gupta's driver parked the car in a lot at the foot of a multi-storied apartment building.

"Here we are," Balaram Gupta said. "The apartment is on the tenth floor."

"Is it like this every summer?" Daniel asked him as they got out of the car.

"Pretty much. I usually go away, but this summer, my wife's not feeling well, and we couldn't leave. I'm afraid that we will spend June in South Asian hell."

"I always thought hell was a western concept," Daniel said.

"It is when you die," Gupta responded, "but for our brief stay on earth, there's no greater hell than life on the Indian subcontinent during the early summer."

"At least it rains," Daniel said.

"Yes," Gupta laughed, "for days and weeks at a time, until the streets become rivers, and whatever's not tied down winds up floating into the Arabian Sea. It's not just rain we have in Mumbai, but a rush of water descending to earth like your Niagara Falls. I've heard wise men say the Hindu gods cry all summer, I've heard them say the gods will continue to cry until people stop messing with the earth."

"You think people will stop?" Gita asked.

"No," Gupta said. "That's why everything's got to be tied down, that's why the monsoons will continue until the last human being either dies or moves to another planet."

"At the end of time," Daniel said dryly.

"Perhaps," Gupta replied. "But, don't worry. We'll all be there, you, Gita, Bob and Diana, my wife and myself, we'll all be there, and we'll laugh ourselves into a state of divine nothingness."

"I'd like to do that now," Daniel chuckled.

"Don't let me stop you," Gupta said. "Don't let me stand between you and your spiritual enlightenment."

"I won't," Daniel said. "I promise you, I'll never hold you accountable."

✳ ✳ ✳

The well-appointed apartment was decorated with antique Portuguese and Dutch Colonial furniture. There was a large rosewood table at the center of the dining room with a heavily-carved skirt and lion's paw legs, a table, which could easily sit a dozen people, was surrounded by twelve

Regency-styled ebony chairs. Standing against a wall was a monumental sideboard crafted in rosewood. The rest of the furniture, whether it was an assortment of chairs, a center and sofa table, a hallstand, beds and dressers were all hand-carved from teak.

On the walls, there were nineteenth century Company School paintings done by Indian artists for the Raj, scenes of British caravansaries, of finely drawn animals and various architectural landscapes, and standing in select apartment niches and on pedestals were tenth and eleventh century South Indian Chola Dynasty stone and bronze sculptures of different divinities.

"My father was a student of the Raj," Gupta said. "He also worked for the British government and collected art and antiquities."

"I can see," Daniel said.

"I've made arrangements for us to have dinner this evening," Gupta said to them, "at an excellent Chinese restaurant in the Taj Mahal hotel." He walked towards the door.

"There's a great deal we have to discuss with you," Gita said to him.

"Here's my card," Gupta said. He handed it to Daniel. "If you need anything, don't hesitate to contact me." He shook both their hands. "I must go, now. Is eight o'clock good for you?"

"That'll be fine," Daniel said.

"I'll pick you up."

"Thank you, Mr. Gupta," Gita said.

"Balaram's my name," he replied. "Americans call each other by their first names. So, please call me Balaram."

"We'll see you at eight," Daniel said.

"Goodbye for now," Balaram Gupta said. "Don't go out in this heat. It'll cool off a bit later this afternoon."

※ ※ ※

Gita had read that sixteen million people lived in Mumbai. Somewhere in this warren of activity, she thought, Prema and Renu were being held captive by sexual predators. Even if she did find them, could she, single-handedly, combat Mumbai *gundas*. Could she really help them to escape? The first thing was to find them, then tackle the rest.

Daniel's mind also grappled with the complexity of the situation. Though he had no watermark by which to gauge the horror of teenage girls in Mumbai brothels, he told himself that the child living in Gita's sisters was like the child in all of us — a precious jewel hidden beneath life's horrors. Renu and Prema were now trapped in a world so full of man's inhumanity that no one could fully understand how it continued to thrive; they've become disposable commodities that entertained creeps who don't care about anything but their own pleasure.

"We'll find them," Daniel said with determination, but beneath his stolid composure, there was serious doubt. He walked over to Gita and put his arms around her.

She kissed him on his neck and mouth. He returned her kiss and they lay down on the bed in one another's arms. Gita started to cry — her taut body was full of fear. Daniel massaged her neck and back.

"Just listen to your breathing," he said to her in a soft voice, "to the inhalation and exhalation." He continued to gently massage her neck and back until Gita fell asleep.

✳ ✳ ✳

The sun's fiery reds and oranges burst through the heat's haze and ignited the Arabian Sea. Daniel stood on the apartment's terrace watching hawks and kites glide in a cloudless sky. He also looked at people on the sidewalk bordering the beach: a man jogged, crowds gathered, children chased each other; and he heard the loud cries of merchants trying to sell tourists postcards and souvenirs. People were beginning to leave the secretive world of apartments and residences, and Mumbai came to life.

"We'd better get ready to meet Balaram," Daniel said.

"Okay. I'm going to shower." Gita walked towards the bathroom, stopped, and went to the window where Daniel was absorbed by the human panorama down below. "Do you think he can help us?" She asked.

"I don't know. But, we'll find out tonight."

"I can't lose hope. No matter what Balaram says I've got to find them."

"I don't know how we're going to do it, but we will."

After Gita went to the bathroom, he poured himself a shot of straight scotch and sat on the couch, sipping it slowly. It was getting dark outside. The Mumbai lights were like a giant decoration mimicking the stars.

So this was India: the land of enlightened *nagababas* and spiritual adepts, the land of the Bhagavad Gita, the Vedas and The Ramayan — the land of child trafficking and sexual depravity. Daniel promised himself that he would do whatever was necessary to help Gita find her sisters, but, at the moment, he couldn't imagine how this would get done...

＊ ＊ ＊

The Golden Dragon restaurant at the Taj was full of local Mumbai glitterati enjoying an evening meal after suffering through the stifling daytime heat. A number of business travelers were scattered about the room trying to catch a glimpse of Bollywood celebrities. The waiter brought them dim sum appetizers, one after the other, the dainty morsels of shrimp and duck and pork wrapped in dough. The background buzz of dinnertime conversation, the occasional loud voice that rose above the others, played on Gita's nerves. She resented this wealthy crowd — even if she was now one of them — who seemed oblivious to the city's dark heart.

"Bob told me why you're here," Balaram said to Daniel and Gita. "I mean the odds of finding your sisters are one in a million."

"But there's a chance," Gita said. She lowered a quarter-eaten shrimp ball to her plate.

"Some possibility if Prema was trafficked a month ago," Balaram answered, "but, Renu, I don't know. In that world, it depends on the crime ring. She could be anywhere. Three or four years are a very long time."

He studied Gita's drawn and unhappy face, took a deep breath and sipped some red wine, and quickly looked at Daniel whose stoic expression revealed no emotional upset — a stoicism that pleased Gupta.

"Trafficking is a criminal business that has been run by entrenched mafia in India for generations," Balaram said. "It demeans my country and touches every part of the Mumbai underworld. The *gundas* force young girls to sleep with countless men. They make tens of millions of rupees, and discard disease-ridden children like filthy dishrags. They kidnap these kids from villages or buy them from peasant families in Nepal, India, and Burma, then bring them here. It's a mega-business run like drug cartels. There are thousands of young girls working as prostitutes on Falkland Road. The upper echelon police and government officials are paid handsomely to mind their own business and the brothels operate without shame or fear."

"And my sisters?" Gita asked.

"There's no way to know what has happen to them," Gupta said without emotion. He took another sip of his wine and looked again at Daniel, but saw no sign of nervousness. He thought that this stoic brother-in-law of Bob Marshal must have been trained in the martial arts.

"The authorities are complicit?" Daniel asked.

Gupta lifted a shrimp dumpling with his chopsticks, put it in his mouth, and chewed slowly. "You have to realize something: cops in this city make just enough money to keep their families off the streets. When the *gundas* slip them *lakhs* of rupees under the table, it's more money then most of them see in a year. They become silent partners in organized crime. If a newspaperman or an aggressive cop makes any noise about the brothels, the life of the reporter or the policeman is worth about as much as a water bug. The *gundas* and the high-ranking police and government officials will make sure the squawker is killed or beaten to a pulp."

Balaram paused for a moment, took another sip of his wine, and looked at Daniel and Gita to see if they wanted to hear more.

"I made a promise to find my sisters," Gita said breaking the silence.

"If they are in a house on Falkland Road, there's little chance of finding them," Gupta responded. "It's a drug-infested labyrinth where street after street of AIDS-infected girls work in brothels, one slimier than the other."

But, he knew other houses that catered to wealthy clients — even people from the West. If Prema happens to be a beautiful teenage virgin, she'd be worth a great deal of money in upscale brothels on Governor Road.

"Where's Falkland Road? Where's Governor Road?" Gita asked. She put her chopsticks down and stared at Gupta.

"Falkland Road is a few miles from Colaba in the middle of a Mumbai ghetto, and Governor Road's not far from here," he said after pouring some red wine for Daniel, Gita and himself. "Governor Road is a well-landscaped street on which a number of Raj mansions are set up like private clubs catering to the sexual needs of the very wealthy. Though it borders on this neighborhood, don't be fooled. These brothels are guarded, secretive, and dangerous places from which none of the girls can escape. The whole business is done by word of mouth. Rich men in this country know exactly where to go to get what they want."

He folded his napkin, looked carefully at Gita and Daniel, and decided that Bob's brother-in-law understood the dangers, but his wife was determined to get herself killed. Was this what my good friend wanted me to do? It wasn't easy for him to speak this way, but he had to tell them the truth. He didn't want to paint a false image of what they were up against.

"I could bring you there tomorrow evening when it cools down," he said to Gita.

"That's too late," she replied. "I want to go first thing in the morning."

"I thought you'd at least take tomorrow to think over what I've said."

"My sisters lives are at stake," Gita answered. "There's nothing to think about."

"The *gundas* are a tight-knit family that protect one another," Balaram responded in a stern voice. He could never tolerate people intent on doing the impossible.

"I have a plan," Gita said. "I have an idea that could work."

"It better be a good one. Rotten people smell rotten food easier than we do," Gupta said impatiently. He finished the wine in his glass.

"Can you bring me a few saris?" Gita asked. "I don't have time to shop."

"Yes," Balaram said. "My wife has a closet full of them."

"I'd like you to take me to Falkland Road first thing in the morning."

Gupta shook his head sadly and said, "Of course." He picked up a shrimp ball with his chopsticks, put it in his mouth, and chewed it slowly lapsing into a deep, but clearly nervous silence.

Gita and Daniel noticed the change. "Is there something wrong?" Daniel asked him.

"A year ago, my niece was killed by the *gundas*," he said in a serious voice. "They want virgins. The sons-a-bitches want them because wealthy people with AIDS pay a fortune to sleep with these girls. There's an idiotic belief in India that you can cure venereal disease by sleeping with a virgin. My niece was a sixteen-year-old virgin and that was the reason she died."

"I'm so sorry," Gita said.

"I've never heard anything like that," Daniel said taking Gita's hand. "These people are the worst shits on earth."

"Pretty close," Balaram said. He stood up. "I'd also like to see those bastards get their due." He offered to pay for the check, but Daniel said no. Balaram replied in a muted voice, "I'll be back in an hour with a couple of saris," and he walked slowly to the restaurant's exit.

"Let's get out of here," Daniel said. "I need some fresh air."

They left the restaurant and sauntered through the grand lobby of the Taj Mahal Hotel, so caught up in their own thoughts, they didn't notice the majesty of the place — its extensive inlaid marble flooring, the MF Husain painting behind the reception desk, the large bouquets of bird of paradise flowers, and the buzz of guests seated on stylish furniture in every corner of the room — all of it so remote from the seedy world of child prostitution that it would stretch the limits of Daniel and Gita's imagination to connect the wealthy men that frequented this place with Falkland or Governor Roads.

After they exited the hotel via its front door, crossed the street, and slowly walked on a sidewalk that bordered the beach, Daniel asked Gita to tell him her plan. He had already decided that no matter what it was, finding her sisters was much too dangerous and he wouldn't let her do it.

"Balaram gave me a better idea," she replied. "Tell me what you think. My rich Nepalese uncle has AIDS, and I'm looking for a virgin to cure him. That might turn up Prema."

"If she's still a virgin," he said sarcastically.

"Let's hope so."

"Let's hope she's still alive and that we can find her, and perhaps she'll lead us to Renu. But, this is a large bustling city, Gita, and dammit, she could be anywhere. I mean, she could be held in some prison for the Maharaja of Diddly-Twat whose prick is infested with worms. Do you understand there's no telling where Prema is or if you'll ever see her again? We're up against your deepest hopes and Gupta's harsh realities."

"I have to go alone, Daniel, so please don't even think of coming with me," Gita said with determination. She stopped walking and stared at him.

"But you heard Balaram. Life is cheap in Mumbai brothels."

"No one's going to believe a word I say if I show up with a rich, handsome American on my arm."

"What should I do? I'm not used to feeling helpless."

"Go to the police or the consulate," she said. "Maybe Bob and Balaram have contacts there."

"The police are complicit," Daniel said angrily.

"Balaram might know an honest cop," Gita said.

"You mean more to me than anyone on earth and you're asking me to stand by and watch you go blindly into a snake pit."

She took both his hands in hers, pressed them together and said reassuringly, "I'm a survivor, Daniel, and I know how to deal with these people. I've learned to live by my wits."

"This isn't the Kathmandu streets," Daniel replied. "These brothels are run by mafia goons that murder children for the hell of it. They'd kill you without blinking an eye."

"What do you know about the Kathmandu streets?" Gita asked him angrily.

"Nothing," he responded. "I'm sorry. I'm just afraid of your going there alone."

"Trust me, Daniel. When you live in a Thamel courtyard with beggars and thieves, a sixth sense for danger comes quickly."

"Did I come to Asia to watch you kill yourself?"

"But, my sisters."

"Dammit, I'm married to you, not your sisters."

"My mother went against my father's will and saved my life," Gita said. "Do you know what it is for a Nepalese wife to go against her husband's will?"

"I'm beginning to find out," he replied.

"If it wasn't for my mother I might be dead today or living in a Mumbai brothel."

"You might die there anyway."

"At least I'll try to fulfill her last wishes."

"Your mother had no idea what she was asking you to do."

"She loved her children and wanted them to have a good life. Isn't that enough. What else did she have to know?"

"Nothing, I guess," Daniel said with resignation.

CHAPTER TWENTY

Another hot Mumbai morning, just like the one the day before, except that Gita was now in the car with Balaram Gupta being driven to Falkland Road. Dressed in a floral silk sari, she had a red *tikka* on her forehead. She decided to wear the bracelet Daniel had given her for their anniversary. "It will impress the brothel's Madam," she thought while dressing. She might even be able to use it to buy Prema and Renu's freedom.

The sun's relentless heat beat down on the Mumbai streets. Traffic moved at the pace of a tortoise. There was a nonstop blare of horns — a symphony of street sounds played by an orchestra of frustrated drivers trying their best to navigate their way through a dismal situation.

"Does the noise ever stop?" Gita asked Balaram.

"The beeping of horns is integral to India's ambiance," he shrugged his shoulders and went on to tell her that if the government passed a law forbidding it, the sudden, deep, wellspring of silence could possibly be too much for the citizens of this country to handle.

They drove on a road surrounded by Mumbai shantytowns — a neighborhood in which tens of thousands of rural Indian and Bangladeshi migrants lived in squalor — a hopeless melting pot of humanity that had little or nothing to live for but day-to-day despair. People washed themselves in dirty puddles of water; barefoot children chased each other in the mud; women cooked, young girls brushed each other's hair, and old men tried to clean the miserable four-foot by four-foot plot of open space they called home. Balaram informed Gita that countless young girls disappeared from places like this every month. Traffickers also kidnapped little boys, crippled them, and forced them to beg. Sometimes they'd cut out a child's kidney and sell it to a hospital in need of organs.

Balaram knew that Daniel wouldn't approve of him being so frank about life in Mumbai. But, what choice did he have. Perhaps graphic images of Mumbai's underbelly would make Gita change her mind. But her face was stoic and her eyes were determined, and Gupta decided that this woman was a little mad: nothing he could do or say would change her mind. He had seen this expression before in the eyes of men and women who fought to rid their country of tyrants. He knew that life and death were the same to them. They had a mission; they would succeed no matter what the cost.

"Imagine trying to teach these people birth control," Gupta said to Gita. "Sex might be the only pleasure they have on earth."

If the by-product was a couple of kids crawling about in the mud, he went on to tell her, what difference did it make to them? They didn't know how to read or write and they lived in a crowded, disease-infested slum where they were preyed upon by hunger, filth, and every kind of bacteria and virus, and traffickers, who plucked the youngest and most beautiful of them out of the anthill, and turned them into slaves.

An endless stream of people moved in and out of narrow passageways that gave entrance to a dense cluster of soot-covered huts. They spread out as far as she could see. It reminded her of the poverty she once knew on the streets of Kathmandu. People there also slept on the streets; and cows and goats and dogs fed on piles of garbage that littered the sides of many roads and alleyways.

"And the authorities do nothing about this?" Gita asked.

"The government has forgotten they exist," Gupta replied. "It flexes its muscles with nuclear weapons, but couldn't give a shit whether these people live or die. Gandhi was the last politician who cared about them. He lived with them, learned from them, tried to make a difference. But how many Gandhis are there in the world? One comes along every five hundred years."

"There's something you ought to know," she said to Gupta in a dead serious voice. "I've lived on the streets, and know the desperation in these people's lives."

"You've what?" Gupta asked. She was educated… cosmopolitan…he was taken by surprise.

"I know what it's like sleeping next to piles of garbage," she said to him. "Does that shock you?"

"A little," he smiled. "I would never have suspected."

"Not many people would," she replied. "But, that's a past life. Tell me something, are we far from Falkland Road?"

"Just a few minutes."

The streets were average Mumbai streets lined with shops and narrow sidewalks packed with streams of pedestrians. The buildings were covered with soot. They were tired wooden structures leaning on each other like wounded soldiers limping home from war. Balaram made a right turn and said, "This is Falkland Road. The side streets are also full of brothels."

"Let me out," Gita said.

"Are you crazy? There's nothing you can do here."

"Please, stop the car," she said in a more determined voice. "I want to walk around."

"I'll come with you."

"No, Balaram. I need to do this alone."

"This is one of the most dangerous places in Mumbai. Women disappear here all the time."

"Like my sisters," she said. "They could be in one of these houses. I'm not going to find out if you're with me."

"Okay," he sighed. "I'll wait for you in the shade over there. If your sisters are in this shit hole, you'll never find them."

"I can ask the girls on the street. Maybe they'll tell me."

"Don't be naïve. Do you think any of these girls give a damn about your sisters? They're all frightened parakeets. Once they become Falkland Road prostitutes, they're rarely, if ever seen again. By the time a girl's twenty years old, she's been tortured and abused and she's slept with thousands of laborers, truck drivers and locals."

His attempt to scare Gita fell on deaf ears. The very thought that Renu and Prema might be two of the hundreds of girls dressed in brightly colored cheap saris and standing in every doorway, increased her determination. Some of the girls peeked out from behind barred windows and others were caged in storefront displays. They resembled featherless peacocks in a garbage dump. There were Nepalese, Burmese and Indian girls selling sex to any comer. Many of them looked no more than twelve years old.

"Please, wait for me here," she said to Balaram.

Gita got out of the car and walked along Falkland Road. Girls were crowded in doorways, on corners and leaning out of second and third-story open casements, girls painted with layers of mascara, rouge, powder and red lipstick, girls with vacuous eyes and dry skin, like lean and hungry made up manikins that were sold to horny men for the equivalent of a dollar or two.

"I could have wound up here," she thought. "I could have been one of these girls."

By now she had memorized Prema's face from studying her photograph — a pretty face with large soft brown eyes, clear skin, high cheek bones and a smile that touched Gita's heart. The only photo she had of Renu was taken when her sister was barely thirteen.

After Gita looked at all the prostitutes on the street and found no sign of her sisters, there was disappointment, but also a strange sense of relief. She walked down a narrow passageway into a warren of old, dilapidated buildings. On both sides of the street, caged girls were displayed in shop windows like hungry animals pacing back and forth in search of prey — half-starved and withered creatures lost in a void located somewhere between a life of torture and venereal disease, and the task of pleasuring horny men. Her legs limp, and her heart pounding, Gita was almost convinced of what Balaram had told her: it would be impossible to find her sisters in this lair of prostitution. But no matter how difficult it becomes, she thought, I have no choice but to continue my search.

The faces of myriad young prostitutes on both sides of the street had no resemblance to either Renu or Prema; and as Gita walked deeper into the warren, she noticed a group of Nepalese girls standing on a street corner. She approached them cautiously.

"I'm looking for someone," Gita said in Nepalese.

"Here," one girl laughed. "In this place! This is Falkland Road, sweetie. No one is ever found here, at least, not by a beautiful girl like you who looks like she should be out shopping in a fancy store."

"What do you want her for?" another girl asked.

"She's my sister," Gita said and showed them a photo of Prema. "She came here about a month ago."

The girls circled Gita like a flock of hungry crows approaching the carcass of a dead animal.

"She could be in that house," one girl pointed and said in a singsong voice, "or that one," another said, "or around the corner," another chimed in. "You can take me," the first girl said putting her arm around Gita's waist. "I'll be your sister and I'll be her sister too. We're all sisters."

"No, I mean my real sister," Gita said. She removed the girl's arm.

"Look lady," another girl interjected taking in Gita's stylish elegance, eyeing her from head to toe — sari, handbag, shoes, and transfixed by the diamond bracelet. "Do you want my advice?"

"What?" Gita asked.

"Get your pretty little ass out of here before one of the pimps sees fresh meat and turns you into the living dead."

They turned and walked away from Gita, but she could hear them cackle and joke with each other. In every cage, prostitutes banged on windows, pointed at her, giggled lasciviously, and waved for her to join them.

Dazed and bewildered, she quickly ran to the car, got in, and said to Balaram Gupta, "It's horrible, just horrible," burying her head in her hands and trying to blot out the grotesque tableau of lost young women she had just witnessed.

"I know," Balaram said. He handed her a bottle of Bisleri. "Here. Drink some water. I tried so hard to stop you from seeing all of this — it's the worst side of the city I love, the city where I was born...my home."

"I can't give up, Balaram. You said there are houses that cater to the rich?"

"Yes, but not on Falkland Road."

"Where are they?"

"Not far from the apartment where you're staying," Balaram said. "I'll take you there."

She wished Daniel were with her. She wanted him to put his arms around her, to hold her, to protect her from what she had seen. Gita remembered how powerless she had been before meeting him and felt more appreciative than ever for his strong, steady presence in her life. The Falkland Road nightmare — its horror, its seediness — the caged girls displayed in shop windows like exotic birds without wings, coming on to lecherous men gaping at them from the street, the grimy push carts selling *dahl* and *chapattis*, and the cry of despair in the glazed eyes of every person inhabiting this neighborhood was no longer an idea, but all too real...

"Here we are," Balaram, said without enthusiasm. He parked the car. "This is Governor Road. It's a private playground for male members of the Mumbai elite."

There were large Victorian houses on both sides of the street built by the Raj in the late 19th century. They were stone and brick structures, two, three, and four stories high, beautiful buildings with neoclassical stained glass windows, circular driveways, carved wooden doors, turrets and steeples right out of a Pre-Raphaelite fantasy world. They had originally been mansions built for wealthy British businessmen, but were now owned by the Mumbai *gundas* who operated them as brothels.

"Can you drop me two blocks from here?" she asked Balaram.

"Yes, of course," he said.

Gita took a mirror from her purse, examined her face and hair, and thought that if the gods were kind to her, she'd find Renu and Prema in one of those houses.

"Please, Balaram, wait for me here." Gita said to him when he parked the car.

"It's very dangerous to go in there by yourself," Balaram said. He was now getting visibly upset at Gita's disregard for his warnings.

"Just two hours, please, two hours. If I don't return at the appointed time, give me another hour, then get Daniel and go to the police."

"Are you sure you want to do this?" Balaram asked her.

"Yes."

"But these people..."

"I know how dangerous they are. I also know it was my mother's dying wish for me to get my little sisters out of Mumbai."

"I'll wait," Balaram said, "but be careful. I don't think you have any idea who you're dealing with."

"No Balaram, I don't," Gita said with a courageous smile. "I made a promise and have no choice in this matter."

CHAPTER TWENTY-ONE

On Governor Road, the trees were parched and limp brown leaves clung to branches like half dead flies caught in a spider's web. Two starving dogs sniffed for food in empty garbage cans. A cow lay on the sidewalk and obstructed the entrance to the first brothel on the street.

When she approached the gatehouse, a *chowkidar* stepped out and asked Gita to state her business. He immediately noticed the fine silk sari Gita wore, the diamond bracelet on her wrist, the gold marriage band, the sublime beauty of the girl, and he decided that upper crust Nepalese ladies have no place in a brothel.

"How can I help you?" he asked her in Hindi.

"I'd like to see the *Gharwalli*," Gita said.

"Madam is not here. Come back later."

"I won't have time later."

"If you want to work, there are no positions open for married ladies," he said looking at the gold band on Gita's finger.

"I've come about my uncle."

"Your uncle?"

"Yes, he's very sick. He needs a virgin."

"That's expensive."

"He will pay fifteen thousand US dollars for the right girl," Gita said.

"Wait here a minute."

The *chowkidar* recognized that this lady could be a very special client. To his knowledge, even the most beautiful virgin wouldn't fetch what she had just offered. He went into the gatehouse, made a telephone call, spoke for a few moments, and told Gita to follow him.

His name was Sadiq. He'd been a *chowkidar* in this house for over ten years. It was a good steady job for him and took care of his wife and children. In Mumbai, where so many people lived on the streets, he thanked Lord *Siva* everyday for it. He'd seen numerous girls come and go, some were young and beautiful and pleasing to the brothel's customers; some he liked very much, but Madam, she forbade him to touch them. In truth, most didn't stay very long. When the clients tired of them, Madam put them in a cage on Falkland Road.

Sadiq knocked at the entrance door. It was an eight-foot high, imposing structure carved in a Gothic style with gargoyle faces and Victorian-like figures of nude women — a door most likely crafted by an Indian artist in the late nineteenth century, a door that spoke of great wealth and history, but a door, in Gita's mind, that separated her from Prema and Renu who could be held captive on the other side.

When the door opened, Sadiq introduced Gita to a middle-aged, somewhat heavyset Indian woman who had once clearly been beautiful, but who was now a brash businessperson running the brothel.

"This is Uma," Sadiq said. "She's the *Gharwalli*."

"Go! Go!" the woman said impatiently to the gatekeeper. She would call him when he was needed. And in a probing voice, she asked Gita what was wrong with her uncle.

"AIDS," Gita said.

"Then fifteen thousand dollars isn't enough," Uma said once she closely inspected Gita's elegance. "After the girl services your uncle, she's useless. We'll have to send her to Falkland Road."

"That's a lot of money," Gita responded. "I don't think my uncle will pay more."

"Thirty thousand dollars is the best price for a guaranteed virgin. They are in high demand," Uma said.

"I'll offer you twenty-five thousand dollars," Gita replied. She was repelled by the perverted exchange between her and the *Gharwalli*. How could the life of a young girl be treated like junk in a flea market? It's business, that's all. It's like any other commercial venture.

"Thirty, that's it," Uma responded angrily. "Please, I'm busy. I don't have time to waste on this."

"I'll do it," Gita said. "If it's the right girl."

"If a beautiful woman like you ever needs a job," Uma said in a cheerful voice knowing she got the best of this elegant Nepalese lady, "I'd be happy to find a place for her in my house."

"It's not my line of work," Gita answered with bitter sarcasm.

The interior of the house retained its Victorian elegance with fine pieces of nineteenth century rosewood and teak furniture, silk curtains, and French and English bronze statuary on tables. In the living room, a number of South Asian girls, perhaps seventeen years old and younger, dressed in elegant silk saris, all with long flowing black hair, stared at Gita as she entered. They assumed she would be joining them later.

Gita followed Uma upstairs to a small office on the first floor with a desk and two chairs.

"Where's the money?" Uma asked abruptly without inviting Gita to even sit down.

"I'll give you this bracelet as collateral when I choose the girl," Gita said pointing to her anniversary gift. "It's worth at least fifteen thousand dollars. Then I have to get my uncle to agree."

"You've seen some of the girls," Uma replied after looking at the diamond bracelet on Gita's wrist. "Are they beautiful or not?"

"Yes, they're beautiful, but are they virgins?"

"No," Uma laughed, "but they please some of the richest men in Mumbai."

"I need to find the right one," Gita said.

"There's got to be someone in my inventory that'll appeal to your sick uncle. Tell me what type of girl turns him on."

"A Nepalese girl, preferably Tamang," Gita replied, "fourteen years old or younger, and unlike the girls you've shown me, she's got to be a virgin. No matter how sick my uncle is, he'll say no if he doesn't like her."

"The money will be paid before your uncle sleeps with the girl," Uma said.

Angry, and quite sick of this woman's greed, Gita stared at her for a brief moment, then, she turned to leave.

"Wait," Uma said. "What's the matter?"

"We agreed on thirty thousand dollars," Gita said to Uma. "That's a lot of money to pay. There are many houses on this street. For thirty thousand dollars, another *Gharwalli* will treat me with a little courtesy."

"Please sit down," Uma said. "I apologize for being so abrupt." If she leaves, Uma thought, there goes my commission.

"A new girl came the other day from Nepal," she said to Gita, "a real prize that we've promised to a government official, but we can always find him someone else."

"I'd like to see her," Gita said and sat down.

"Madam Lakshmi will tell me if she's still a virgin," Uma said. She picked up the telephone. "Where is your uncle now?"

"At the Taj Mahal Hotel."

"Hello, Lakshmi, my angel," Uma said into the phone. "How are you? May the gods give you a thousand young virgins in the New Year...Me, too...I don't have your luck. How's the little Nepalese princess? Good... good. There's someone here you should meet. Can I bring her over? Okay. I'll see you in a few minutes."

Years of living and working in brothels had clearly taken a toll on Uma. She was adept at trading in human life and pleasing her superiors — a liaison between the men who frequented her house, the girls who serviced them, and Madam Lakshmi, whom Gita later learned was the chief *Gharwalli* on the street.

"There are many girls in this house," Uma said with some persistence, knowing that she wouldn't have to split the commission if this fine lady chose one. "Let me show them to you before we meet Lakshmi."

Gita and Uma returned to the parlor. The assistant *Gharwalli* lined up an assortment of girls between thirteen and seventeen years of age. One after the other, they paraded before Gita who pretended to examine each of them.

"What do you think?" Uma asked.

"Not my uncle's taste," Gita said when she didn't see either of her sisters.

"Then let's go," Uma replied. She tried to hide her disappointment. "Lakshmi's house is just across the street."

"Did you ever think of taking up the trade?" Uma asked Gita with a sly smile. "A beauty like you could attract a wealthy clientele. You'd get very rich."

"I'm rich enough," Gita, replied in a dismissive voice. She had grown tired of Uma's chatter.

"One can never be rich enough," Uma's grating voice responded.

They crossed the street to a four-story mansion with balconies and trellises and a very large teak front door. Uma opened the door and motioned for Gita to enter. A small group of girls greeted them in a parlor decorated with Anglo-Indian furniture, lamps, prints and statuary, each girl from a different part of Asia, beautiful, and less than seventeen years old.

"Would your uncle have sex with one of these lovelies?" Uma asked.

"There's still not a virgin in the bunch," Gita replied after she saw that none of them were Prema or Renu.

"I can think of any number of men that would pay big money for you," Uma said, "and you're not a virgin."

"I'm not here for me. I'm here for my uncle. He's sick and he needs a girl right away."

Most of the girls watched a Hindi movie on television. They sipped cheap wine, and smoked *bidis* — the thin inexpensive cigarette filled with tobacco flake and wrapped in a tendu leaf. A young Burmese girl stood up, took a bow, and danced the same steps the actress danced on the television screen. The others clapped their hands and shouted while the

Burmese girl shook her hips and ass. Moving gaily around the room, she sat on each girl's lap, sipped wine from their glasses, kissed them, hugged them, put her fingers on each of their breasts, uttered loud and explicit sexual cries, and moved in a circle around Gita — her hands touching Gita's hair, her tongue sticking in and out of her mouth — she cawed like a bird seeking its mate.

"Don't pay her any mind," Uma said. "Two of her clients canceled last night, but this evening will be busy. There's a political convention in Mumbai and you never know who is going to show up."

She asked Gita to take a seat.

"I'll be down in a second. I've got to talk to Lakshmi."

"Hey! Look at this one," the Burmese girl shouted at the others in Hindi. She continued to move to the music and simultaneously touched Gita's face, hair and sari, and examined her wedding ring. "Praise the goddess, she's a married lady," the girl said, "with a beautiful sari and large black eyes." She stopped all movement and intently looked at Gita. "Is your husband good to you?" she asked.

"What do you mean?" Gita responded.

"You know what I mean," the Burmese girl giggled. "Does he fuck you all night? Does he make you squirm and shout and want more?"

"Every night," Gita said dryly. "How old are you?"

"Fifteen," the girl replied.

Gita touched the girl's face with her hand and stroked her hair. "Where are your mother and father?" Gita asked.

"In Burma," the girl answered, "in a village near Rangoon."

"Do you like it here?"

"It's better than the streets," the girl answered. "At least, I have food and a place to sleep."

"I guess," Gita replied.

"Can I brush your hair?" the prostitute asked Gita. "It's so long and soft and beautiful."

"If you'd like," Gita said. "I'll watch the Hindi movie and you can fix my hair."

She's just a child, Gita thought, whose parents sold her to traffickers like my father sold Prema and Renu. But children don't belong in brothels or on the streets or in any place other than where they can be loved and be taken care of. The thought of some fifty-year-old slimebag paying to have sex with this girl...

"Madam Lakshmi wishes to see you," a South Indian girl with long black hair, black skin, large brown eyes, and wearing a dark blue silk sari, said to Gita. "Follow me."

They climbed a flight of steps leading from the parlor to the first floor and entered a large office. Gita was greeted by Lakshmi — a heavyset Nepalese woman with a hardened face that spoke of a long history in Mumbai brothels. Now the head *Gharwalli* of six houses on the street, she reported solely to Mustapha Khan, the brother of the *gunda* kingpin who ran the entire organization.

Khan had taken a strong liking to Lakshmi's transparent beauty when she first arrived in Mumbai. He never allowed syphilitic or AIDS-ridden clients to touch her. In time, she became his mistress. He made her an assistant to the *Gharwalli*, and a year later, chief *Gharwalli*, and Lakshmi no longer had to service any of the brothel clientele. The only person she slept with was Khan. His love for her was so strong he couldn't see the obvious changes that had transformed a sweet fourteen-year-old girl into an overweight, stern taskmaster who looked well beyond her years. Becoming Khan's mistress and chief *Gharwalli* ended her life as a prostitute. Better to sleep with him, she figured, than a battalion of strangers every week.

"You're not a working girl," Lakshmi said to Gita observing the beautiful sari and diamond bracelet.

"Didn't Uma tell you why I'm here?" Gita asked.

"Yes, yes, of course," Lakshmi said in her most polite voice, "but one can always hope for a little extra benefit."

"Thirty thousand dollars is a lot of benefit," Gita said. "I need a virgin for my sick uncle."

"I don't run a hospital," Lakshmi said with some impatience.

"Then I'll look somewhere else," Gita said, and started to leave.

"Not on this street."

"There are many houses."

"Yes, but every one of them reports to me. Now tell me, my fine lady, what's wrong with your uncle." She motioned for Gita to sit down.

"He's got AIDS," Gita replied without moving.

"Then thirty thousand dollars isn't enough."

"What do you want?"

"Sixty thousand US dollars. Not a paisa less."

"You doubled the price," Gita said.

"My little virgin will cure him. Isn't his life worth sixty thousand dollars?"

"I have to see the girl."

"She's Nepalese like you and me."

"That's good," Gita replied. "He won't sleep with an Indian or Burmese woman. How old is she?"

"Come. I'll show you," Lakshmi said.

Gita followed her up the steps to the fourth floor. They walked along a corridor that had room after room on either side. The hospital green walls were covered with filth and grease, and Gita could smell the stale, dank odor of mold and must.

"In here," Lakshmi said. She opened a door and they entered a room the walls of which were covered with soot and gray peeling paint. A dim light bulb hung from a cord attached to the ceiling. A young, half-naked Nepalese girl sat on a wooden cot, very frail, frightened, and biting her fingernails.

"Leave me alone," the girl said in Nepali to Lakshmi. She spoke in an icy voice that was far beyond her years. "Stay away from me. Where's my mother? My father? I want to go home."

"This is Maya," Lakshmi said to Gita. "She'll come around."

Gita tried to control her own anger.

"Maya, say hello to the lady," Lakshmi said.

The girl didn't move until Lakshmi grabbed her by the hair.

"Be nice to the lady," Lakshmi said. "You'd better listen to me when I talk to you."

"Do you think your uncle would like her?" she asked Gita. "Maya's a twelve-year-old Nepalese virgin."

"She's not beautiful enough," Gita said softly.

"Then I'll show you another girl."

They left the room and walked down the corridor. Lakshmi opened another door and they entered a room where a wisp of a Nepalese girl, almost boy-like, with a flat chest and virtually no hips, lay asleep on a bed.

"How old is she?"

"Thirteen," Lakshmi said. "She's a guaranteed virgin who will cure your uncle."

"My uncle told me that the girl has to be Tamang, less than fourteen years old, and very beautiful," Gita said. "She's got to resemble my aunt who he married over forty years ago."

"Is your aunt still alive?"

"No. That's the problem. He misses the young bride he first fell in love with."

"But he has AIDS."

"Yes, I know," Gita shrugged.

"Why not let him die?"

"I love him," Gita said. "He's been kind to me all my life."

"Your uncle's nuts," Lakshmi said impatiently.

"Yes, I know, but he'd spend sixty thousand dollars for the right girl."

"Come with me," she said to Gita.

They returned to Lakshmi's office and Gita was handed photo albums of every prostitute on Governor Road. "I'm the keeper of the books," Lakshmi boasted with a cynical smile. "Look through the lot. It will be faster, a lot easier, and if you find one that resembles your late aunt, if she's a fourteen-year-old virgin, I'll let you see her."

This is a strange kind of business, Lakshmi thought, but she's rich and its easy money, and what do I give a damn if she looks through those albums. It just saves me a lot of time.

"I'll make some tea," Lakshmi said.

Gita studied the photos carefully, but none of them resembled Prema or Renu. When Lakshmi returned with the tea, Gita pointed to photos of three Tamang girls and said that they must be older than fourteen.

"These girls are no longer virgins," the *Gharwalli* said. "They got sick and were sent to Falkland Road."

"I guess I will have to disappoint my uncle." Gita got up to leave.

"Come with me," Lakshmi said.

Frightened that she'd lose sixty thousand dollars, it was worth one more attempt to please this difficult, but very wealthy woman. Khan would be pissing mad if this deal fell through.

"I'll show you a fourteen-year-old jewel worth sixty thousand US dollars. She's been reserved for an Indian minister, but I can find him someone else."

At the end of the corridor, Lakshmi opened a door without knocking. When Gita entered, to her horror and surprise, she recognized her little sister Prema seated naked on a bed — a teenage girl with long beautiful black hair, tiny breasts, soft skin, and large dark brown frightened eyes. Her body was covered with welts and bruises, and her hunched over vacuous stare went right through Gita.

"Help me," Prema said to Lakshmi. "I want to go home. I want to be in my village. Why are they beating me? What do they want?"

Lakshmi, who had played the mother role to offset the beatings the girl had received from other members of the brothel, took the child's hand and said to her, "They want you to be kind to the men that come here."

Gita's mind and heart froze and she could barely speak when she recognized that the young girl was her sister pleading with this monster.

"She's just a child," Gita blurted out to Lakshmi.

"That's what you want," Lakshmi replied with a twisted smile on her face. "She'll cure your uncle of AIDS."

"I don't care," Gita said. "She's so young, so beautiful."

"Then we'd better go," Lakshmi said. "You're wasting my time."

"No," Gita said. "I'm not going. Not without her." She sat down next to her sister. "Maybe, I can help you."

Prema, who had no recollection of Gita, pushed her away.

"Do you know her?" Lakshmi asked.

"She's my littlest sister."

"Your sister?" Lakshmi said in an astonished voice.

"Yes," Gita answered.

"What do you want?" Lakshmi asked.

"I want to take her with me."

"What's your name?"

"Gita."

Lakshmi just stared at Gita.

"There's really no sixty thousand US dollars, is there?" Lakshmi asked.

"I can offer you plenty of money," Gita said.

"No amount is enough from someone who tries to make a fool of me," Lakshmi said. "Many of my clients are going to enjoy sleeping with you and your sister."

"Put your clothing on," Gita said to Prema. "We're leaving this place."

Prema pushed Gita away again.

"Leave me alone," she screamed. After wrapping her arms around Lakshmi's legs, she pleaded for the *Gharwalli* to help her.

"Where do you think you are going to take her?" Lakshmi asked.

"Get out of our way," Gita said.

"Calm down, my little lovely," Lakshmi said with a sinister smile on her face. She gently undid Prema's arms from around her legs. Then she grabbed Gita by the arm and pinned her against the wall.

"Uma told me you offered collateral," Lakshmi grinned. She looked greedily at Gita's bracelet. "I like that bauble on your wrist. It'll look very chic with a dress I just bought." She pushed Gita onto the wooden bed, took a cellphone from her pocket, dialed, and said, "Ali! Come to room nine. Bring Mohamed!"

Almost immediately, the door opened, and two six-foot thugs entered with guns in hand. "I want you to beat her just enough to get the fight out,"

Lakshmi said to them. "She's going to bring a good price. She and Prema will service the elite of Asia."

"How much money would it take to let us go?" Gita asked Lakshmi.

Lakshmi walked up to her, laughed an almost deranged and hideous laugh, and spat in Gita's face.

"There is no amount of money," Lakshmi finally said. "No one makes a fool of me and gets away with it."

CHAPTER TWENTY-TWO

Balaram believed that Americans lived in a sheltered world far from the horrors of Falkland Road, the scars of war, and economic blight. Perhaps the World Trade Center tragedy had taught them a few lessons but the rest of the planet's bubble had burst a long time ago. Now they had learned what the rest of us have known for years: there is no safety zone, no place to hide, and no secure womblike cell that insulates people from edgy terrorists who choose to blow themselves up along with thousands of innocent people in the name of God. One has to be conscious of good and evil lurking in every corner. Americans are always shocked when they discover that repressed and neurotic young kids who live in small towns have stashed arsenals in their own homes and use them to kill fellow students. It happens all the time. Why are they surprised? Is it because they live in lily-white, well-cushioned safety nets as real as Walt Disney's animated movies? Then they make war in the wrong places. They stir up an asp's nest and are surprised when snakes bite them.

Balaram looked at his watch for the hundredth time.

"It's taking so long. Where the hell is she?"

He got out of his car and walked towards the brothels, stopped, looked at his watch again worriedly. He would give her another few minutes. Surely, she'd come back soon.

Balaram returned to the car, tried to read the newspaper, but he was growing more and more nervous, and he looked for Gita in the direction of the brothels.

I shouldn't have let her go, he thought. She doesn't know her way around the underworld well enough to deal with Lakshmi and Khan.

Suddenly, he threw the newspaper away.

"Three hours," he said to himself after he looked at his watch again. "Where is she?"

Gupta cursed his own stupidity for allowing this obsessed girl to walk into hell. He opened the car door, but quickly changed his mind and decided against going to the brothels.

"Gupta! You're an idiot!" he said. "She could get killed because of you."

Balaram Gupta had walked a tightrope since he was a teenager. To him, there was no voice of reason when you've lived your life on the political edge — a place where the mad trained the blind to be a high wire act in a tragicomic circus. When he and Bob Marshal were in their early twenties, they had fought with Tibetan freedom fighters in their struggle against the Chinese. They had incited Burmese students to riot against a dictatorial Government; they had trained Hindu soldiers in Kashmir and been involved in the internal politics of most countries in South Asia.

Gupta never understood the motives that drove countries to war. When he tried to make sense of each side's position, he always came up empty. People just killed each other and would continue to kill each other until human life became extinct. One had to endure the insanity of the world and be prepared for any crisis.

He eventually became rich playing one political group off another, accepting large payoffs for his services. The only person he refused to squeeze was Bob Marshal, a longtime friend, who had saved his life many times over. Now that Gupta was retired, he turned down all political commissions. He had had enough of the world's intrigue. The only dramas he wished to endure at this point of his life were in the cinema and on TV.

When Bob asked him to help find Gita's sisters, Gupta reminded Bob that it was Falkland Road. Almost no one has ever been found on Falkland Road. He didn't believe for a second that Gita's sisters would surface if they were among the thousands of sex workers that lived and worked in Mumbai's red light district.

"Come on, Gita, where the hell are you?" he blurted out.

He got back into his car, started driving, thought of telephoning Daniel, but decided it was best to talk to him in person. After a few moments, he considered calling Mohan Chowdhury, the police commissioner. But, he knew that was a waste of time and dangerous. It was no secret in Mumbai that Chowdhury was on the brothel's payroll.

※ ※ ※

Daniel paced the floor of Gupta's apartment. Too upset to sit still, he decided to practice different martial arts warm-up routines. He needed to rid himself of mounting fear and anger that made him mad enough to tear apart all the furniture in the room. He lit a cigarette, put it out, poured a shot of straight scotch, and telephoned Bob Marshal but was unable to get through. He seriously considered calling his father. Seconds later, he decided it was best to keep the family out of this. An archetypal male hunter, Daniel rarely called on family, business associates or friends if he felt he could do something by himself.

The phone rang. It was Bob Marshal.

"She went with Balaram to find her sisters," Daniel explained. "I haven't heard from either them in hours."

"That's what I was afraid of," Bob said. "Your wife's a gutsy lady, but in real danger."

"You have no idea of how frightened I am. Tell me what to do."

"Have you called the police?"

"What about them?" Daniel answered angrily. "Do you think they're going to help?"

"I don't know," Bob said, his voice now choked with emotion.

"I should have gone with her to Falkland Road to kick the shit out of those cocksuckers," Daniel said.

"And get yourself killed," Bob said. "This is South Asia, Daniel. No one in the West can figure out what goes on in the minds of these people. They believe in things we've never heard of in America: karma, ancestral ties, gods, demigods, you name it; they bathe in holy rivers and burn dead bodies at shrines. This is fucking South Asia. I've lived here for over ten years and still haven't a clue as to what the hell is going on."

"So what do I do?"

"Just wait," Bob said. "Balaram's a good guy. He'll take care of Gita."

He hung up the phone and paced the apartment floor. Could he wait forever in this godforsaken country for Gita to get killed while he stood by and did nothing? He kicked a table and punched his fist through a sheetrocked wall, then walked out onto the terrace and studied the slow moving almost ant-like people on a sidewalk that bordered the beach. He tried to calm his mind, but found himself thinking what good were all his Sensei's wise words and philosophies if Gita was going to die?

The sound of the doorbell made Daniel jump. He ran quickly to open the door and expected to find Gita and Balaram.

"Where is she," Daniel asked Gupta who was standing alone in the corridor.

"She left me in the car and went to the brothels on Governor's Road," Balaram said.

"Are you out of your mind?" Daniel shouted.

"She asked me to wait three hours for her. If she didn't return, I was supposed to get you."

"There was no sign of her?"

"I don't even know which house she went into," Balaram said. "She's a stubborn lady, Mr. Gold."

"Yeah, I know, but why the fuck did you let her go there alone."

"There was nothing I could do," Gupta responded. "Your wife was determined to go there by herself."

"Shit!" Daniel said. "Take me to the police and if that doesn't work, then the American Embassy."

Daniel stormed out of the apartment. Gupta followed him and they took the elevator downstairs.

* * *

Daniel's legal mind found no explanation for the sudden turn of events that had so deeply affected his life. It was as if a tornado had uprooted houses and trees in a pastoral setting, leaving behind nothing but desolation. He tried to use every skill his Sensei had taught him to quiet his mind and emotions — and like a samurai making ready for battle, he needed to calm himself and focus his entire attention on outmaneuvering the enemy.

He and Gupta were driving on a Mumbai boulevard. When the car stopped at a red light, a beggar put his half-eaten leprosy-scarred hand against the window. Daniel and Balaram ignored him.

"Ten rupees," the beggar said. There was a pitiful expression on his face. "Eat...I...am...hungry...ten rupees...not so much money. I have little daughter. She...hungry too." He placed his other hand near his mouth. "Ten rupees...hungry."

Daniel took a few ten-rupee notes from his pocket. He opened the window, and gave them to the beggar who promptly put them in his shirt pocket and walked quickly into dense pedestrian traffic that moved up and down the street. On Balaram's side of the car, Daniel saw a teenage girl with a badly broken arm that had never mended. She held an infant on her chest. She raised the fingers of one hand to her mouth as if she were hungry — a teenage girl in ragged clothing with unwashed matted hair, a dirty face, and half-starved, stared at Daniel until the light turned green.

The overwhelming presence of poverty made its way into Daniel's psyche and he wondered how great wealth and indigence could live so near to one another. He had never seen poverty like it before, not in Harlem, Bedford-Stuyvesant, South Central Los Angeles, not even while trekking through small villages in Nepal, he had never seen poverty so oppressive, so intense, so full of despair.

"The beggars are like mosquitoes," Balaram said. His voice cut through

Daniel's thoughts and brought him back to the present. "I know the police commissioner. He's also like a mosquito. I mean he'd suck your blood for twenty rupees. He's as corrupt as they come and on the brothel payroll. He just built himself a beautiful house."

"Is there anyone else we can talk to?"

"I doubt it," Balaram said. "But I can get you an invitation for dinner at the police commissioner's new house. He loves to show off his wealth by entertaining foreigners, and you being the brother-in-law of an American Ambassador would greatly please him."

Balaram pulled the car into a parking lot in front of a nineteenth century Anglo-Gothic Revival building constructed by the Raj. It was now used as the headquarters of the Brihanmumbai or Mumbai police. Set on a well-landscaped street with palm and banyan trees, a constant flow of people moved in and out of the front door.

"I have many friends here," Balaram said to Daniel before they got out of the car. "Maybe luck will be on our side."

Upon entering the somber and majestic building, they found a large queue lined up in front of a registration desk.

"Wait a minute," Balaram said. "I see a friend. Come with me." Daniel followed him across the building's rotunda.

"Vishnuji," Balaram said in English to a police officer dressed in a well-decorated uniform. "It's been a long time. Are you still drinking Kingfisher at the club?"

"With or without you, my friend. Although I miss our happy hour laughs. Where have you been?"

"You know, my wife's not been well."

"Sorry, old chap. I hope it's not serious. Send her my best."

He introduced Daniel to Vishnu Ramaswami, the Assistant Chief of Police. He was a middle-aged man in a well-pressed uniform sporting an assortment of medals on his chest, with salt and pepper hair sticking out from beneath a policeman's hat. When Daniel shook Ramaswami's limp hand, he could feel a cold sweat that made him question the man's integrity. Never once, throughout the entire conversation, did the Assistant Police Commissioner look either Daniel or Gupta in the eye. When Balaram told Ramaswami about Gita, the latter asked Daniel in a serious voice if it was his wife.

Daniel replied with a nod.

"Governor Road can be a dangerous place. We'll get on it right away. Just come with me."

He took them upstairs to a room marked Missing Persons in which a clerk sat behind a desk.

"Atul will help you," Ramaswami said in English. "It's so nice to see you, Balaram. I hope your wife gets well."

"She'll be fine."

"We should have a Kingfisher at the club," Ramaswami replied. He shook Gupta and Daniel's hands and left.

There were three desks in the room. Behind one of them sat the clerk Atul who greeted Daniel and Balaram. Following procedure, he asked both of them for identification.

"No doubt America is a great and powerful country, Mr. Gold," the desk clerk said in English after looking at Daniel's passport. "I have two cousins and a brother that live there. Do you know Flushing? My brother tells me it is paradise on earth."

"My wife is missing," Daniel said ignoring the policeman's banter.

"Sometimes a missing wife is not a bad thing," the clerk said chuckling to himself.

"Sometimes a mouth without teeth is also not such a bad thing," Daniel said.

"No reason to get upset," the clerk said. "I was just making a joke. If your wife is missing, the Mumbai police will find her. Rest assured. But first I have to make a report."

"To whom?" Daniel asked.

"My superiors, Mr. Gold. They will take care of everything."

"Where are they?" Daniel asked.

"At lunch."

"I want to see someone in charge, now," Daniel said.

"I am in charge at the moment," the clerk said imperiously. "There's no one else here. But, it's no problem, Mr. Gold. Tell me how your wife disappeared. Where was she last seen?"

"On Governor Road," Balaram interjected.

"What was she doing there?" the clerk asked incredulously.

"Looking for her sister in a brothel," Daniel said.

"Is she American?"

"Nepalese-American," Daniel replied.

"No problem, Mr. Gold," the clerk said with a big smile. "I will report this to my superiors and they will find her. Just tell me where you are staying."

Daniel wrote down his address and telephone number in Mumbai.

"We solve cases like this all the time," the clerk said. "If you are a friend of Mr. Gupta's, we will do everything to help you." He stood up and shook Daniel and Balaram's hands. "I really want to visit Flushing, Mr. Gold. Is it as beautiful as my brother says? Is it really paradise on earth?"

Daniel was so filled with anger he turned away without saying a word.

As they left the police station, Daniel asked Gupta if he and Bob had no better connections than this supercilious prick.

"We do," Balaram said, "but they're not going to help you. The only way to get your wife and her sisters out of the brothel is to go there and get them yourself."

"You mean just walk in and ask for them."

"No. But I have an idea and it just might work."

"And that jerk upstairs?" Daniel asked.

"I don't know," Balaram replied about the desk clerk who had already consulted with Vishnu Ramaswami. The Assistant Chief of Police had told him to throw Daniel's report into the trash.

CHAPTER TWENTY-THREE

The brothel's fourth floor was used to torture girls until they submitted to a life of prostitution. The girls were starved and beaten, drugged, and threatened by men whose sole occupation was the transformation of beautiful, young women into seasoned sex workers to service the needs of a wealthy clientele. The torture was nonstop for days at a time. If a girl refused to submit, Ali and Mohamed would rape her repeatedly. If they were virgins, and therefore valuable commodities to the brothel, they were never raped. Instead, the torture continued until their resistance broke down and they were forced to succumb to a life of sexual slavery.

Gita sat naked on a small wooden platform bed. The walls of her windowless room were covered with gray peeling paint-like prison walls without bars and heavily streaked, and dimly lit by a lone hanging light bulb — the room was airless, musty and humid. Gita could barely breathe. She sat with her back against the wall, her hands tied, her mouth gagged, and her body covered with bruises. Mohamed and Ali sat next to her on bentwood chairs chain-smoking cigarettes. When Ali removed the gag from Gita's mouth, she bit him.

"You little bitch," he said to her in Hindi. "I'll teach you how to behave." He smacked her in the face and put his hand between her legs. "When I'm finished with you, the tigress will become a lamb. The rich and famous will pay good money to crawl between your legs."

"I'll die first," Gita said.

"That's okay," Ali said, "but before you die, Mohamed and me will fuck you a thousand times."

"Do whatever you want," Gita said, "but I'll never work for you."

"This is going to be fun," Mohamed said to Ali. "I like to screw wild animals."

Lakshmi entered the room. Her face was like a sinister mask created by a primitive people to hide the devil. She reminded Gita of paintings she'd seen as a child of Mother Kali in her most evil form — the cemetery goddess slaying the souls of the living dead. She's less than human, Gita thought, she's evil-incarnate — a pool of blood that drowns the world.

"Have you had enough?" Lakshmi asked in Nepali with a big frozen smile. "Most of the girls crack after one hour with Mohamed and Ali."

"Yes, I've had enough," Gita said to her, "but I'm not going to be one of your whores."

"The alternative is easy," Lakshmi went on in a calm voice. "There'll be no disease, no abuse…just the pleasure of servicing my clients."

Gita spat in Lakshmi's face. The Gharwalli didn't move. She stared at Gita with cool and calculating eyes, and slowly wiped off the spit.

"I won't forget that," Lakshmi said.

"I won't forget this slime putting his hands between my legs," Gita answered. "I also won't forget wiping your spit off my face."

Lakshmi walked towards the door.

"Come," she said to Gita in a muted voice that seethed with anger. "I want to show you something. Your sister Renu's almost ready to be sent back to Nepal."

Did she say Renu…could she also be here? Gita thought. How is it possible that the three of us are imprisoned in this place, together, at the same time? She was too stunned to move. Ali grabbed her by the arm and forced her to get up.

"When I talk to you," Lakshmi said, "you listen. Now come! She's in the next room."

"Who are you?" Gita asked.

"Someday I'll tell you," Lakshmi answered with a frozen smile.

Renu lay on a wooden bed curled up fetus-like, and wrapped in a cotton sheet. She couldn't have weighed more than eighty pounds. She was pale, and her dark eyes looked like they were pasted on her face. Her skin was flaking and her head was partially bald and thin strands of hair dropped to her shoulders. Toothless, half-starved and frightened, there were needle marks in every vein of her legs and arms. She looked more dead than alive.

"Renu," Lakshmi said. "It's mother Lakshmi. I've brought your sister Gita. I'm sure you'll be happy to see her again. Now you, Prema, and Gita are together."

"What have you done to her?" Gita asked.

"There's heroin in her veins. I mean she has a taste for it. Isn't that true, my pet?" Lakshmi asked Renu.

The last time Gita had seen Renu she was milking a goat behind the hut in their village. It was the day before Gita and her mother went to Kathmandu. She was a beautiful child, lithe and strong, and she loved to dress up like the goddess Parvati. It was her way of speaking to Lord *Siva*.

"I'm nobody's sister," Renu said. "I'm the wind. Have you ever met the wind? It speaks in whispers." She didn't even look at Gita, but gazed at the head *Gharwalli.* "Oh, hello mother Lakshmi. Isn't it time for another needle? I'm getting cold, you know. It's no fun being cold. Then there's the pain. I told you about the pain. It hurts me so much everyone in the house feels it. I don't want the other girls to feel it. All I need is another needle, mother Lakshmi, please give me a needle so the pain goes away."

"Tonight," Lakshmi said.

"When is tonight?" Renu asked. "The pain is so strong I hope tonight isn't far away."

"It's just a few hours from now, my sweet," Lakshmi said.

"Don't wait too long. I'm so cold. The wind is also cold, mother Lakshmi. Please take care of the wind."

"I'm going to send you back to your village," Lakshmi said. "Your father and mother will welcome the wind with open arms."

Her mother's dead, Gita thought, and her father's mind is gone.

"Thank you, mother Lakshmi," Renu said. "You're so kind to me."

Gita put her hand on Renu's face.

"My darling sister," Gita said. "What have they done to you?"

"No!" Renu shouted. "Don't touch me. Take your hands off my face. Who is she? Please *ama*, get her out of here." Renu curled up on the bed sobbing, "No. No. Keep her away from me."

"I will my child," Lakshmi said.

"Your child," Gita said angrily.

"Yes, you heard her. She calls me Mother Lakshmi. I take care of the wind."

"No! This is horrible," Gita said through her tears.

"The same thing is going to happen to you if you don't service my clients," Lakshmi said in a cold and indifferent voice.

"You're the buffalo demon," Gita said.

"And Durga will slay me," Lakshmi laughed.

"Yes, she will slay you."

"Not before I get you to sleep with a battalion of Indian businessmen. Do you think I'm playing around? If you don't obey me, I'll get Ali and Mohamed to fill your veins with heroin."

"And Prema?"

"The ex-Defense Minister's coming tomorrow. He's got AIDS and he'll pay me a lot of money to cure himself of the disease."

"And kill my sister," Gita said.

No, not right away, Lakshmi thought without saying a word to Gita.

First I'll put her in a cage for a year or two on Falkland road. When the disease gets bad, I'll send her back to her father in Nepal.

✳ ✳ ✳

Lakshmi hated Khan, the brothel, and most pointedly her father, who had sold her to traffickers when she was a teenager. No day passed without her plotting some kind of revenge. Her idea was simple: buy her younger sisters for little or no money, service them to hundreds of brothel clients, get them hooked on drugs, then dump them on the doorstep of their father's hut. Disgrace him in the eyes of the whole village. Turn him into a buffoon and let him be the laughing stock of all his moronic friends.

When she first arrived in Mumbai, Lakshmi was more dead than alive. Lobsang had brought her down a dark alley at the rear entrance of a brothel — an alley that stank from rat and mice shit and rotting garbage. She knew that she had to change her name to Lakshmi — a goddess who helped her survive the nightmarish pain inflicted on her by traffickers.

Lakshmi had learned to play the brothel game by pleasing its wealthiest clients with her natural beauty and strong body. She did it with so much cunning that Khan took notice and began to favor her. In time, he made her his mistress. Slowly, but surely he gave her more and more influence in the running of the brothels. When Khan raised her to the position of chief *Gharwalli* overseeing all the houses on Governor Road, Lakshmi finally had the power to negotiate with traffickers. She sent two of them to her village in Nepal knowing that her father would sell her sisters. They returned with only Renu, her father refusing to sell ten-year-old Prema.

"Where's Gita," she asked the traffickers, not trusting them.

"The old man said his most beautiful child died many years ago."

"Just as well," Lakshmi said. "It's one less sister I have to worry about."

A few years later, wily, and knowing her father would need money, she sent the traffickers back to Rumla, and they delivered Prema to Governor Road.

But, Gita is still alive, Lakshmi thought. The traffickers must have lied to me or my father was protecting his little goddess? She laughed a dark, almost demonic laugh, and told herself that it really didn't matter. "The gods have been kind to me. Now, I have all three of my sisters in the brothel."

Lakshmi opened the top drawer of her desk and removed a family photo in which she was standing next to her father — next to him were Renu, then Sivan, Gita and her mother. Prema had not as yet been born.

They were all smiling with their arms around one another.

After all these years, she thought, I can now turn my father's precious daughters into wild animals — like he turned me into an animal. I'll make sure his soul never rests.

"I was your child, once. I loved you so much. I kissed your feet and hands," she said to the photograph.

And her father was the blessed one — a god on earth to Jamuna. How could he have sold her to a brothel for eight thousand rupees? She'd never forget her mother crying and her father bragging to his friends that his daughter would send him thousands of rupees. It was the last thing Jamuna heard before she left the village.

"But Jamuna won't send you rupees," she said out loud to the image of her father in the photograph. "Lakshmi will send you the filthy bodies of her AIDS-infected sisters. Your three daughters will beg at your door, then shame you in front of the entire village. You will have no rest."

CHAPTER TWENTY-FOUR

Gupta had told him the best time to go to the brothel was noon the next day, but Daniel could only think of Gita imprisoned there and hadn't the patience to wait.

He tried to get Daniel to understand that every politician, gangster, corrupt police officer and diplomat went to Governor Road in the evening, and Khan's thugs were all over the place. They partied all night.

"We've got to wait. I know it's hard, but noon tomorrow is the best time. The brothel will be slow. It'll be easier to find her."

But how could he wait? There was no telling what has happened to her. His mind fabricated sordid images of her trapped in the clutches of Mumbai *gunda*. But, mostly, he had no idea of what to think. He was left with an empty, almost hollow feeling. A strange, but stagnant voice inside him kept saying: "She'll be alright. Everything will be fine." A part of him believed this, yet, he still worried about where she was and what he could do?

Daniel put himself through a series of karate drills to loosen his muscles and quiet his mind. Balaram Gupta looked on and remembered his own CIA training — the daily martial arts, the target practice, the instruction in dismantling and building weapons, in sword and knife fighting — all so necessary when dealing with dangerous political enemies and terrorists. Now, those days were over. He was too old to seriously consider fighting the tyrants of the world. He and his wife wanted a little peace and quiet: a trip to Manali, to Thailand, or to Paris, a little time on the beach, some golf, good restaurants, anything but the war on terrorism, anything but ferreting out evil in a dangerous world.

Daniel's well-trained, Balaram thought, but he doesn't have any martial arts experience outside of his dojo. It's going to be his first foray into living hell. He'll find out the value of his karate training and how to apply his Sensei's wisdom in a dangerous world — and maybe save Gita's life.

* * *

The sun's fiery red ball settled quietly in the West, and Mumbai nights,

155

more frantic and crowded than Mumbai summer days, guided people into a seething beehive of human activity that throbbed until early hours in the morning. The brothel was coming to life. On the main floor, a steady flow of male traffic moved in and out of the front door. Every room was occupied. Some young Indian sex workers dressed in stylish silk saris resembling colorful flowers in a vase were seated in the living room.

Upstairs in her room, Lakshmi and Khan were in bed. Having just finished making love, he lit a cigar and asked her to bring him a glass of whiskey. He covered his large, bulbous belly with a cotton sheet. He stretched his pudgy arms and flicked cigar ash on the floor, took a few sips of Chivas Regal and told Lakshmi that he wanted to make love to her until he was ninety years old. It was so good. Not like his goddamn wife. He couldn't stand to be in bed with her. He couldn't even stand her smell.

"You haven't slept with her in years," Lakshmi said.

"I'm not missing anything," he answered.

"How do you know she's not good?" she asked him.

"I don't," he said and flicked another ash on the floor. "But I also don't want to find out."

It was too big a price to pay, Lakshmi thought.

Khan asked her to get him another shot of whiskey.

"She called me a few hours ago," Khan said. He took the quarter-filled highball glass of whiskey from Lakshmi and downed it in one gulp.

"Your wife?" Lakshmi asked.

"Yes, my pain-in-the-ass wife. She's worried about our daughter."

"What's wrong?" Lakshmi asked.

"I don't know. But I'll have to go home tonight and find out."

"The daughter studying in America?" Lakshmi asked.

"Yes," Khan replied. "Her Harvard education is putting me in the poorhouse."

"I'd like to meet her one day."

"You think I'd bring her here?"

"No," she said, sadly. "I don't think you'd bring her here."

Khan had been a *gunda* front man for twenty-five years. He oversaw the running of the brothels as well as many other businesses owned and operated by the organization. He was five-foot-eight, fifty-three years old, and well over two hundred pounds. He had puffy hair, his cheeks were full-blown, and with his short stocky legs and large belly, he was a bloated human specimen that smoked Cuban cigars and wore white linen suits and a white bow tie.

"Tell me about the new girl," he said to Lakshmi. He sat up on the bed, stretched his arms and legs and scratched his belly.

"She's worth a lot of rupees," Lakshmi said, "but it'll take a little time to get her ready."

"Is she Indian?"

"No. She's Nepalese. She's from my village."

"Not another sister? That would make three."

"Yes," Lakshmi answered.

"Just remember, no heroin. I let you get away with Renu, but this one's to be trained without dope. No wealthy client wants an addict."

"Heroin works well," Lakshmi said with a bitter smile.

"I know faster and better ways of getting rid of people. If she's doped, the only clients we can sell her to are workmen and untouchables."

✳ ✳ ✳

From his terrace, Daniel looked down at the slow moving lights of boats dotting the Arabian Sea. It was like a black hole — a vast pool of darkness surrounded by high-rise condos, by a continuous stream of car headlights moving from one destination to another on a half-moon road bordering the beach — the pulsating rhythm of Mumbai's night life, so breathless, unabated, and distant — every human being, he thought, touched by their own little soap opera that afflicted minds and hearts in a personal way — different than Daniel's, but just as dark, uncomfortable and full of grief. He checked his watch for the fiftieth time; he wanted to go to Governor Road with or without Gupta.

"Listen to your breathing," Daniel remembered his Sensei saying. *"It will calm your fears. It will give you the strength to fight your enemy."*

I can borrow a gun from Gupta, Daniel thought.

He quickly negated that idea. If they searched him when he entered the brothel, his game plan would be up before it started. He'd never find Gita. His best and only resource was years of martial arts training.

"The mind is your enemy," his Sensei once said. *"If it's quiet, you'll be able to fight. If it's noisy, then you'll have to battle yourself before you even begin fighting your opponent. Focus the mind. Its energy is your friend if you keep it from being scattered."*

My mind is like a wild beast that won't shut up, Daniel's thoughts continued. It howls every moment and I can't make any sense of anything. I was a happily married man on a second honeymoon and now my wife could be a prisoner in a brothel. How could this have happened? Where is the logic? There's none — not even a hint of anything that made sense. I feel like a piece of tumbleweed bouncing about in a tumultuous storm.

※ ※ ※

Nine o'clock that night. Daniel walked along the beach. In the distance, he saw the lit Gateway to India that once welcomed sea voyagers to a subcontinent ruled by the *Raj*. Beggars asked him for rupees while vendors tried to sell him postcards and plastic trinkets of gods and goddesses. The more money he gave out, the more indigents gathered around him. They were like a force of nature that kept at him until he had to push them all away.

His Sensei had told him that the greatest samurais feared neither life nor death. One couldn't exist without the other. There were no enemies, just obstacles; and these samurais were taught to fight every battle with an open heart.

But Sensei's wife was never trapped in a brothel, Daniel thought. He never had to fight this kind of battle.

Dozens of homeless people slept in doorways, beneath trees, and on benches, some without blankets, but all of them resting quietly. Daniel wondered how they could sleep so well. Were they relaxing after a busy day? He didn't know. His head buzzed with nervous energy and his entire body felt like it was in a state of shock. He was certain that it would be impossible for him to sleep tonight.

"Nighttime brings out high-level and important slime bags that frequent the Governor Road brothels," Gupta had said to him earlier.

He told Daniel about a man who went to Governor Road at midnight to look for his daughter. The following morning, the police found him dead in an alleyway near the beach. A little restraint would benefit them. Their best shot was tomorrow at noon when brothel business comes to a virtual standstill.

"Look," Balaram said. "Gita might walk through your apartment door at any moment with her sister and all this worry is for nothing."

Daniel didn't know what would happen tomorrow, but his love for Gita was so strong that he had to find her. Years of his life were spent looking for a source of happiness only to realize it existed at the center of his own heart — a place where Gita lived, a place where she'd always be.

CHAPTER TWENTY-FIVE

A group of Saudi businessmen arrived at the brothel, followed by six teenage boys, the sons of Mumbai CEO's, quite drunk, and full of vigor. They had come to "sow their wild oats" with young, exotic Burmese beauties who catered to their every whim. By midnight, many of the men had come and gone. A few wanted to stay and party. Others arrived, and the brothel stayed busy until the early hours of the morning.

Lakshmi ran a respectable house. If clients caused unnecessary problems, if they were too drunk or rowdy, if they disturbed the low-key and understated vibe, bouncers asked them to leave.

In a soundproofed room on the fourth floor, Mohamed and Ali had tied Gita's naked body to a chair and beat her with wooden sticks until her breasts and thighs ached and her body was covered with black and blue welts. When she refused to scream or move they squeezed her nipples until the pain was unbearable and knuckled pressure points all over Gita's body. But, she never, not for a moment, gave voice to the rage brought on by such intense suffering.

From a far corner of the room, Lakshmi watched them torture Gita. She had witnessed the transformation of many innocent girls into full-fledged sex workers; and had never forgotten the time, fourteen years ago, when Lobsang had raped her in Nepalgunj. But Gita's transformation had special significance to Lakshmi who was obsessed with paternal vengeance.

"Do you want to spend the rest of the night with them?" she asked Gita in Nepali with a twisted smile on her face. "I can arrange it. I can also arrange for them to rape you for days on end. There's nothing they'd like better."

The pain was so intense that Gita had to struggle to keep herself from screaming.

"There's always more," Lakshmi went on in a sadistic voice. "We can torture you until your will breaks. If that doesn't work...well...you saw your sister Renu. Heroin makes unwilling girls good bait for untouchables. If none of that works," she went on in a cold and threatening voice, "I can always have them kill your little sister Prema. I'd like nothing better. No one makes a fool of me and gets away with it."

"Kill her?" Gita gasped with horror.

"Why not?" Lakshmi said. "The traffickers bring beautiful girls here every day. She's easily replaced."

"But she's only a child," Gita said angrily, "a beautiful child with so much to live for."

"Then give her the opportunity to live. All you have to do is sleep with my clients."

"Never," Gita said. She tried to scratch and kick Ali. "Do you hear me? You'll have to kill me first."

"If that is what you want, I can arrange it. But I'm sure that a few more hours with Mohamed and Ali will change your mind."

She grabbed Gita by the throat and said, "What a beauty you are! Almost like a goddess. These boys are certainly going to enjoy fucking you."

"Never!" Gita said again gasping for air. "I'll never be your slave."

"Let me know when she comes around," Lakshmi said to Mohamed and Ali. She threw Gita to the ground and stared at her with a frozen smile on her face. "I've got to go. There's some other business I must take care of."

After Lakshmi departed, Ali and Mohamed tormented Gita all night. The intolerable pain and the thought of them killing Prema forced her to relent.

"Tell Lakshmi, I'll do whatever she wants," Gita said to them. "I can't take it anymore. I just want to sleep."

"Let her," Ali said to Mohamed. "We'll get Lakshmi in a few hours."

※ ※ ※

An interminable night — dreamless and sleepless — a night crawling with vengeance that made it's way from a small village in Nepal to a brothel in Mumbai — vengeance and profound suffering that wracked the minds and bodies of Gita, Prema, Renu, Daniel and Lakshmi.

When dawn's first light filtered through the window of Lakshmi's bedroom, she rose from her bed, lit a stick of incense and placed it before a statue of Kali.

"For years I've dreamt of this," she said to the statue, "and now my father will pay for what he did to me."

※ ※ ※

Gita lay naked and awake on a wooden bed when Lakshmi opened the door to her room.

"You did a great job," the *Gharwalli* said praising both Mohamed and Ali. "The scars and bruises will heal in a few days and her body will be prized by many men."

"It was a long night," Ali said laughing.

"The rich will enjoy you," Lakshmi said to Gita in Nepali. "You will make my house even more famous."

"You're the cemetery goddess," Gita said.

"Really," Lakshmi answered with a wry smile. "Well, I'm also your sister."

"My sister?" Gita asked incredulously. "What are you talking about?"

"Don't you remember your sister, Jamuna? I waved goodbye to you when the trafficker took me from the village."

Gita looked at Lakshmi with horror. She couldn't for a moment believe this was true. Could last night's torture have affected her senses?

"I'm your sister who was sold by our father to girl traffickers," Lakshmi said in a half-crazed but darkly muted voice, "your sister who had been raped and beaten and forced to sleep with hundreds of men, your sister who was smart enough to become the *Gharwalli* of this place, your sister who will make our father pay with the lives of his own daughters."

Gita didn't know what to make of the half-crazed voice and frenzied look of a person who must have endured an unimaginable life. When she heard the name Jamuna, when she so vividly remembered the last time she saw her sister...Gita gasped, and stared at Lakshmi.

"It can't be," Gita said. "It's too horrible. Tell me it's a dream."

"No, it's not a dream, " Lakshmi answered. "It's a nightmare, and I've lived in it for more than half my life. Now that all my sisters are Mumbai prostitutes, they will also live in this nightmare until I send their disease-ridden and soulless bodies back to our father."

"But, his mind is gone," Gita said, "and *ama* is dead. Your vengeance has no purpose."

"Don't tell me that," Lakshmi replied angrily. She paused for a moment, and said, "If I can't take it out on *bah*, then I will take it out on every son-of-a-bitch in our village who let him sell me."

CHAPTER TWENTY-SIX

It was a fresh morning, cloudy, and a little cooler, a morning offering a sense of new possibilities. Daniel and Balaram sat at the breakfast table in a den off the main dining room in Gupta's guest apartment. Although the maid brought papaya, orange juice, scrambled eggs, samosas, toast, jam, butter, and black tea, Daniel had no appetite for solid food. He sipped the orange juice and had some black tea with milk. He couldn't stop thinking that Gita had been gone for almost twenty-four hours. He and Balaram solemnly discussed the necessary steps they'd have to take to execute their plan.

"The *Gharwalli* treats the girls like starving dogs, but extracts as much money from clients as possible," Balaram told Daniel. "You'll have to bargain with her like you'd bargain with merchants in the *Ch'or* Bazaar; and be certain she shows you every girl in her Governor Road inventory until she comes up with Prema, Renu or nothing."

Balaram suspected that if either of the sisters were in a brothel, Daniel would surely find Gita there as well.

"But don't trust Lakshmi. She's disarming and smart, and remember she was just another prostitute until Khan fell in love with her and made her his mistress."

"Who's Khan?" Daniel asked.

"He and his brother run the whole deal," Balaram answered.

"How long have you known the *Gharwalli*?" Daniel asked.

"I've known Lakshmi for ten years and Khan even longer."

"They won't do you a favor?"

"Lakshmi? Khan?" Balaram smirked. "It would be easier to get something from a leper on the streets."

"What do you know about him?"

He told Daniel that Khan was driven around in a chauffeured Mercedes, smoked Cuban cigars and lived in a Mogul-styled mansion in the Mumbai suburbs. He and his brother ran their filthy businesses to pay for it all. They had an army of thugs that took care of all the dirty work — drugs, protection, and prostitution. They also had a go-down somewhere in the Mumbai suburbs that they had filled with weapons.

The subjection of young girls to inhuman torture was an ordinary activity for him. He murdered, raped, kidnapped, stole, and bribed, and he was never held accountable. Every night, he returned to his palatial estate in the suburbs and congratulated himself on a day well-spent.

Khan was extremely rich, cheap, and selfish, and he cared about no one but Khan. Lakshmi seemed to be the only person who could get anything out of him.

"The Mumbai authorities don't do anything," Daniel said.

"That's a laugh," Balaram answered. "You met them. Politicians invite him to the weddings of their children, to cocktail parties, awards ceremonies, and to the homes of the wealthiest members of Mumbai society."

Khan and his brother were big contributors to charitable organizations such as cancer and heart disease foundations, even orphanages from which they plucked children and used them in their prostitution ring. Their legitimate businesses were part of a complex network they'd created to shelter themselves. They were able to function openly because the powers that be simply winked whenever they discussed them in private. Nearly everyone knew the real source of their fortune, but no one had the courage to confront them. It was a running joke, not a serious matter.

"The few times police officials have tried," Balaram said, "their dead bodies were found floating in rivers."

Daniel pushed his food away, stood up, and said to Gupta, "You mean Gita's in the hands of those slimebags and we're having a leisurely breakfast. Come on, Balaram, we've got to go now."

"Trust me, noon's a better time."

"I don't give a shit," Daniel said. "Something could happen to her."

✳ ✳ ✳

Lakshmi sat crossed-legged in front of a Kali shrine in her bedroom, lit incense and a candle, and chanted the goddess's name many times. She recited prayers to *Siva*, the great god of death and rebirth, of change, of movement and power, the lord of the dance who made all things possible. But her prayers were drowned out by thoughts of the future, and by images of her three sisters sitting in a ring of fire, their faces scarred, pitted, and unrecognizable — a *Dashain* present for her father, Lakshmi laughed out loud. "I'm sure he would love that," she said to the small bronze image of Kali sitting in the shrine. "You know how long I've dreamed of this? From the moment I realized that Mumbai was nothing more than a bottomless hell for me."

＊ ＊ ＊

Prema was still curled up in fetal position on a metal-framed single bed in her cell-like room — her delicate fist pounding the foam mattress; and she shook with fear, not knowing what to make of the two women who had just been there. Her entire body was wracked with pain that increased every time she took a breath — her chest so tight she wanted to scream to the goddess that this wasn't her village…her mother and father weren't here…there were no temples in which to pray. She was afraid of the strange voices that she heard in the hallway; she was afraid of the men Madam Lakshmi said she had to be nice to; she felt empty, alone, and frightened of anyone who came into her presence; and this new woman, whoever she is, frightened her when she said, "I am your sister." Why did she say that? Who was she really? Prema had no idea if Mumbai was in Nepal or India, but she felt that all her youth and innocence was being drained from her fourteen-year-old body.

She watched a lizard crawl across the ceiling and followed the movement of the green, four-legged creature as it made its way down the wall and disappeared through an open window to the street; and she wondered how a lowly lizard could crawl with such ease out of this prison while she was unable to escape from Mohamed and Ali's terrible beatings. Her whole body broke out in a sweat.

She wouldn't do what they wished of her, no, never would she listen to them.

"Mother Kali, please tell me why I am here?"

＊ ＊ ＊

Daniel studied the Victorian mansions that had been built by the English in the nineteenth century — the wealth of Governor Road — the sophisticated architecture and well-manicured lawns designed by landscape architects over a hundred years ago. It was difficult to equate the upscale neighborhood with the businesses being run inside its houses. But, on closer inspection, he spied young Burmese girls sitting in the mansion windows. They puckered up their lips, blew kisses at him, and lifted their saris to reveal shapely legs.

No *chowkidar* was on duty at the gatehouse of the brothel where Gupta had told Daniel he'd find Lakshmi and Khan. He decided to go directly to the front door, knocked, waited a moment, and when it opened, a middle-aged Burmese woman in a floral print silk sari greeted him.

"I want to see the *Gharwalli*," he said to her.

"I am Nitra," she replied, "the assistant to the house *Gharwalli*. Come with me." Daniel followed her into the mansion.

"We have best girls on the street," Nitra said to Daniel. "Just look. Take your choice. They give you good time. What you want? Half day, whole day, week, month, hour, just tell me what you want. Maybe you busy man and only want half-hour. Maybe you want two or three girls. That okay too. Just little more expensive, that's all. Take your choice. There are no better girls on street."

"I want a girl for three days," he said. "I'll pay good money for the right one."

"What about her."

Nitra pointed to a young girl who sat cross-legged on a chair. "She a beautiful Burmese girl. I guarantee, she also a good fuck. Come highly recommended. Not expensive."

Daniel studied the faces of the girls sitting in the living room.

"Is there anyone else?" he asked.

"Just look. Here's an Indian one," Nitra said.

A beautiful, dark-skinned, South Indian girl in a blue silk sari, like an ancient Hindu statue stood on the stairwell. "She clean...no disease. She show you good time. She more expensive than Burmese girl, but she very beautiful, almost like goddess."

"And you?" Daniel asked Nitra.

"No, you no want me," Nitra said smiling. "Me used up, old lady. You want beautiful young thing."

"Is there anyone I haven't seen," Daniel asked.

"Yes, we have many girls," Nitra said.

"If I can't have you, then I'll have to go to the house next door," Daniel said.

"I'll get the *Gharwalli*," she replied. "Just stay here. Maybe you'll decide that one of these girls will please you."

✳ ✳ ✳

The smell of Mohamed and Ali had defiled and disgusted Gita — the *bidis* dangling from their mouths, their saliva dripping on her belly, their tongues on her thighs and in her crotch, the pinching of her nipples, the grisly smiles on their faces and their nonstop laughter as they forced her to spread her legs and dangled their penises over her. A thousand baths couldn't wash it away. And Daniel? The man she loved. Could he ever find her; and if he did, would he want to touch her again?

And then there was Renu...poor Renu. She had to see her again; she had to do something to help her. Gita couldn't shake the image of needle marks on her sister's emaciated arms and legs; she couldn't get Renu's voice out of her head. "The wind is cold..." and would Mother Lakshmi shoot some dope into her arm.

Gita wiped her tear-filled eyes, took a few breaths, rose, and walked to the door, opened it with trepidation, stepped into the corridor, found Ali sitting there — a thali tray on his lap, and shoveling food into his mouth with a *chapatti*.

"Where do you think you're going?" he asked her in Hindi.

"To see Renu."

"Not without Lakshmi's permission."

"Then get her."

"I'll get Lakshmi," he said, "but you wait in the room."

She re-entered her room and sat on the wooden bed in deep thought. Daniel will never touch me again; I will always be an outcast and *Sati's* easy now that the demon Lakshmi had sentenced me to living death. At that moment, Lakshmi and Khan entered the room.

"You want to see Renu," Lakshmi said to her.

"Yes," Gita answered.

"The girls only socialize downstairs."

"But, Renu's sick. I thought I could help her."

"Only heroin can help her," Lakshmi said with a sneer.

"Can I talk to her?" Gita asked.

"There's nothing to say."

"She's your sister, too."

"No, not my sister," Lakshmi said. "She's the daughter of my father."

"But, she's dying."

"Yes, I know. I'm sending Renu back to the village to let him take care of her."

"He can't. I mean...his mind is gone!"

"That's not my problem," Lakshmi said.

"But Renu is your sister," Gita said incredulously. "Prema is your sister, I am your sister! What happened to you? Who turned you into a stranger — a monster?"

Khan walked up to Gita and took her face in his hand.

"Your sister's a beauty," he said to Lakshmi. "I wouldn't mind having her for myself."

"She's worth a lot of money to the brothel," Lakshmi said.

"Is that all you think of?" Gita asked her.

"What else?" Lakshmi said.

"A lady like her would look good on the arm of a powerful man," Khan said as he held Gita's face.

"I have a husband," Gita said.

"What's his name," Khan laughed. "I'll get Mohamed and Ali to take care of him."

"None of your business."

"You are our business," Lakshmi said.

"I think good business," Khan laughed as he let go of Gita's face. "If you don't cooperate with us, Ali and Mohamed will rape you every day."

Gita stared at Khan's short, stubby legs, big belly, and puffy cheeks.

"What kind of a man are you?" she asked him. "Would you let your own daughter work as a prostitute?"

"She's at school in America," Khan said bursting into laughter. "Not so bad, eh? She will never be a sex worker. I would kill anyone who tried to do that to her," he laughed again taking pleasure in the bitter irony.

"May the goddess make her pay for your crimes," Gita said. "May she pay for the lives of all the whore-slaves you torture and fuck and force to work in this pigpen."

Khan slapped Gita across the face.

"Don't you think every girl in this place of yours has a father and a mother?" she screamed at him.

"I don't want to hear another word from you," he screamed back. "You will be ready to work tonight…if not earlier. Lakshmi will make phone calls as soon as we leave."

"Can I at least see Renu?" Gita asked. She cared less about herself than her sister and still believed there was something that might be done to relieve Renu's pain.

"In the living room downstairs," Lakshmi said.

"She's too drugged to go downstairs," Gita, said. "If you're afraid I'm going to do something, then come with me. I just want to see her for five minutes."

"It's okay," Khan said. "Go with her. Then get her ready to work. I don't care if she's covered with bruises, arrange for someone to sleep with her tonight."

※ ※ ※

Renu's cell-like room was dark and dank, and the smell of alcohol flitted through the musty air. Gita and Lakshmi could barely make out Renu's naked body on a wooden bed. When Gita called to her, there was no answer; and when Lakshmi turned on the light, they saw Renu lying face down in a puddle of her own vomit. She had a tourniquet around her arm.

"Renu," Gita said. She poked her sister's shoulder. "Wake up." But Renu's body had gone cold. There was no pulse or heartbeat and her short lifetime of suffering had come to an end.

"She's overdosed," Lakshmi responded in a cold disinterested voice. "One less headache for me."

"Renu, my little sister," Gita said crying. "She's also your little sister, Jamuna."

"It happens all the time," Lakshmi said calmly as if the death of Renu was just one more bothersome detail. "Now I have to get rid of the body."

Lakshmi's knew that this was Khan's work. Her voice covered up a deep anger she felt for the son-of-a-bitch who had betrayed her. She had told him that traffickers were going to bring Renu back to Rumla next week and she would finally get her revenge. But, now this...

To avenge my father, she thought, I must wait for Gita or Prema to disintegrate into hopeless human wrecks.

"Get back to your room," Lakshmi said to Gita. "I will take care of Renu."

"You already have. You've killed her."

"The same thing will happen to you if you don't obey me."

"Renu called you mother. Did she not obey you?"

Lakshmi didn't answer.

"She did nothing to you," Gita said angrily. "She did nothing to anyone."

"Ali," Lakshmi cried. He was just outside in the corridor. "Take Gita back to her room. Then, you and Mohamed get rid of the body."

CHAPTER TWENTY-SEVEN

Seated alone in her room, seething with anger, knowing that it was Khan who had killed her sister, and wanting revenge, Lakshmi remembered how many times Khan had said to her that he would never mess with Renu. But, he just couldn't mind his own business.

She telephoned him.

"Yes, hello," Khan answered.

"What happened to Renu?" Lakshmi asked.

"I gave her the overdose. It's cheaper than supporting her stupid habit."

"I thought so."

"Ali and Mohamed will get rid of her."

"It's already taken care of."

"Okay," Khan said. "Then, I'll see you later in the evening."

Lakshmi hung up.

He stole fourteen years of my life, she thought, and the least he could do is not interfere with my revenge by ridding the brothel of another expense. The cheap bastard! I manage the brothel and I make a fortune of rupees every year for him and his brother.

She promised herself that when the time was right, she would make him pay for killing Renu.

There was a knock at the door.

"Now what?" Lakshmi said out loud in an angry voice. Her thoughts were full of vengeance. There was another knock. "Yes! Yes! Come in. It's always something at the wrong time."

When Nitra entered, Lakshmi asked in an imperious voice what she wanted.

"Sorry to bother you, Madam Lakshmi," Nitra said timidly, "but a rich American is in the living room. He wants a girl for three days."

"I'll be there in a moment," Lakshmi replied. The telephone rang. "Okay, okay," she said to Nitra. "You can leave now."

It's always something, she thought, and picked up the phone.

"Yes, hello…hello…yes…just leave Renu there. A dirt lot's the perfect place. The police will bring her to the morgue. Just another dead junkie they'll have to bury."

Just another dead junkie, she mused. Renu was like every other piece of garbage she'd dumped on dirt lots. But, Renu was also the seed of her father and deserved to die at his feet — his junkie daughter who finally returned home.

"Oh, stop it!" she said to herself. "Shit Lakshmi, stop it. You never gave a damn about these girls before."

She poured a shot of straight whiskey, drank it in one gulp, went downstairs, and introduced herself to a very handsome, young foreigner inspecting girls in the living room. Self-assured and well-built he appeared, from her appraisal, to have money.

"I'm Lakshmi," she said to him, "the *Gharwalli*. I see you are interested in finding a girl."

"Yes," Daniel replied.

"You look like a man of taste," Lakshmi said. "My girls should please you."

"I'll know the right one the minute I see her," Daniel replied.

"There are five girls sitting here that the wealthiest men in Mumbai would desire."

"None of them turn me on," he said.

"Not her or her or her," Lakshmi said. She pointed to the last girl sitting on the couch. "Look at this sweet Burmese thing."

"She's not to my taste. I'd be willing to pay two thousand dollars a day for three days, but only if it's the right girl."

"None of my girls leave the brothel if that's what you have in mind," Lakshmi said. "We have beautiful suites upstairs."

"That's okay," he said.

"Where are you from, Mr...?

"Freeman, Daniel Freeman. I'm from New York."

"American, huh, I like Americans. We have many clients from the States," she boasted.

"If I find the right girl, you'll have one more," Daniel said.

Gita could be somewhere in this house, he thought. The very notion tested the limits of his self-control. It took every second of his martial arts training to reign in his anger.

Daniel understood immediately that this woman cared only about money. Her business sense was no different than a horse trader selling a mare. She took advantage of the twisted need in sexually-starved men who sought out teenage girls. How many times had he read about this kind of degeneracy in magazines and newspapers? But to be standing here, to be staring it in the face, to think that his wife might be somewhere in this brothel, made his stomach knot and his thoughts turn deadly.

"I run many houses on this street," Lakshmi said with a cold business-like smile. "There's also Falkland Road if you have a taste for a village girl with lots of experience. You come with me."

They went from brothel to brothel, each a well-kept emporium full of beautiful young women from all over South Asia, and each catered to the tastes of wealthy Indians and foreigners. She introduced him to girl after girl but none pleased him.

"You're a difficult man," Lakshmi said to Daniel.

"Not if you show me the right girl," he said.

"I've shown you a hundred of them," Lakshmi said impatiently.

"I need one so fresh and beautiful that Krishna himself would fall for her."

"Krishna," Lakshmi laughed nervously afraid that she would lose the American's money. "I don't think he would be as difficult to please as you."

"Then I'll have to forget about it."

Lakshmi suddenly realized that there was one woman here more beautiful than all the rest and Khan had said that he wanted her to start to work tonight. If this American likes Gita, she thought, I would not only get money, but also my revenge on *bah*.

"I will show you three special girls, Mr. Freeman. One of them is more beautiful than any I've had in years. She just arrived yesterday and I was saving her for the CEO of a Mumbai corporation. I can always find him someone else. But, come, let's go back to my house."

"Where's she from?"

"Nepal."

The intense Mumbai heat and humidity made Daniel sweat so much that his cotton shirt was soaked through and through. He was getting impatient, a little edgy — something he promised Gupta would never happen. The shits that run this place, he thought, would rather have tens of thousands of dollars than a young girl. I can give them that for Prema and be finished with this business.

"I'll arrange a showing," Lakshmi said to him after they entered the brothel's parlor. "Just wait here for a few minutes."

Two young Burmese prostitutes were told to enter a room with a small one-way glass panel on its door; and Lakshmi went to Gita's cell, put make-up on her face to hide the dark spots, made sure that most of the black and blue welts were covered, dressed her in a sari, and threatened her with another night of Mohamed and Ali if she didn't perk up.

"Everything aches," Gita said.

"I don't give a damn," Lakshmi answered. "I have a very important client who will pay serious money for someone as beautiful as you."

If Gita doesn't please him, Lakshmi thought, I don't have any other options. Then, what? Khan bitching at me for lost money; a month of harangues and no sleep — threats to kill Gita and Prema and a flock of new girls — some prettier, but mostly blind sheep herded into this hellhole.

"You'd better make this guy horny," she said to Gita. "If you don't, a visit to *Naraka* will seem like paradise before I get through with you."

Nitra brought Gita to the room where the two Burmese girls were waiting, and Lakshmi got Daniel.

"There are three girls on the other side of this one-way glass door panel," she said to him. "Whichever one you like will be bathed, scented, and gotten ready for a night of lovemaking."

After Lakshmi parted the window's curtain, Daniel pretended to look casually into the room. He saw Gita there, and at first, he thought, how wonderful to see her alive. But what have they done to her? How could she be working as a prostitute? The very thought ignited a deep anger in him and he wanted to kill every son-of-a-bitch in the brothel. "But, you've got to stay calm," he said to himself. "That's the only way out of this situation."

"Let's go into the room," Lakshmi urged Daniel. "There are no more beautiful girls in Mumbai."

"No," Daniel replied. He continued to stare at Gita.

"Just tell me which girl would help you forget your problems. The one on the right in the green sari?"

"Not her," Daniel said.

"Then the one in the middle?" she said pointing to Gita.

"Perhaps," Daniel said in a quiet voice.

"And the last one?" Lakshmi asked.

"No," Daniel answered. "She's not my taste."

"The middle girl is as beautiful as Radha," Lakshmi said.

"Yes, she is," Daniel, concurred. "She's the one. Tell me about her."

"There's nothing to tell," Lakshmi said. "Her name's Gita. She came here yesterday and asked for work. Who knows why these girls come?"

Lakshmi could already taste the commission that Khan would give her. Well aware that money like this didn't come along too often, she said to Daniel, "Mr. Freeman, you've made the perfect choice. Just go downstairs and wait a few minutes in the parlor. Nitra will get her ready to please you."

Take it a moment at a time, Daniel thought. Have patience, listen and act when the time is right, and don't arouse any suspicion.

"I'll be downstairs," he said to her.

Lakshmi and Nitra went to the *Gharwalli's* bedroom. From her closet, they chose a beautiful hand woven floral print silk sari, some rosemary and myrrh essence, coconut and papaya creams, kohl and henna. "Now let's get Gita," Lakshmi said happily. "Her first client's waiting for her in the parlor."

✳ ✳ ✳

Lakshmi took Gita by the arm, and with Nitra, the three of them walked quickly through the corridor, down the steps to a room on the second floor. It was decorated with nineteenth century English prints, a large Indo-Portuguese four-poster rosewood bed and an antique Amritsar carpet on the floor — a room the brothel used when it entertained special clients.

"I want you to bathe her, scrub her, massage her with these creams and oils, then dress her in this sari, and prepare her for the gentleman."

Now for Mr. Freeman, Lakshmi thought with a greedy smile, and six thousand beautiful US dollars. Most Indian men, no matter how wealthy, would pay three thousand rupees to sleep with one of her girls. A deal like this didn't come along too often. When she squeezed her cut out of Khan, Lakshmi could use it to send her sisters home. She'd see if the villagers adored these beauties after discovering the sluts they'd become.

"First-time clients have to pay cash up front," Lakshmi said to Daniel. They were in her office. "It's house policy. No exceptions."

Daniel reached into his pocket, pulled out a wad of hundred dollar bills, slowly counted sixty, added a five-hundred-dollar tip and gave the money to Lakshmi. I'm buying my own wife, he thought with disgust. But he needed to play the game to its end, and when Lakshmi said to him that he gave her too much money, he replied in a voice that covered up his anger. "It's no mistake. There's a little extra because you found a girl as beautiful as Radha."

"You're a very generous man," Lakshmi said. "Let's hope we do business again."

"We will," he answered in a muted voice.

"Good," Lakshmi said. She was impressed with Daniel's free-spending habits and stuck out her right hand for him to shake.

"Where's the girl?" Daniel asked, too disgusted to touch her. He moved towards the door.

The smile disappeared from Lakshmi's face, and Daniel, once again, saw those cold dispassionate eyes. She pulled back her hand and answered, "In room number two on the second floor."

✳ ✳ ✳

"Like Radha being prepared for *Sri Nathji*," Nitra said laughing. She ran water for Gita's bath, and ordered her to get in. Within twenty minutes, she had transformed Gita into the image of a goddess waiting for her lover. "I will tell Lakshmi," Nitra said and left the room.

On a carved rosewood coffee table, there was a small bronze vase, an unopened pack of Marlboro cigarettes, two cigars and a box of wooden matches. She picked up the bronze vase and set it down on the floor next to the bed. Gita reasoned that she could use it to protect herself from whatever shithead came into the room.

The wise men in her village had told her there was no such thing as death. The soul moved from lifetime to lifetime until it learned what must be learned. It would be better to reincarnate as an innocent and beautiful baby then spend the rest of her life as a slave to this brothel.

When the door opened and she heard footsteps, all Gita could think about was the moment Mahesh Bhahadur *Rana* raped her in Kathmandu. She had made a solemn vow that a strange man would never touch her again. She bent over, hid her face in her lap, grabbed the bronze vase with her right hand and prayed to Lord *Siva*, "Take me into your heart; take me to the place where you dance. I'm your child who wants to come home."

"Gita," Daniel said softly.

It's Daniel's voice, she thought, but Gita didn't move. It could only be a sign that her senses were deceiving her, that Ali and Mohamed's beatings had damaged her mind. She tightened her grip on the vase. "Stay away from me," she whispered through her tears.

"Gita," the voice said again.

"Go away," she cried. "If you touch me, I'll kill you."

"It's Daniel," the voice said again.

"Daniel?" she asked with her head buried in her lap. How could it be? She slowly lifted her face and gasped when she saw him in the center of the room. "Are you real?" she said. "Let me touch you."

"Yes," he said. "I'm very real."

Gita ran her fingers over his face. She wanted to be sure he wasn't some deranged figment of her own imagination. Was it a dream, a vision? Would he disappear if she awakened? She didn't trust herself after a night of torture. Her heart was pounding, and tears flowed like a river from her eyes. He put his arms around her and they embraced each other in rapt silence, neither sure what to say, but both grateful to be together, to feel the love that flowed between them.

"We'll find a way out of here," he whispered to her.

"Just embrace me, my love."

She couldn't get close enough to him. She pressed her face against his chest, touched his arms and legs, and tried to convince herself that it was Daniel in her arms. "You're a crazy man," she told him in a hushed voice. "How did you get here?"

"Lakshmi showed me every girl on Governor Road until I found you."

"This is a very dangerous place," she said.

"I know that," he replied.

Not only had Balaram warned him, but he also saw armed *gundas* just about everywhere in the brothel. He knew it wouldn't be easy for them to get out.

"We'll talk soon," he whispered. "Let's just hold each other, then you can tell me what happened."

❋ ❋ ❋

The Kali altar was Lakshmi's sanctuary — a place where she could sit quietly and mull over the events of the day. Everything she'd dreamed about for years had been given to her — Prema's virginity would be sold to the ex-Defense Minister. Gita was well on her way to becoming a sex worker. At last she could repay her father for this miserable life. There was only one regret: she wouldn't be present to witness his moronic friends throw him and his daughters out of the village. *Bah* would become an outcast, just as she had been an outcast and pariah all these years.

Maybe she should go back to Nepal and look him up, she thought bitterly. She could tell him how good her life has been in Mumbai, how successful she'd been at her profession. She could show him what eight thousand rupees bought — a vile world of rape and dope and whoring and beatings — a one-way ticket to hell.

"There's nothing left of me, *bah*," she said out loud, "nowhere to go, no one to talk to, no meaning to my life anymore, and I was once your little girl. I loved you so much. You were like a god to me. And now, my despicable father, take a look at your daughter Jamuna who everyone calls Lakshmi. I've come a long way in my life. But, you know something *bah*, the best of all is revenge. Nothing I know of could make me happier."

She imagined herself standing proudly before her drunken father — her mission completed, the old man disgraced. She'd have the last laugh, and that laugh would be loud and clear. It would touch the clouds like her kite once did when she lived in Rumla and *bah* would be finally punished for the miserable life that she lived in Mumbai.

And Khan, she thought with a bitter laugh, who slept with her on Mondays, Wednesdays and Fridays, who'd repeat like a parrot that he loved her every time he came, who had never taken her to a restaurant or the cinema or to his house. She was at the bottom of his list of priorities. What difference did it make that he pulled her out of the prostitute pool? She was still an inmate in his prison. She was certain that he'd kill her as quickly as he killed Renu if she ever crossed him.

He's less than an animal, she thought, and death means nothing to animals.

What about Gita's husband? Lakshmi's thoughts continued. What can he be like? Did she enjoy making love to him? Was he kind to her? Did he miss her? Was he in Nepal? India? Lakshmi had never found out where they lived. It might be fun to invite Gita's husband to meet Daniel Freeman. He'd never touch her again after the American.

Lakshmi had succeeded in a world where it was almost impossible for a woman to get ahead. She had power, enough money, and she stood above the other girls in the brothel like an army officer who commanded troops. No one dared to disobey her.

But how did Gita get so rich? She wondered. How did she escape from Rumla? And that diamond bracelet? She took it from her pocket and examined the stones set in gold. "It must be worth a fortune," Lakshmi said to herself. "Did she steal it from someone? Where did the bitch get jewelry like that?"

The gods had given Gita beauty and the talent to dance. Now they've given her diamonds. But once Gita serviced an army of men, she'd no longer have the strength to keep secrets from Lakshmi. There would be no more diamonds for the little goddess.

"I could always get Ali and Mohamed to get answers for me," Lakshmi laughed. She put the bracelet back in her pocket.

Lakshmi kneeled in front of the Kali altar, lit a candle, and some incense. "Teach me something," she said to the statue. "You have given me what I wanted and yet it has taken me nowhere. Now what? What do I do now that my revenge has run its course?"

✳ ✳ ✳

Somewhat calmer, Gita put her head on Daniel's shoulder. He kissed her cheeks and eyes, ran his fingers lightly over her supple midriff and gently massaged her thighs and legs.

Gita winced in pain, moved away from him and kept the sari closed. She didn't want Daniel to see the bruises on her legs.

"It must have been terrible," Daniel said. "What did they do to you?" He gently opened the sari and saw the welts and bruises on her thighs and shins.

"Oh, Daniel," she cried out in fear. Her sobs were now so deep that he took Gita in his arms and tried to calm her. She didn't know if he'd ever touch her again after what Mohamed and Ali did.

"Can you still love me?"

"My darling," he said as he covered her bruises with gentle kisses.

"I'm sorry, Daniel," she said still crying.

"For what?"

"For all of this."

"For better or worse," he said. He ran his fingers through her hair and kissed her on each cheek.

"What are we going to do?" she asked him.

"I'll get you out of here," Daniel said.

"It's not going to be easy," Gita responded. "I mean Lakshmi's thugs are everywhere."

Gita began to cry again.

"What is it?" he asked her.

"My sister Renu died today from an overdose of heroin."

"Renu? It can't be." He shook his head in disbelief. He paused for a moment and asked her about Prema.

Gita's tears were now sobs that came from a place so deep within her that she choked over her words and blurted out that Prema was also in this house.

"But how did you wind up here?" Daniel asked.

"When Lakshmi found out that Prema and I were sisters," she said in a voice that was barely a whisper, "it so infuriated her she promised to get revenge. 'No one makes a fool of me and gets away with it,' she said. 'Both you and Prema will fuck the elite of Asia.'

"Her goons tortured me for hours on end but I wouldn't submit. She threatened to have them rape me. 'If torture and rape don't work,' Lakshmi said, 'I can always kill Prema.'

"It's beyond words, Daniel, a nightmare beyond anything I could ever have imagined, and the worst of it," Gita sighed almost unable to continue, "is that Lakshmi's my older sister."

"Lakshmi?" Daniel asked incredulously.

"All she rants about is vengeance," Gita said.

"For what?"

"Our father sold her into prostitution. Now she wants to send her AIDS-infected sisters back to Rumla and shame him in the eyes of the village."

"She wants to wipe out your entire family," he said in a muted but angry voice.

"Yes," Gita replied, "she's become the demon buffalo. The incarnation of everything evil on earth."

It was *man's inhumanity to man* played out not on some theater stage, but right before Daniel's eyes — a surreal world so bizarre that human beings treated each other worse than rabid dogs.

"These people are driven by other things as well."

"What?" she asked.

"Money. Large bundles of US dollars."

"You don't know her," Gita said. "She's obsessed with vengeance. She'll take your money, then have Ali or Mohamed put a bullet in your head."

In his legal practice, he had dealt with every kind of corporate sleaze and discovered that they always trip themselves up. The shits that run this brothel couldn't be much different.

"Trust me, I'll be careful," he said to Gita. "I've had to negotiate with some of the craftiest CEO's around the globe, and I've won. The first thing in the morning, I'll go to her office and buy your freedom."

"And Prema? I can't leave without her."

"Little Prema, too," he said as he embraced her.

"I love you with all my heart," she said. She felt safe in his arms. For the first time since Lakshmi discovered that she and Prema were sisters, the future had some possibility.

There's no more powerful weapon on earth than money, Daniel thought, and I'll use it to buy our way out of this place. He took his cell-phone from his pocket and dialed Gupta.

"At least I found Gita," he said into the cellphone, "but it's a mess. You're right. These people are the worst cocksuckers on earth. Even you would find it hard to believe."

"Now the real problem begins," Gupta responded. "Getting the both of you out of there alive."

CHAPTER TWENTY-EIGHT

Many clients had booked select girls for the entire evening. At midnight, Syrian diplomats blocked a suite of rooms on the second floor. They asked Lakshmi to make sure that a number of young Burmese girls would come to their party. At two in the morning, some Bollywood big shots hosted their Hollywood counterparts for a few hours. All in all, it was a busy evening. Even Khan broke his routine and told Lakshmi he'd come to her quarters later for a spell of lovemaking.

After an intense day, Lakshmi needed time to sort things out. She told Nitra that her head hurt, returned to her room, took a few aspirins, and tried to clear her mind of the image of her dead sister Renu. In her own distorted way, Lakshmi believed that she was like a mother to the girl. "I was the only person in the brothel Renu trusted," the *Gharwalli* said to herself. "Didn't she call me Mother Lakshmi? She was the wind and I kept the wind from getting too cold; and she'd always thank me for taking away the pain." But, the wind has been snuffed out by Khan, Lakshmi thought. It cost too much money to keep it blowing, he said. So he killed the wind and I'll never see my junkie sister again. We had a bond, didn't we, a connection to each other that's gone, and Renu, dear sister Renu, you were my father's daughter and had to be sacrificed to teach him a lesson. I've told myself hundreds of times that I once loved you very much, and in the next breath, I cursed *bah* for sending me to this place. I'm like a dog biting the people that it once loved the most, a dog that will never be happy until every living soul has rabies. What is the purpose of all this? King Khan and his whorehouse on Governor Road. How many times have I told myself that it's just plain madness for me to keep on living.

When Khan first admitted that he was in love with Lakshmi, she got drunk on that love and celebrated her union with him. She could hardly believe that someone in the world actually could feel that way about her. But the lightness of being died a quick death when Lakshmi realized that his love went no further than him sleeping with her three times a week.

Better to have gone to Falkland Road, she thought. At least I would be dead by now. At least I wouldn't have had to deal with the inner workings of this brothel; at least I would be free of the foul stink of revenge that motivates my every thought and action. I'd no longer have to spin on the same merry-go-round I've been spinning on since the day I arrived in Mumbai.

She looked at her watch.

Khan would be there in an hour. After they made love, he'd want some whiskey to help him sleep. But, this time, she decided to put a draft of poison in his glass that would kill him instantly.

"His sleep will be permanent, she thought with a bitter smile. I'll never have to feel his filthy hands on me again. I'll never have to listen to him complain about his wife or see his pompous ass walk through the brothel. His brother will most likely kill me, but, so what? Could death be any worse than what I have to live with now?

※ ※ ※

A night of torture had reduced Prema to an empty shell. She was curled up on the floor in the corner of her room and could barely move. Mohamed and Ali had choked the innocence from her young mind and body.

I'll do whatever Mother Lakshmi asks, she thought, if that will keep them from ever touching me again. Anything is better than their filthy hands all over my body...

Mohamed and Ali knew that she was a teenage virgin stripped of the will to live. "She's ready for the Defense Minister," they told Lakshmi. "There's nothing else we have to do."

※ ※ ※

"Can I get you something to drink?" Lakshmi asked Khan after they finished making love.

"Some Scotch."

She put on her robe, walked over to a cabinet, opened the door, and took out a bottle of Chivas Regal.

"We fit well together," Khan said to her. "I've taken good care of you all the years you've been my mistress."

"Yes, I know," she said, thinking how easily Gita could be her replacement.

"It's a whole lot like love," he teased.

Love, she thought, and laughed to herself. Romance in a tightly guarded prison with no way out.

Lakshmi poured scotch into a couple of glasses. She reached into the pocket of her robe, took the cap off a vial of poison, and thought, all I have to do is pour some of this liquid into his drink. What is stopping me? Why am I so stupid? Why are my thoughts more powerful than my actions?

"Can I have the Chivas?" Khan asked her.

"Yes. Yes. I'm coming."

Just a few drops…it wouldn't take much to do the job.

She replaced the vial's cap without pouring any poison into Khan's glass, put both glasses on a tray, and walked over to him.

After toasting each other, Khan laid down on the bed and fell asleep.

She stared intently at Khan's sleeping body, and thought, what a fool am I? Even now, it would be so easy to stab him in the heart. I'm nothing but a coward and resigned to live in this brothel for the rest of my life. Just look at how quietly he sleeps — this man who has murdered hundreds of people, this thief and slave owner who lies there like a newborn babe, like a pillar of society, just look at him; and my soul is tormented, so full of hatred, so much in need of revenge that I can barely get a few moments of rest every night.

She removed a photo of herself and her father from a desk drawer and studied it for a long time. "At some point, it's all got to end," she said to herself. "Death will be a welcome blessing to every one of us."

CHAPTER TWENTY-NINE

So many noises filtered through the deep silence — footsteps in the corridor, a television in another room, night birds and crickets, Gita's breathing, and the relentless voice in Daniel's head plotting methods of escape. Unable to sleep, his razor-sharp mind created numerous equations that might work, but every one of them led him back to the same answer: money is a universal god and it will buy both Gita and her little sister their freedom. It's the quickest and most sensible path out of here. It's what created this hellhole in the first place, and Lakshmi and Khan must worship at its altar. He decided to offer them enough to get their attention.

When the first traces of dawn came through the window, and brought with it the morning sound of birds flitting in trees, of cars driving past, and the voices of people talking in the brothel corridor — a new day, and a new purpose — dreams and thoughts of freedom and a voice in Daniel's head saying no man should enslave another. I've lived in an insulated world where money and power blind people to life's injustices. Gita has opened my eyes and I'll never be the same after seeing all of this.

A knock at the door: a servant entered the room with their breakfast — tea, toast and scrambled eggs. "Compliments of Madam Lakshmi," she said and left. Gita and Daniel nibbled at the food, neither having much of an appetite; and after the maid took the dirty dishes away, there was another knock at the door. This time it was a ragged and unkempt Lakshmi with large black bags under her eyes, a wrinkled sari, and an overall countenance that appeared ten years older than the day before.

"Do you like her?" she asked Daniel. "Isn't she a beauty? A girl like Gita comes along once in twenty years." She put her hand on Gita's face and smiled. "If the goddess sent me a hundred girls like her, I'd get very rich."

Her pompous nature angered Daniel, but he simply smiled at her, and said, "I like her so much I need to talk to you."

"About what?"

"Buying her from the brothel."

"One night did that?"

"Yes," Daniel answered.

"Maybe she is the wife of Krishna," Lakshmi said. "There are still two more nights to go."

"Hopefully, many more after that," Daniel replied.

"We'll talk in my office a little later. I'm sure you realize that Gita's a valuable commodity."

"I think so," he said.

"But don't be in such a rush. There's plenty of time to discuss this."

Lakshmi had never met a client who wanted to buy one of her girls. They all came to the brothel, shot their load and returned to family and friends — men out for a night of fun — something they couldn't get at home where sex had dried up and they'd spend half their time fighting with their wives and kids and the other half sitting in front of a television set.

If Mr. Freeman wants to take a girl home, Lakshmi thought with a smile. So what! She only wished it wasn't her sister. Lakshmi had plans for Gita and it had nothing to do with her going to America.

"You are a very interesting man. First the gratuity and now you want to buy Krishna's wife. If you come to my office, we'll discuss the matter," Lakshmi said to him, closing the door behind her. She liked being on equal footing with rich Americans.

"I could easily ring that woman's neck," Daniel said to Gita.

"Be careful when you meet with her," she answered. "Don't trust a thing she says."

The more I know about the workings of the brothel, he thought, the better my chances of finding alternative ways of freeing Gita and Prema.

"I'm going downstairs for a few minutes ," he said, "to negotiate with her and familiarize myself with this place."

He kissed her gently on the lips.

"Be careful," she said.

"I will," he replied and left.

The brothel's interior was like a photo from a book on fine Anglo-Indian design and architecture. The constant buzz of uniformed maids who dusted, vacuumed, mopped floors, polished brass and silver, removed cups, glasses and plates, served *hors d'oeuvres* and cocktails — an upscale service that attracted many wealthy clients.

In the common area, Balaram Gupta sat on a couch and chatted with Lakshmi. They appeared to be old friends. He had a beautiful young girl perched on each knee, a cigar in his mouth and a cocktail in his right hand. He nodded his head at Daniel as if he were greeting a stranger.

"What will it be, Mr. Gupta?" Lakshmi asked him.

"I want something Burmese," Balaram answered.

At a nod from Lakshmi, Nitra went upstairs and returned with four teenage Burmese girls. After examining them, Balaram commented that the quality of the brothel has gotten better.

"Nothing but the best for you," Lakshmi said. "Which one do you want?"

The girls gathered around him.

"Lakshmi, dear, as always, you make my life very difficult," Balaram said laughing.

"Why not take all of them," Lakshmi replied.

"I thought the brothel caters to repeat customers," Balaram said. "The four of them would be the death of me."

He examined each girl, flirting with one, feeling the waist and thighs of another, blowing into the ear of a third until he finally chose a silk-skinned young lady about fifteen years old with perfectly formed breasts and hips.

"This one will do," he said to Lakshmi after pinching the girl on her bottom.

"You have exquisite taste," Lakshmi replied.

"How much for her?" Balaram asked.

"Five thousand rupees for an hour."

"I'll give you twenty-five hundred rupees," Balaram said.

"After ten years, you're still the same cheapskate with good taste," Lakshmi said with an irritated laugh. "Okay. Okay — four thousand rupees."

"No, no way," Balaram shook his head. "Thirty-two hundred rupees. Take it or leave it."

"That's thirty-two hundred rupees for one hour, not a second longer," Lakshmi said.

Balaram put his arm around the girl.

"It's a deal," he said to Lakshmi.

"Go to room number three," she replied. "When you're finished, bring the cash to my office."

✳ ✳ ✳

Khan was seated behind a desk in the brothel office when Daniel and Lakshmi entered. He didn't rise, nor did he shake hands with Daniel, but offered him a cup of tea.

"No," Daniel replied. "I've just had breakfast."

The conversation quickly turned to Gita.

"Girls like her don't come to Governor Road that often," Khan said. "If she makes love the way she looks, she has to be priceless."

"She is," Daniel said.

"And you want to buy her from the brothel," Khan said with a sinister smile.

"Yes," Daniel answered him. "Both she and her sister."

"She told you about her sister?" Lakshmi asked.

"This morning, when we got up."

"Then make us an offer," Khan said in a cold and calculated voice.

Daniel had negotiated deals in corporate offices around the world, but this was beyond his experience. He studied the faces of Khan and Lakshmi and tried to find a weak point — something he could get his hook into that would make this work. He saw greed and inhumanity in the leather-like visages of his adversaries; he saw short fuses and intolerance, and he recognized that protracted negotiations were off the table. He had to act quickly. These people would kill Gita, Prema, and himself without second thought. His first impulse was to crush the skull of the overstuffed scumbag in a white linen suit who called himself Khan. But, he resisted, and after a moment's pause, he said,

"What are Gita and her sister worth to you?"

"A fortune," Khan said feeling confident. "You can't replace girls like that."

"I'm a very rich man," Daniel responded. "You name your price and the money will be wired to a bank account anywhere in the world."

"Let us think about it, Mr. Freeman," Lakshmi said. "One never knows what you Americans are going to do next."

"Right now I'm feeling generous, but, I tell you, that could quickly change."

"Give us a little time," Lakshmi said. "I mean you've paid for three days."

"It will take just one phone call for my banker to transfer the funds," Daniel said.

"There's no rush," Lakshmi said. "Go back to Gita and enjoy her. We'll meet again later this morning."

Daniel decided that it would not be smart to push at the moment. His gut told him to give them a little time to come up with a price. Money took precedence in their lives and they couldn't pass up a deal like this.

"I'll be back in a few hours," he said and left the office.

✳ ✳ ✳

The Assistant Chief of Police, Vishnu Ramaswami, sat on a bench in the waiting room and read the *Hindustani Times*. He instantly recognized

Daniel who had just left Lakshmi's office — Gupta's friend, Ramaswami thought, who was looking for his Nepalese wife. He put the newspaper down, thought for a moment, then got up and knocked on the door.

"The two girls are worth at least US fifty thousand dollars each," Khan said to Lakshmi after Daniel had exited. "But I hesitate to sell them."

He explained to her that in a few years, Gita could bring in double to triple that amount of money; he calculated that Prema, at fourteen years of age, if handled properly, and if not given to the ex-Defense Minister who has AIDS, could easily make the brothel a fortune. But, his brother would be pissing mad if Khan turned down one-*lakh* dollars on a very small investment.

"But they're not yours to sell," Lakshmi said to Khan.

"What do you mean?" he asked her.

"We have an agreement," she said. "These two are my personal property. I want to dispose of them as I see fit. We can always get other girls."

"I've had enough of this nonsense," Kahn said angrily. "A hundred thousand dollars is too big a return on our investment. We can't afford to lose money like that because you want to send Gita and Prema back to Rumla. My brother and I don't give a damn about revenge unless it's our own and Freeman will wire the money to a bank account outside of India."

An intense argument was in progress when the Assistant Chief of Police knocked on their door.

"Come in," Lakshmi said.

Ramaswami entered the office. "I'll come back if it's not the right time," he said.

"No, come in, Vishnu," Khan said. "What can we do for you?"

"I've come to pick up some money," he replied in a respectful voice. "The pledge you made to help my family."

"How much?" Khan asked.

"Two *lakhs* rupees."

"For what?"

"Do you have to ask that question?" Ramaswami said. "Some people at the office don't like what you do here."

Khan reached into a desk draw and pulled out two bundles of rupee notes and tossed them to the Assistant Chief of Police.

"Here," he said. "Don't spend it all at once."

Ramaswami shook his head and rose.

"Thank you Mr. Khan," he said.

"Our best to the officers at the station," Lakshmi said.

"By the way," Ramaswami said after he put the money in his jacket pocket. "Did Daniel Gold find his wife here?"

"Who's that?" Khan asked.

"The American who just left your office," Ramaswami said. "He filed a complaint at Missing Persons yesterday."

"That's not Mr. Gold," Lakshmi said. "That's Daniel Freeman."

"Gold, Freeman. It doesn't matter what name he gave you?" Ramaswami said. "That's the same American who came to the police station to report that his Nepalese wife was missing. He told my clerk that she went to a brothel on Governor Road to look for her younger sister. On my orders, Atul threw the report into a trash basket."

After the Assistant Police Commissioner departed, Khan pulled a gun out of the desk draw. "That son-of-a-bitch," he said. "Does he think he can make an ass out of me?"

"Let me take care of this," Lakshmi said to Khan. She took the gun and put it in her pocket.

"You'd better," he replied. "It's your family that's made this mess."

"You just let me take care of it," Lakshmi said. "Don't get in my way."

✳ ✳ ✳

Here, it's simply a matter of life and death, Daniel thought. There are no laws. Human beings are eliminated with the same ease as it takes to swat a fly.

"Daniel," he heard a voice whisper. "It's me." Balaram Gupta stepped out of room number three. "It's a miracle Gita's still alive. Did they torture her?"

"Yes," Daniel replied." He paused for a moment, and said, "I see you're friends with Lakshmi."

"I get around."

"Maybe too much," Daniel said.

"I can't stand her. The bitch speaks from both sides of her mouth."

He told Daniel that an ex-Minister of Defense had paid Lakshmi a handsome sum of money to sleep with a virgin. "Is that Gita's little sister?" he asked.

"Yes," Daniel replied.

"Then we've got to do something right away."

"I'm negotiating to buy Gita and Prema from the brothel."

"How much?" Gupta asked.

"Whatever deal they want. The ball is in their court."

"There's a slim chance it will work," Gupta said. "I know how she and Khan think. No matter how valuable Gita is to you, she's that much more valuable to the brothel. They'll try and squeeze you for everything you're worth."

"We'll see."

"Did you see the man sitting on a bench reading a newspaper outside of Lakshmi's office?" Balaram asked.

"No."

"It was the Assistant Chief of Police we met at Brihanmumbai."

"What the hell does he want?" Daniel asked.

"Probably *baksheesh*," Balaram answered. "He clearly recognized you and I've got a feeling that he's in bed with Khan and Lakshmi."

Balaram touched his pant leg where he had strapped a gun. "I've brought a good friend with me."

"Okay, but let's hope it doesn't come to that," Daniel replied.

⁂ ⁂ ⁂

Though Lakshmi couldn't stand Khan, he was all she had, and she knew that the moment he turned on her, the cops would find a dead *Gharwalli* in a trashcan.

She needed to think…to consider her options….

The precarious nature of her own situation was clear to her. Khan could easily keep her from avenging *bah*. But that was the least of it. Lakshmi also knew that when Khan reached his limit, without a second thought, he'd replace her with Nitra or one of the other girls in the brothel.

The telephone rang.

"Yes," she said. "Who is it? The ex-Minister of Defense is here? Tell him I'm busy now. I'll be down in fifteen minutes."

In her fourteen years at the brothel, Lakshmi had never met an AIDS patient who'd been cured by a virgin. She'd often wonder who put such nonsense into their heads. Without a second thought, she had arranged for countless girls to sleep with men who had AIDS. It was simply good business for the brothel. But Lakshmi couldn't remember one client getting well.

"It's your world," she said to the statue of the goddess Kali in a distracted voice. "You've created it. All I ask is for you to teach me how to live in it and keep from losing my mind."

✳ ✳ ✳

It didn't matter to Daniel how much money Khan wanted, he would buy Gita and her sister's freedom. There was nothing to do now but wait an hour or so for their answer.

"She'll never do it," Gita said.

"Maybe not," he replied, "but Khan's the boss and dirty money runs this place. That bastard won't screw up a good deal."

"What if they don't accept?"

"Then we do it another way."

"What other way?"

He wasn't sure, but, Balaram was here, and he'd definitely help them.

"There's not a lot of time," he said. "The ex-Defense Minister is coming today and Prema's going to cure him of AIDS.

"It's horrible," Gita said.

"I know...I know," Daniel replied. He was visibly upset. "I'll go and see Lakshmi and Khan again. Maybe they've made up their minds."

✳ ✳ ✳

Khan ordered Mohamed and Ali to get Gita and Prema and bring them to Falkland Road. He also told them to kill Freeman if the American made any trouble. Without saying a word about it to Lakshmi, he leaned back in his chair, placed his feet on the desk, took another puff from his cigar, and decided that he would spend the next few days at his estate.

There was a knock on the door and Daniel entered.

"Mr. Freeman," Khan said sarcastically, "or should I say Mr. Gold. What do you want here? Your wife?"

"Yes," Daniel answered. The time for charades was over.

"Then Vishnu Ramaswami wasn't lying," Khan said.

"Name your price," Daniel interjected.

"There's no price...no deal," Khan replied.

"They're my father's children," Lakshmi said, "and my father sold me to this place."

"Shut up!" Khan said to Lakshmi. "I don't want to hear another word out of you about your sisters or your father or any of the miserable shits in your goddamned family." He lowered his voice and spoke to Daniel. "You lied to me, Mr. Gold. I don't like people who lie."

"I'll give you a hundred and fifty thousand dollars for the two girls."

"You must be very rich," Khan said. "Gita did well for a village girl."

"I'm rich enough."

"No you're not," Khan said.

Patience, Daniel reminded himself. Don't overact. Don't give away your power.

"These girls mean nothing to you," Daniel said. "You have thousands of them, but a hundred and fifty thousand dollars in a foreign bank account is a lot of money."

"I don't want your money," Khan said. "Gita and Prema are going to Falkland Road."

"Not if I have anything to say about it."

"You should mind your own business," Khan said coldly.

"You forget that Gita is my wife."

"A pity, Mr. Gold. You seem like a very smart and capable young man. How did you manage to get yourself involved with a Mumbai prostitute?"

Daniel walked towards Khan.

"Not another step," Khan said. "I have eight men outside just waiting for me to call them."

At that moment, Gita screamed in the hallway.

"No! Take your hands off of me. Daniel! Daniel!"

Daniel's leg flew up in the air and he kicked Khan in the chest, and with one stroke, he hit him on the neck with his forearm and knocked him to the floor. He ran out of the office. He saw Mohamed and Ali dragging Gita and Prema to the staircase. Mohamed drew a gun, but before he could use it, Daniel kicked the gun out of his hand and knocked him unconscious. He spun and kicked another thug, then smashed another one into a wall. More *gundas* came up the stairs and Ali pointed a revolver at Gita's head.

"Don't move," he said to Daniel.

"If you as much as scratch her," Daniel said to Ali, "they'll have to scrape your blood off this shithole-of-a-brothel's walls."

"Just stay where you are," Ali said.

"What are you going to do now?" Khan said to Daniel. He stood outside the brothel office door holding his neck and grinning sadistically.

"Let them go," Daniel heard Balaram say.

"This is none of your business," Khan said to Gupta. "Stay out of it or you're going to get hurt."

"No one's going to get hurt," Balaram, said.

"Don't be a busybody, Mr. Gupta. It's not a healthy way to live."

"There's no reason for any of this," Balaram replied. "If the police come there'll be an investigation. Just let them go."

"The police are in my pocket," Khan laughed. He nodded at Ali, and with one swift shot, Gupta was hit in the shoulder.

"I told you to mind your own business," Khan said. "If you open your mouth again, Ali will kill you. And you, Mr. Freeman, or should I say Gold. Your wife is going to fuck untouchables on Falkland Road. That's my payback for trying to make an ass out of me."

In the office doorway, just behind Khan, with eyes rolled back in her head and streaks of makeup on her face, Lakshmi stood as motionless as a bronze statue on a pedestal. She had a gun in her right hand.

"You're my sister," Gita said to her.

"Our father was a pig," she replied to Gita in a strained voice.

"But what about *ama*? She asked me on her death bed to free Prema and Renu from this place," Gita said.

"She did nothing to keep him from selling me," Lakshmi said in barely a whisper.

"She was a Nepalese village woman. What power did she have?"

"She saved your life."

"Yes," Gita said. "She didn't want to make another mistake."

"*Ama* should have saved me." Tears rolled down Lakshmi's face.

"I wish I could change it," Gita said. "I wish she could have stopped our father from sending you here."

"She didn't."

"But, you're my sister, Jamuna," Gita said. "No matter what has happened, I still love you."

"It seems that all you care about is your husband and your American way of life."

"You can come to America too," Gita said. "You, Prema and I can live in the States."

"It's too late. There are no happy endings in my life."

"Take them away," Khan said to Ali. "Take them to Falkland Road and lock them in a cage."

It's the right moment, Daniel thought, and if I don't act now, there might never be another chance.

He grabbed Ali by the arm and forced him to drop the gun, and without a pause, Daniel bent his right knee, pivoted his left foot and roundhouse kicked Ali in the jaw, knocking him unconscious. He jumped again and spun, kicked another thug in the chest, and grabbed two knife-wielding *gundas* by their throats and threw them down a flight of stairs.

"Daniel," Gita cried. "Lakshmi's got a gun."

"Shoot him," Khan screamed. "Be fast and shoot him."

Lakshmi stood like a statue near the office door — her leather-like face, steely eyes, and large body casting shadows across the room — and she fired at Daniel, but intentionally missed him by many feet. When Khan bent over to get Ali's gun, Lakshmi, with a steady hand, shot him in the back, and he fell to the floor in a dead heap.

"Please put the gun down," Gita said to Lakshmi. "I beg you."

But Lakshmi didn't listen. She moved quickly towards Gita and grabbed her around the neck.

"Everyone stay where they are," she screamed. "If one person moves, I'll kill her."

"You don't know what you're doing," Gita said.

With a glazed look in her eyes, Lakshmi fired the gun at the ceiling. The loud noise made Prema cringe and stick her fingers in her ears.

"Sister," Lakshmi said, "what a joke. I've been hurt so much there's no more room for sisters. My father took my life away, and why should I care about you being my little sister? I can kill you. Then I can kill Prema, and I'd never have to hear the words father or sister again." Lakshmi paused for a moment before she continued in a singsong voice, like a lost child in search of her home. "No little sisters, no fathers, no more brothels... nothing, nothing at all. I'll find a place where there's soft earth and blue skies over small villages and crows, water buffalo, cows and chickens... where I can live in peace.

"So many people dying," she continued. "It doesn't matter anymore. Who's next? To kill once is to kill a thousand times. The goddess told me to take revenge," she laughed. "I can hear her now screaming at me to avenge myself. But, when did I ever listen to the goddess? When did she ever care about my life? When I was a child, my father said he loved me. But he lied. A father doesn't sell his daughter." Lakshmi waved the gun above her head. She laughed a high-pitched crazed laugh and tightened her grip around Gita's neck. "The sky is full of crows that come every morning to eat my flesh. Oh my Father! I once loved you so much. You were like a god to me. Where are you?"

She aimed her gun to Gita's head.

"No, don't," Daniel, screamed.

"Why not?" Lakshmi said. "One day she's going to die, anyway."

Daniel rushed towards Gita, but before he could reach them, Lakshmi moved the gun from Gita's head to her own, pulled the trigger and dropped to the floor, her tortured soul instantly put to rest. There was a moment of profound silence in which no one dared move. Then Gita knelt in front of Lakshmi. She whispered in a prayer-like voice, "Rest, Jamuna. The goddess will take care of you. I promise, my sister, the sad memory of you and Renu will remain in my heart."

"And me?" Prema's frightened voice screamed in Nepali after she threw herself on Lakshmi's body. "Mother Lakshmi's dead? Sometimes she was nice to me, like I was her child. Where should I run? Tell me where should I go?" she sobbed. "Don't let Ali and Mohamed ever touch me again."

"We won't. You're my little sister," Gita said in Nepali. She put her arms around Prema, and gently lifted her off Lakshmi's body. "You're coming with us."

"Where?" Still shaking, unconvinced, and after a month of betrayal, deeply untrusting, she challenged Gita. "If you're my sister, then bring me back to my village. I want to see *ama*, I want to go home."

Gita couldn't tell her that *ama* was dead. It was too soon and Prema had been traumatized enough. She'd tell her, but only when the time was right.

"We have to get out of here right now," she told Prema.

"*Ama*," I want *ama*," Prema said. "I can't stand the pain anymore."

"There will be no more pain for you, Prema, I promise," Gita said softly. "This is my husband, Daniel. We'll take care of you."

Gita motioned for Daniel to sit down next to them.

"Tell her that she's family; tell her that I want her to come live with us," Daniel said to Gita. He kneeled and put his arms around both of them.

Gita translated.

"Where?" Prema asked. "In my village?"

"No," Gita said, "in America."

"Does *ama* know?"

"It's what *ama* wanted, it's what she asked me to do."

"Where's America?" Prema asked. "Will Renu be there?"

"No, my precious," Gita said haltingly. "The goddess has taken Renu."

"Renu's dead? No! No! It's not true."

"Yes. All we have is each other, and I promise, by everything sacred, no one will ever hurt you again."

There was blood all over Balaram's face and jacket. He knelt and told them they didn't have a moment to waste. They had to get out of the brothel. In fact, he emphasized, they had to get out of Mumbai and India.

"Hurry, follow me now," Gupta said to Daniel and Gita. He gave Gita a clean handkerchief. "When we get into the car, tie it tightly around my wound. It will help slow the bleeding."

"You need a doctor," Daniel asked.

"No," Gupta responded. "It's nothing my wife can't patch. But, we need to move now, please, Gita, tell your sister there's not a moment to lose."

Gita translated for Prema.

"Stay close. Follow me," Balaram said — and the four of them went through the brothel office out a back door, down a flight of stairs to a secluded alleyway behind the house where he'd parked his car.

"It's best that you drive," he said to Daniel. "I'll be your navigator."

Daniel drove the car into the crowded Mumbai streets. There were bicycles, scooters, taxis, cars, trucks, and countless people wherever he looked.

"Nothing has changed," Daniel said to himself with a smile. "Life continues in Mumbai just as it did before."

In the back seat of the car, Gita spoke to Prema in Nepalese about village life when they were both younger; she spoke about the temple where she used to dance a sacred dance taught to her by their mother. Gita's voice helped to calm Prema who was by now so relieved to be out of the brothel that she took her sister's hand. She wanted to see *ama*, and her Aunt Gauri, and to worship once again in the village temple. How can I tell her that *ama*'s dead? Gita thought. It's too soon. But Prema insisted that Gita bring her to Rumla. She wouldn't go to America without first speaking with her mother.

"I was in our village last week," Gita said to her in a gentle voice, "and *ama* was very ill. A few days before she died, *ama* made me promise to come to Mumbai and help you escape from that horrible place."

"*Ama's* dead?" Prema asked.

"Yes, my sister, but she also saved your life."

"There's a flight to Delhi late this afternoon," Balaram said to Daniel. He took out his cellphone, called a friend at a travel agency, and made reservations for Daniel, Gita and Prema on that flight. "I also booked the three of you on an Indian Airways flight late this evening from Delhi to Kathmandu."

"What about a passport for Prema?" Daniel asked.

"Call Bob and tell him to arrange it with the Nepalese Consulate. They can deliver it to Prema at the airport. All you have to do is get a photograph of her."

"Where?" Daniel asked.

"A friend of mine has a shop on the way to the airport," Gupta said.

"How's the shoulder?" Gita asked.

"It's okay. I'll live."

At the Colaba apartment building, Balaram asked them to tell Bob that he would be coming out of retirement. He was going to do something to put those *gunda* shits out of business. But for now, they all had to leave Mumbai, and his driver would pick them up in twenty minutes.

Gupta told them that Prema was one child among thousands imprisoned in that red light stink hole. Something had to be done to free those kids. He hadn't forgotten his niece and other young women like Renu the police have found dead in trashcans and dirt lots.

"We'll see each other again," Daniel promised. "We'll do something about changing this."

CHAPTER THIRTY

The car pulled into the driveway at the Marshal's residence a little after midnight, and Gita led Prema up the marble staircase to Sara's room. She smiled when she saw her sister's reaction. Gita knew that Prema had never seen a house like this before, and her wide-eyed expression was similar to Gita's own when she first came to live here. There were no huts like this in Rumla, Prema told her, nothing so big and full of furniture and with steps that seemed to go up to the sky.

After Gita kissed and hugged her sister good night, she went to the bedroom where she had spent the last of her teenage years. It was a sweet haven for Gita, one that brought back memories of an enchanted time, when her life had changed. She had arrived there a frightened street kid just out of an orphanage. Now she was a married woman living with the man she loved — the man whose child she would bear, and with whom she'd spend the rest of her life.

She could hear Daniel, Diana and Bob talking downstairs in the den. I should join them, she thought, but Gita couldn't resist laying down on top of the orchid and white-striped comforter and savoring its familiar sweet scent, letting her body be caressed by the plush satin fabric just as it had when she was a young girl who thought she had no future. She mused about Prema who slept peacefully in Sara's room, and despite the horrors of a brothel, how she and Daniel had emerged with a stronger love for each other than ever before.

"Gita," she heard Daniel's muted voice call her from downstairs. "Diana's made some tea."

Gita rose from the bed and walked towards the door. She paused for one last look at her old room — a lifeboat that had kept her secure throughout a turbulent time; and gently closed the door. She peeked into Sara's room and saw Prema sleeping on her back with outstretched arms. No longer was her little sister curled up in a ball hiding from the horrors of life. Gita smiled, and thought, that even in her sleep, Prema was welcoming the future and whatever it held in store.

Now for my husband, Diana and Bob, she mused.

Her eyes were fixed on Daniel, and then, as if they were the lens of a camera, she zoomed in on Bob and Diana, and with fleeting thoughts of her own misplaced rage which mercifully had given way to forgiveness and understanding — Gita welled up with tears of happiness and completion. She would never forget *ama* walking around the village in the post-dawn light — her dying mother who said in a weak voice, "My daughter is alive. She's come home to me."

As she came to the den's entrance, Gita heard Daniel talking to the Marshals about what he'd seen in Mumbai. He would start an NGO and help to free those kids from the brothels. He knew that in time Gita and Prema would also want to do something to help the children; that Balaram Gupta was well acquainted with the underbelly of India and planned to come out of retirement.

The room grew silent when Daniel and the Marshals noticed Gita. Smiling, she walked towards them — her family — she wanted to embrace them all.

Made in the USA
Charleston, SC
31 July 2013